A PRISONER'S CINEMA

A PRISONER'S CINEMA

stories

Justin Lee

For information, contact support@passage.press.

Hardcover ISBN: 978-1-959403-47-0
eBook ISBN: 978-1-959403-92-0
Audiobook ISBN: 978-1-959403-93-7

Cover design by J.D.M.

Library of Congress Control Number: 2025944738

Passage Publishing
Los Angeles, CA
www.passage.press

Printed in the United States of America

1 3 5 7 9 10 8 6 4 2

For my mom and dad.

CONTENTS

GODS AND SPIDERS

"Rarely does one know beforehand when the music will come," said Drazen's father. "It is selective, capricious." He sat with his legs crossed on the floor of his study, assembling his kaval, which was large, roughly ninety centimeters, and of a lush, low register. It was one of three possessions which Mehmet Dizdarevic had retained from his life in Srebrenica. The other two were a Swiss wristwatch, which had been his father's, and his son. The kaval had been his grandfather's, from whom he first learned to play. "The music is deep, melodic," he said, "and it is a construct of emotion, a melancholy hanging in the air."

Drazen watched his father carefully twist the segments together and run a scarred finger over the bone ferrules and down the length of the boxwood pipe. He found it interesting that though his father was a man of letters—a poet and translator, to be precise—he interpreted his experience through music. Mehmet pressed the mouthpiece to his lower lip and blew gently. An antique oil lamp, perched on the smallest of the study's bookcases, vibrated as the rich note filled the room. Mehmet lowered the instrument and smiled at his son.

"You hear the music in those rare moments that transcend the ordinary, those moments that make all others seem hollow. Gilded moments. For me, the greatest of these moments occurred when I was courting your mother."

Drazen, who was sitting in the study's reading chair with his chin on his fist, leaned forward and focused on his father. Mehmet, when he spoke of Zudha, spoke of her as he spoke of all things from before his expatriation: in a dark whisper, his copper eyes lost in remembrance. He would not answer Drazen's questions about her. All the son knew about his mother was that her name was Zudha, and that she had died in the war, shortly before his fifth birthday. He should have memories of her but does not. Once, when he was eleven, Drazen found his father curled in his reading chair, muttering fragments from a dream. Zudha's name was spoken several times in the midst of an indiscernible mash of English and Bosnian. He had gently patted Mehmet's hand until he roused with a start and glared in confusion at his son. Drazen asked him what he had been dreaming of. "Nothing! What concern is it of yours? Leave me, now." As far as Drazen was aware, it was the only time his father had ever spoken harshly with him. Now, however, he was speaking openly, his voice full and deep in the husk of his accent.

Mehmet continued, "She was quite beautiful, your mother. Hair like mahogany, the sort of full lips that begged kissing. She drew many eyes. I discovered the music the night I proposed marriage. We were alone in the hills outside of town, walking to a place of ours, a rocky clearing where we would lie and stare at the night sky.

"She was Catholic before our marriage, not Muslim like so many of the young girls, and so we had more freedom together. Still, we were careful about our little sojourns.

"The moon was glowing through the pine branches and the whole forest quivered. I took her hands and proposed in the dark

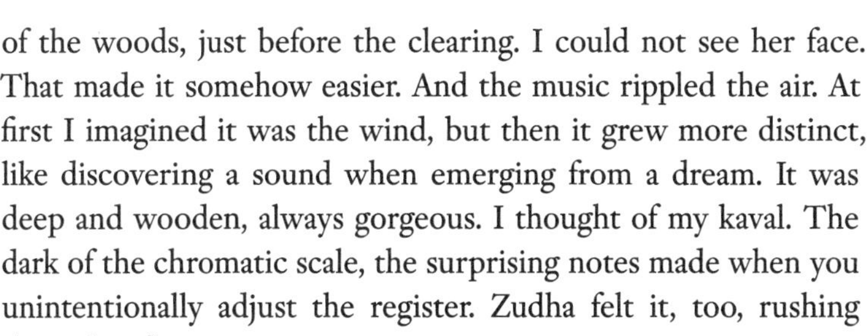

of the woods, just before the clearing. I could not see her face. That made it somehow easier. And the music rippled the air. At first I imagined it was the wind, but then it grew more distinct, like discovering a sound when emerging from a dream. It was deep and wooden, always gorgeous. I thought of my kaval. The dark of the chromatic scale, the surprising notes made when you unintentionally adjust the register. Zudha felt it, too, rushing through us."

Mehmet again set the kaval to his lips. He played a tune of his own composition, which he called, simply, "Memory." It was familiar to Drazen, sad and beautiful, a permanent aural fixture in their home. Now, however, it did not strike him as quite so mournful.

"I love you, son," Mehmet said, drawing back from the pipe. "I know how rarely I speak of your mother, and this is difficult for you. I know it displeases you. I speak of her now only because you have decided to propose to Alexis, and that is so very significant. Zudha, she is my only point of reference for such things. I—" His jaw worked for a moment and fell still as his eyes clouded with emotion.

Drazen watched his father and imagined that some crushing memory was working through his mind. He conjured images from his readings, his attempts to piece together some meager shape of what might have happened to his family so many years ago: hordes of little Bosniak boys lined up with their defeated fathers and brothers against the black lips of ditches; women bused off to refugee camps where, amidst the shanties and fuliginous mists, they were raped, defiled, humiliated by Mladić's men; dead bodies compressed in vile, orgiastic tangles. He longed to see inside his father's mind, to give true form to his past. Whatever happened to his mother had been unspeakable. Mehmet closed his eyes and leaned back, resting his hands on the hardwood. He was fifty-eight, but looked seventy, his gray-white hair withdrawn over a leathery scalp, his eyebrows absurdly black. He was grizzled in the way Eastern European men can be—that look of having seen conflict, whether they actually have seen it or not. Mehmet seemed to be waiting for Drazen to question him about his mother. For a single, horrific moment, Drazen thought he could discern the thump of his father's heart through his thin shirt. This unsettled him and he shut his eyes and rubbed them with the heels of his hands. When he opened them, his father was staring at him.

Drazen knew a dark mystery shook its oily mane about the holds of Mehmet's soul, daring him to induce its revelation. But he could not.

Mehmet seemed to guess at his thoughts. He smiled weakly. Drazen imagined a silent thankfulness rippling from his father like heat above a candle.

He wondered if this was, for its gravity, a gilded moment. But he heard no music. He closed his eyes. Then it came, dark, crisp, resonant: His father had once again set the kaval to his lips.

"We're early," said Alexis.

"Yes."

"Should we go in and wait for the show?"

Drazen shut the car door and looked at the building, at the flecks of gold disappearing from the glass and metal framework as the sun extinguished itself in Lake Michigan. The Rothrup Memorial Botanical Gardens sat just south of Rocky Gap Park, flanked by a dark tangle of pine and aspen. They had come at Drazen's suggestion. The performing hypnotist, Viktor Radenovic, was an old friend of his father's. Although he had fled the Balkans around the same time as the Dizdarevics, Drazen had never met him. He was eager to do so now and perhaps speak to him privately, to learn about his mother.

"Let's walk the shore for a bit," he said.

They skirted the side of the gardens and made their way onto the sand. Drazen rolled up his pants and removed his socks and shoes and Alexis took off her heels. They walked up the beach, the nightglow of St. Joseph at their backs, the wet sand packing beneath their bare feet. Occasionally they stopped to test the water with their toes, listening to the gulls swooping and murmuring over the waves in the veiled distance.

Drazen slipped a hand into his pocket and felt the velvet box that held the ring. He had been carrying it around for more than two weeks, waiting for the appropriate moment. Alexis scorned the saccharine, the extravagant. So Drazen was waiting for a small unplanned moment of private warmth. He believed he'd recognize it when it came, as his father had.

He watched her kick up a spray of water. The pale skin of her calf shone in the moonlight. His heart lurched at the sight of her. Alexis's beauty was such that Drazen often wondered if she were a nymph. The ensuing daydreams were simple: Alexis would suggest they walk together through a lush wood, where she would turn to him, kiss him, her eyes twinkling with impossible colors, and then simply dissipate into nature, melting into the bark of a slender tree or else falling in a ghostly splash against the stones of a brook. He believed that such a thing, were it to occur, would feel quite natural. Even now, looking into the deep beauty of the great lake, he nearly expected her to walk into the waves and never return.

She came to him from the water and rested her forehead on his chest, taking his hands, and began to hum a sweet soft improvisation that Drazen felt vibrating against him. This put him in mind of Mehmet's music. He would know the right moment—his gilded moment—when he heard the music. He strained to hear in the lick of waves some undertone of chorus, in the whisper of wind some melancholic accompaniment. But there was nothing.

He considered kneeling in the sand and doing it anyway. Perhaps her humming was music enough. The ring was a live round in his pocket.

He thought of his father, how he might lie when asked to describe the music. He didn't want to lie, but neither did he want Mehmet to know he had heard nothing. He might take it as an omen.

Mehmet was intensely secretive. His former life had died in Bosnia with Zudha, and he intended for it to remain tucked in the soil. In many ways America had meant rebirth: a renewed career, a faith moderated to the point of agnosticism, an unfettered future for himself and Drazen. Yet the zombies of the old world haunted him on occasion. Drazen saw it most in Mehmet's superstition: his refusal to do laundry on Tuesdays, how he quickly covered his mouth when he yawned—so the devil didn't reach in to snatch his soul—other foolish things.

"What is it?" asked Alexis.

"What is what?"

"You've got that look. You're trying to make up your mind about something."

"What if I am?"

"Tell me."

"I think we've dawdled and missed the start of the show. I'm deciding whether I want to go back or spend the rest of the night out here with you."

"Well, decide."

"Come on," he said. She took his hand and they headed south.

It took them fifteen minutes to arrive. A warm, strange light reared from the structure's heart, an amber-green lambency that gave the gardens the look of a luminescent jellyfish sitting on the floor of a black sea. Shadows, tall figures of men, flickered through the manufactured canopy.

They crossed onto the broad patio stretching the west side of the gardens and brushed the sand from their feet and put on their shoes. The glass doors of the patio were locked, and so they pressed their faces to the windows. Exotic ferns obscured their view. Past the vegetation a warm glow could be seen.

They walked to the main entrance. The parking lot was nearly filled. A cold thrill tore through Drazen as he opened the door for Alexis. It was as if the building were charged with a foreboding, mystic energy. The atrium, away from which extended the three wings of the garden, was large, surmounted by a low glass vault and filled with a tangible darkness tainted only by a slice of clear yellow light that slipped through the cracked doors of the north wing. A caterer, white-sleeved and black-vested, sat fast asleep, his elbow propped against a long table of hors d'oeuvres.

"Come on," said Alexis, "I'm feeling mischievous." Quietly, with furtive glances at the slumbering caterer, they sampled the food. Alexis discovered several bottles of champagne chilling in ice pails at one end of the table and suggested they toast the man's nap. They did, several times, daring the caterer to stir. He did not.

A murmur rolled from the north wing, reserved laughter, applause, and Drazen noticed for the first time a large sign resting on a tripod a few feet from one of the doors. It was black with gold lettering and read:

The City of St. Joseph
Cornerstone Chamber of Commerce
Presents
Mesmerist Viktor Rađenović
A Fundraiser

His eyes lingered over the man's name, Rađenović, and, even though he had anticipated it, an unsettling sensation possessed him. It was as if time had stilled and folded upon itself, twisting together past and future, canceling, resolving into a dark nothingness. Drazen encountered this sensation in passing when confronted with something of Eastern Europe, a Slavic name or artifact, anything of that lost world. He imagined at such moments as this that something had touched upon that well of emotion that lay boiling beneath him, unreachable.

Alexis hooked her arm around Drazen's, taking care not to spill her champagne. "Come on," she said, "let's sneak in." She reached for the long brass door handle.

He looked through the gap between the doors and saw a warm, aurulent light and the red flicker of a woman's dress.

"Let's wait until intermission," he said. "I don't want to interrupt."

"In that case, let's explore."

They began with the south wing, which was long and, as of yet, populated with only a smattering of exotic flowers, arranged in tiers against the walls (for the gardens were new, having opened the previous spring). Alexis examined a few plants that exhibited colors brilliant enough to be of interest in the dim light sneaking through the glass ceiling. They lingered for several minutes before returning to the lobby and slipping into the west wing.

Inside the air was heavier and much warmer, saturating a microcosmic rainforest. A stone path wound around a central pool, cutting through a startling variety of ferns and other greenery–among which stood a few rubber trees and a small kapok–until opening in a broad stretch before the west foyer. Amber lights fixed above the door illuminated the room. Drazen watched Alexis amble down the path toward the outstretched buttresses of the kapok. He began to follow her but paused before a bunching of Sri Lankan pitcher plants (*nepenthes distillatoria*, the card read). His face darkened as he wondered what startling course evolution–or perhaps providence–must have taken to create these luscious traps. Alexis called to him, snapping the chain of his ruminations. She looked at him over her shoulder, wiggling her hips. He looked at her face, hauntingly half-lit, touched equally in gold and shadow, and felt drunk.

For an instant, only an instant, the half-formed image of his mother's face intruded upon his mind and then dissolved into the ruins of unnurtured memory.

Drazen dismissed the image and the queer sensation that remained in its wake. He went to Alexis and she pulled him behind the tree.

They embraced, leaning against the tree, fading into each other. They kissed. She flicked her tongue at the roof of his mouth and the sensation was so ticklish that he tore away. As if on cue, a garble of conversation erupted from the atrium.

Alexis laughed, a swirl of champagne odor escaping her mouth. "Let's go."

In the now well-lighted atrium they found an active crowd, predominantly baby boomers and older, all discussing the performance with enthusiasm.

"Where'd we find this guy?" said a swarthy, bespectacled man at Drazen's left to another shorter man, who had usurped the caterer's chair to tie his shoelaces.

"He's a friend of Johnson's cousin or something," the man answered. "Supposedly he's been in retirement for years. I'm not sure I believe that, though."

"Yeah, thank Christ it's intermission. Linda would've had me up there making an ass of myself." The two laughed and moved on through the crowd.

"Do you know any of these people?" asked Drazen.

"No," said Alexis. "I'm sure my parents would. You know how small the upper-crust is here. Have you thought about what you'll say to him after the show?"

"Some. It's weird. I know almost nothing about him and yet I want him to share something intimate and horrifying. How do you ask for that?"

"Just ask. You have no trouble being earnest. Just tell him what you want."

After about ten minutes people began filtering back into the north wing.

Alexis and Drazen found seats in the last row of black velvet chairs positioned before the stage. Drazen began to survey the room as the audience settled. The couple to their immediate left appraised them, then resolved to ignore them. No one else seemed aware that anyone new had arrived. Drazen judged the north wing to be larger than the south, though of similar design and proportions. Palm trees traced the perimeter of the room. A man sat in a chair on the small, red-carpeted stage, drinking whiskey from a glass and talking animatedly to a boy of about thirteen. Drazen wondered if the man, clearly the mesmerist Viktor Rađenović, was the boy's grandfather. They certainly had identical granitic jaws and piercing brown eyes. They even wore matching clothes—lightly striped charcoal slacks and vests. Viktor's sleeves, however, were rolled to the elbow, revealing forearms, which, for his years, appeared surprisingly lean. Suddenly, he stood and dismissed the boy. On his feet he was an imposing ogre of a man. His hair was thin and silver, slicked back and carefully parted at the side. He was thick with muscle and possessed not even the hint of a paunch.

"I suppose we should resume straight away," he said, his voice ripe with dissonance—booming and stentorian, yet underscored by compassion. His accent was thick, similar to Mehmet's, Drazen thought, though darker. "I must warn you," he continued, "this portion of the act will differ a great deal from the first. Before, it was about humor, pure joy and entertainment. Now, we will take a serious tone. No more of the puerile, the absurd clucking, the involuntary compulsions, those things so often demanded by sophomoric audiences. Do not misunderstand. Comedy has its place and I do enjoy it, as, clearly, have you. However, you are all mature and I want to share with you things of higher interest. I want to demonstrate to you some of the true power of my art. Things, perhaps, you have never seen before." He turned and motioned to his young attendant. The boy struggled forward with a rather insubstantial leather chair and placed it at the right end of the stage. Viktor thanked him and turned back to the audience. "I will need a volunteer. Only one."

A man a few rows ahead of Drazen raised his hand and was called to the stage. He trundled to the front, an exceedingly fat man with protuberant eyes, and introduced himself to Viktor as Dr. Samuel Goldstein. Viktor assisted the man onto the stage and the act began.

After allowing Dr. Goldstein a brief introduction, Viktor asked him whether he believed in God and the supernatural. Dr. Goldstein answered in the negative, citing perfunctorily a Jewish heritage and a faith that had devolved from lax orthodoxy to curly-haired secularism. After medical school, he claimed, the idea of God seemed quite foolish.

To Drazen, Viktor appeared pleased by Dr. Goldstein's response. He took Alexis's hand as Viktor explained that, foolish or not, tonight Samuel would believe again, if only for a few minutes.

Dr. Goldstein sat back in the chair, at Viktor's request, and began to breathe deeply. Viktor paced the stage for a few minutes, taking sips of whiskey, watching the doctor's body relax. At last he sat down in front of him and removed a golden cigarette lighter from his pocket.

"Now, Samuel, I have something to show you. I want you to watch very closely, and as you watch, discover the great weight of the air in this room." Viktor held the lighter in front of Dr. Goldstein's face and began to pass it over his knuckles, as in a coin trick. The circuit was slow at first, but quickened. "Do you feel it, Samuel? That tremendous heaviness falling upon us?"

Dr. Goldstein nodded slowly, his eyes lost in the bright arc.

Viktor watched his subject for several moments and then said firmly, "Sleep."

Drazen and Alexis shifted nervously against one another as Dr. Goldstein's head dropped to his chest. The man's entire body became flaccid, almost lifeless.

Viktor leaned back, crossed his legs, and took a cigarette from his pocket. He lit it and took a lengthy drag and blew the smoke slowly into Dr. Goldstein's face. He did not stir. Satisfied, Viktor smothered the cigarette on his palm and flicked it aside.

"Are you with me, Samuel?" he said.

"I'm here," he said, voice dreamy and distant.

Viktor leaned forward, his elbows on his knees. "Listen closely. In a moment I will ask you to open your eyes. When you do, you will see nothing. The entire room will be dark. *In the beginning there was darkness*. That is what you will see. The darkness at the beginning of the world. Now, open your eyes."

Dr. Goldstein blinked several times. He looked ahead, his eyes unfocused.

"Tell me what you see," said Viktor.

"Nothing. Everything is black."

"And how does that make you feel, Samuel, the blackness?"

"Cold. Uncomfortable. Like I'm lost at night."

"You feel lonely, yes?" asked Viktor, staring intensely at the doctor.

Dr. Goldstein nodded.

"You shouldn't. You're not alone. We're not alone. What else do you see, Samuel? Do you see anything in the darkness? Shapes, maybe? Do you see shapes in the darkness?"

Even from where Drazen sat it seemed as if the doctor's eyes focused, regaining light. The muscles in his neck tightened in a few spasms, jiggling the folds beneath his chin. "No," he said, with a peculiar hollowness. Then he said it again, and again, and again, erupting into a bewildered stream of negatives.

"What do you see?"

"I don't believe it."

"What do you see, Samuel?"

Dr. Goldstein's speech became fragmentary, tense. He described tall, gray shapes—humanoids filling the room like a cloud.

Drazen discerned movement from Viktor's lips, though the man appeared to be silent, and assumed he was softly suggesting to the doctor what he was seeing.

"Does that frighten you, Samuel?" Viktor said. "Are you *frightened*?"

The man was silent. Many in the audience were wide-eyed, leaning forward, straining to hear.

"Yes," Dr. Goldstein said, and a tear broke free from his right eye. "I am frightened. Why are they here? Why?" His voice was breaking now. He was trembling.

"They're here, Samuel, to see you. To bring you a message."

"A message?" the doctor hissed. "What message? What are they saying?"

"Listen to them. Listen and they'll tell you. Can you hear them? Hear what they're saying about God? Tell me, Samuel. What are they saying?"

"They're angels. They say they're angels. They say God is on his holy mountain. He is watching from beyond the blackness."

"Do you believe that God is watching?"

"Yes, yes. I believe. He's watching . . . always watching. I can't, can't . . . can't escape him . . . everywhere . . . in the darkness."

Mrs. Goldstein was on her feet, and looked to be on the verge of calling out. Viktor turned and watched her for a moment. He turned back to the doctor and said, "It's time, Samuel. Time to close your eyes." He did so, tears coursing. "Now, I'm going to count back from five. When I reach zero, you will open your eyes and you will only remember the very last thing you said. Five . . . four . . . three . . ."

Upon zero, Dr. Goldstein lurched forward, eyes blinking. He was profoundly confused. Viktor took him by the arm and led him down off the stage.

"Thank you, Samuel," he said. "Everyone give Samuel a round of applause. He's been a great subject."

The chamber applauded and Samuel returned to his wife, who grabbed his hand and began to squeeze it compulsively.

Drazen looked at Alexis and found that her eyes were as wide as his own.

Viktor then called for another volunteer. "This time I require a man or woman with a phobia. In particular, a phobia of spiders. In a crowd this size there should certainly be a few."

Reluctantly, and at his wife's prodding, a skeletal, early middle-aged man rose to approach the stage. Viktor received him and, after gathering that his name was George Prince, asked him to describe his phobia.

"Well," said George, "I've been afraid of spiders all my life, really. But I'm not afraid of all arachnids. Scorpions, ticks; they don't bother me a bit. Spiders though, God! I get such panic attacks. I have to get away from people and just stand or sit in an open space. Sometimes I can't get settled unless I read Psalm 23, you know, 'though I walk through the valley,' that one. It's weird." He glanced at Dr. Goldstein—who sat nervously pulling at the folds of his neck—and then to his own wife. "I hardly ever go to church anymore, but that Psalm does the trick."

"Why do you think that is?"

"I'm not sure. There's something peaceful about it."

Viktor smiled and studied George. He scratched his chin and asked, "Do you enjoy your disorder?"

"Are you kidding? Of course not. It's horrible."

"What if I told you we could put an end to it, together, tonight?"

George looked at Viktor, incredulous.

"All you have to do is give me permission to rid you of your fear. Do I have your permission, George?"

George laughed. "Sure, why not. I've got nothing to lose. You couldn't possibly make it worse."

Viktor motioned for George to have a seat and bent down for another sip of whiskey. He then sat George on a deep-breathing exercise while he addressed the audience. He told of a dramatic childhood experience he had in Yugoslavia, involving abuse in a closet full of wolf spiders. He had been trapped by an older cousin, he explained, held down and briefly fondled while he stared into a corner covered with the quiet, scurrying things. He was phobic for years, until, after prolonged therapy, he overcame the fear. George, however, would be much more fortunate tonight. His fear would be lifted in mere minutes.

Viktor sat down in front of George. "To start, George, I need you to answer a few questions for me."

"Okay." George seemed at ease, every muscle relaxed.

"Is it rational to be terrified of spiders?"

"I suppose not."

"Suppose? What are the chances a spider could hurt you, especially here, in this country, in this state?"

"Almost none."

"So, it's completely irrational then, yes?"

"Yeah, it's irrational. It's foolish."

"Good, George. That irrationality, you don't choose it, do you? You've never made a conscious decision to erupt into panic because you saw a garden spider, right?"

"Of course not."

"That's because it's not a decision of the conscious mind. Deep within you, in a part of you not confined by notions such as 'rationality,' this decision is made. George, the subconscious is like a frightened child that never grows up. Tonight, we're going to force it to obey us. How does that sound?"

"Sounds good to me."

Viktor smiled and again produced his golden cigarette lighter. "Now," he flicked the cap and a flame sprang to life, "watch the flame. Focus upon it. See it dance. See nothing but the flame."

George watched the flame twisting in Viktor's hand. Eight minutes went by with George nestled back in the chair, staring, his eyes soft and intent as if witnessing a powerful drama. Viktor began to whisper. The audience strained to hear, but all they could discern was the faint movement of his lips. George's face became more and more placid. Viktor raised a hand to his face, the index and pinky brought together with the thumb, the middle and ring finger pressing lightly against his temple. His arms trembled a moment, and he fought to keep the lighter still. George's eyes closed. Viktor clicked the lighter shut, and continued to whisper for a moment. Then he was silent. He gripped both his knees, leaned toward George and spoke clearly in Serbian. He repeated the phrase over and over, as if an incantation. Then he said in English, "George, are you with me?"

"Yes." George's voice was distant. He was withdrawn almost entirely into himself.

"I need you to do something for me, George."

"Of course."

Viktor asked George to repeat after him. He slowly said something in Serbian.

George repeated the phrase, somehow pronouncing everything with precision.

"Now," Viktor continued, closing his eyes, "you must address your subconscious. Tell it you refuse to be forced into subservience, tell it you are master of your own mind and actions. Tell it you refuse to fear spiders any longer."

George complied. There was genuine anger, along with a mild embarrassment, strung through his voice.

"Now picture for me the most vulgar, reprehensible spider you have ever seen. Describe it to me."

"It's a funnel web weaver. It's in my garage at home. Lots of them there, in the garage. They're large, some of them, the size of drink coasters. Brown hairs. Light brown—no, gray—on the backs."

"What do you feel as you look at it, as you look at them."

"Anger."

"Anger? What sort of anger? Righteous anger?"

"Yes. They don't belong. They're intruding."

"Good. Now, George, I want you to envision all those spiders crawling over one another. Can you see it? Those spiders pattering against one another, trailing silk? It's as if they're just one entity, yes? One writhing, squirming, pitiable mass?"

George agreed, grimacing.

"This mass is that foolish part of your subconscious that makes you act out its own foolishness whenever you see a spider. Do you see that, George? Do you see them for what they are? Wrong ideas?"

"I do."

"Now, George, approach the spiders, approach that vomitous mass. Stand before it. Are you there? Good. Now stomp on them. Press the life out of them. Pound your feet down until you smell their guts cloying the air."

George twitched in his seat.

"Can you smell it, George? Smell their spilled lungs and hearts, their shattered, oozing carapaces?"

George's nose scrunched and his lips drew back against his teeth. "Yeah, I can smell them. They're dead."

"That's great, George. Great that you've banished that weakness from you. Doesn't it feel good, no longer being weak? Tell me how it feels. Does it feel like floating freely in a breeze?"

"It feels wonderful." His voice was loose and distant, mystical.

"Bask in that feeling, George. Delight in it." Viktor stood up, looked squarely at the audience and pressed his finger to his lips, willing them to be silent. He turned to his attendant and said quietly, "Miles, bring me St. Jupiter's Left Hand." The boy nodded and walked a short distance to a black trunk set behind the stage. He returned with a large glass jar, inside of which was a tremendous spider. Viktor received the jar and loosened the lid. Miles handed him a small vial of liquid with a rubber dropper top. Viktor squeezed two drops into the jar, waited for roughly one minute, and then reached in and removed the spider. It sat on his hand, relatively sedate, its legs twitching and hanging over the sides. It had a yellow and gray mottled abdomen the rough size of an elongated chicken egg. Its gleaming black legs were highlighted by ribbons of gold.

"George," said Viktor, now standing before the man, whose eyes remained closed, "I want you to bring your hands together, as if you were trying to catch raindrops."

George did so and Viktor placed the spider in them.

"I'm going to count back from five now, George. When I reach zero, you will open your eyes and you will feel absolutely no emotion about what you find in your hands."

Viktor sat down and began counting back. At zero, George opened his eyes and stared at the blasphemous thing in his hands. He did nothing, merely looked at it, then at Viktor, then back at the spider. Slowly, it began to make its way up his arm. He placed his other hand in front of it and it climbed on. Then George held it in front of him, placing one hand flat after the other, letting the creature walk slowly forward in place.

Viktor took back his spider and addressed the audience, holding it gingerly by the abdomen. "The golden silk orb-weaver, a native of every life-supporting continent. I have named mine St. Jupiter's Left Hand. Strange name, I know, but they are strange creatures. Their webs are brilliantly golden and large enough to ensnare birds, which they are known to eat. While they are quite innocuous, in Taiwan alone they cause up to twenty deaths each year, accidental deaths, of course, from people behaving foolishly to avoid them. I find them quite beautiful." He turned to George, "How do you feel?"

"I feel just fine, strangely enough. A little surprised, but that's all."

"That's good to hear," Viktor said, and then, a little whimsically to the audience, "It doesn't always work, you know."

Everyone laughed and Viktor dismissed George and ordered another round of applause. He slipped St. Jupiter's Left Hand back into its jar.

"Do you think it's real?" asked Alexis.

"I believe so," said Drazen. "If not, those two men are remarkable actors."

"What if they're plants?"

"I think the term for that is 'stooge.' But it'd be an awful lot of work to prepare something like that for a crowd this small."

"If they're not stooges, what are they? How do you get someone to see something that's not there?"

Drazen tried to bluff his way through an answer as the audience was settling. Alexis listened attentively. It was not until the entire room was silent that Drazen realized Viktor Rađenović was waiting for their attention.

"It seems we have a skeptic in our midst," Viktor said, not without some humor. Most of the audience turned to appraise Drazen and Alexis.

Drazen attempted to smile away his embarrassment and was startled when Viktor invited him on stage. He looked at Alexis, who merely raised her eyebrows. On impulse he agreed.

He made his way down the center aisle and stopped before the stage.

"Come on," said Viktor. "Don't be shy."

Drazen stepped onto the stage and Viktor shook his hand. He looked back at Alexis. She was flushed and laughing quietly with her hands over her mouth. Drazen believed she must be amused by the irony of Viktor's mistake.

"What is your name, young man?" said the mesmerist, his arms folded across his chest.

"Drazen."

Viktor's eyes narrowed with interest. "And your surname?"

"Dizdarevic."

"Ah." Viktor raised a hand to his face and tapped a finger against his chin. "Am I correct in assuming you are Bosniak?"

"Yes," said Drazen. "And I believe you know my father."

"*Mehmet*?"

"Yes."

"Ahhh! Excellent. Well, I suppose that changes things. I had planned to get you up here and embarrass the holy hell out of you. How is your father? I was disappointed when he declined my invitation for tonight. I haven't seen him in years."

"He's well," said Drazen. "He's still in Bay City, finishing a new translation of Andrić."

Viktor turned to address the chamber. "I must apologize," he said. "I had not planned on meeting the son of an old friend.

You'll have to bear with me." Then, to Drazen, he said, "What brings you here tonight?"

"My father told me about your show. I work just over in Benton and thought I'd come meet you. Father is very quiet about his past."

"Yes?"

Shit. The words had just slipped out. Drazen sighed. Then he had an idea.

"He's quiet about *before*. Before we came to the states. And I remember almost nothing. I hoped we might be able to talk about the war."

Viktor was silent, seeming to work something out in his mind. "A terrible business," he said at last. "I had several acquaintances in the Army of Republika Srpska. We no longer speak. Makes a man ashamed of his origins." He looked away from Drazen, at the red carpet. "I, too, left because of the war, but for a different reason. I was disgusted." Viktor's face had paled considerably. An aura of whiskey clung to him. "But enough of history," he said, turning to the audience. "Our young friend, unless I misheard him across the room, has doubts concerning the validity of my act. Which is understandable. My profession is overrun with flimflam men. But I assure you, I have not tonight, nor have I ever, employed stooges. Now," he turned back to Drazen, "I have a certain affinity for winning converts."

It occurred to Drazen that he could explain that Alexis, his girlfriend, was the skeptic, not him. But, sensing a unique opportunity, he remained silent.

"Have a seat and learn for yourself what is real."

Drazen sat down heavily in the bare leather chair.

"Are you comfortable?" Viktor asked.

"Enough."

"Usually," Viktor said, addressing the audience and Drazen, "this is where the old performers went into interesting, albeit farcical, descriptions of their trips through the East, where they would describe, in grandiloquent terms, the wisdom of Oriental occult masters. I, however, have never been farther east than Bucharest and will do no such sensational crowd-jazzing. What I know I have learned from books and in the basements of certain private clubs in Belgrade. One does not need to travel to Tibet to discover mysteries, ancient or otherwise. Now, Drazen, what will it take to make a believer out of you?"

"Something difficult," he said.

"To be a skeptic, you must know at least a little about hypnosis," said Viktor. "So pick something you've seen or heard of that you doubt."

Drazen forced himself to remain collected, to appear genuinely unconvinced. "I've always heard about people recovering lost memories," he said. "And I just don't believe that it works."

"What sort of memory would you have me call up?" asked Viktor.

"I want to know how my mother died."

A strange fire sprang up in the old sorcerer's eyes. He was silent for a long while. Finally, he asked, "Are you certain?"

"Yes."

Viktor took out his lighter and sat opposite of Drazen. He looked at the lighter, turning it over in his hands, and then gave it to him. Drazen studied it, noticing a Latin inscription along one side (*de fumo in flammam*, he read, remembering suddenly the bright red streaks of the pitcher plants).

"You just keep a hold of that," said Viktor. "No gimmickry this time."

Drazen made a fist around the golden lighter and rested his arms in his lap. Viktor told him to relax and then simply stared at him.

After only two minutes, Drazen's chin fell against his chest.

Viktor motioned to his attendant to bring him more whiskey. He refilled his glass, drank it quickly, and discarded it. He sighed heavily and resumed staring.

"Sink, sink, my good boy. Down, down, into that place of peace we all go when we need it most. Drift, yes, drift down softly, into that place of wonder, to the place of things lost, of things forgotten."

Drazen rolled his head side to side and mumbled gibberish.

"Are you there, my boy?" Viktor's tone was fatherly.

"Yes," he said.

"Good," said the hypnotist. "There is a door there, an old door with black hinges and a black knob. Do you see it?"

"I see it."

"What do you see? Describe it."

"I see the door and, around the edges, a light."

"What color is the light?"

"It is blue and green, like the sea."

"How does that make you feel?"

"At peace."

"Do you know where the door leads, my good boy?"

"No."

"Would you like to?"

"More than anything."

"It leads to another door. A beautiful door, made of glass and light. Beyond that second door is paradise, Drazen. Would you like to see paradise?"

"Yes. Yes. Yes," he said.

"Are you willing to do anything to see that second door, to enter paradise?"

He responded with a mantra of acquiescence.

"Then you must open the first door, but only when I tell you. Beyond that door is a hallway through which you must pass. There is something in that hallway, Drazen. Do you know what it is?"

"No."

"It's that moment, my boy, my good boy, that moment from your childhood. Do you know the moment I speak of? The moment you have repressed all your life, the moment you have shut out forever."

"I don't know."

"You must know, Drazen. You must remember, or you will never enter Paradise."

"Please," he said. "I must enter Paradise."

"Then open the door, Drazen. Open the door. And remember the worst thing that ever happened to you."

He saw it clearly, in the dark of his trance, a black door so knotted as to appear unfinished. He dragged his fingers across the surface. It felt as if he had touched a hunk of petrified tumor.

He found the knob and turned it. The door opened and he stepped into the humble place of his childhood.

The light was warm, provided by two dim lamps and a row of candles set on the mantel of a small fireplace. There had been a fire recently—the aroma of burnt wood suffused the room. Before the hearth sat a small boy with disconcertingly large eyes. He was playing jacks and casting playful glances at the man and woman sitting across the room on a worn-out couch. They were sharing an elaborate book with gilt edges, perhaps the only extravagance in the small room. On the table, a radio played soft, sweet music.

Drazen was drifting toward the boy, and then, in a wash of color and smoke, he was the boy, tightly gripping a red rubber ball and looking at his parents with love.

"Majka," he said in a near whisper.

Zudha looked up with a smile, delighting in her little boy and his jacks.

This moment seemed to stretch out for hours, blending exquisitely with the sound of the music. Mehmet continued to read nearby, entranced with the book, oblivious to the concert of emotions around him.

There was a knock at the door.

Mehmet closed the book and sat it on the end table, by the lamp. He disentangled himself from Zudha, stood, and crossed the room to a small desk where he opened the top drawer and removed a pistol. His face grew suddenly weary. He hid the gun on the desk, beneath a newspaper, and went to open the door.

He asked the visitor to identify himself, and Drazen heard a deep, authoritative voice, but he couldn't discern the words. Zudha stood quickly and covered her head with a hijab.

Mehmet unfastened the bolt and two men entered, one wearing the forest-green camouflage of the Army of Republika Srpska, the other dressed in simple street clothes. Both carried Kalashnikovs with long clips like crescents.

Then: his mother's face, torn with screaming as a dark shape rushed her. His father on his knees, hands to his face, blood running down his chin. A warm, tacky hand gripping Drazen's neck, the sensation of metal and oil on his cheek. His mother pinned down by that dark shape. Mehmet looking at him, his face unrecognizable. Torn clothing on the floor. Mehmet reaching toward Zudha and the dark shape writhing atop her. Mehmet, bestial, aiming a pistol above Drazen's head. A smell of burning. An indefinite shape sprawled on the floor, outlined in crimson. Mehmet bearing down upon the dark shape, holding the radio above his head. The radio becoming one with the head of the dark shape. Everywhere, everything, buried in red.

Then Zudha was carrying him, his arms around her neck, his head against her breast. He felt her heart hammering inside of her as they went to the bathroom. Zudha took off her remaining clothes and turned on the shower. Parts of her face and neck were bright red. Drazen saw that the redness ran lower, down far past her breasts.

She placed him into the big brass bathtub and climbed in behind. The water was ice cold, but that did not bother her. Everything was hazy inside the tub. Everything seemed glazed in gold.

He looked at his mother. She was beautiful, the most beautiful woman in the world. Her eyes were blue like the sea. She leaned forward and held Drazen. He felt her nipples, hardened by the cold water, digging into his back. The sensation was startling. She rocked with him as the water washed away the blood.

DRAZEN BLINKED and saw a confusion of shapes and colors, heard a frantic voice fraught with uncertainty atop a multitude of murmurs. His mother's face vibrated in and out of focus. It contoured and the light behind her changed. Then he was dry.

Alexis held him, rocking him steadily, trying to calm him. He was pressed against her on the stage, looking into the tortured oceans of her eyes as full consciousness rushed upon him and he realized that she was not his mother.

A PRISONER'S CINEMA

Cal leaned in close to the wall and blew away the detritus left over from his etching. He traced his fingers over the surface of the figure, and tried to smile. Carving on the wall of his cell was a pleasant diversion from the agony of time. But over the past few days it had involved an agony of its own.

In his old cell he had made his art with an etching needle crafted from the iron band of a bed slat. The needle was lousy compared to his tools back at the high school studio; even his students would have scoffed at it. But it was his, and he had made it with care. The guards had confiscated it ("A shiv, Cal? Really?") in a shakedown before transferring him to his deathwatch cell three days ago. He had been left without implement. That is, until in desperation he fashioned a new one from his left thumbnail.

Was there meaning or truth in creating art up to the moment of death? Was this even art? Was he leaving something behind, for posterity? Or would this too be painted over just as the guards had assured him the fine macabre vision in his old cell would be? Cal laughed at the notion of posterity. "*John* Calvin *Cavanaugh*," another murderer might read some distant day and wonder at the startlingly detailed Janus head on the figure beneath the words. Posterity lived in an infinite succession of little bursts of days at the ends of wasted lives.

Cal kneaded his temples with the middle finger and thumb of his right hand. He tried not to philosophize. Philosophizing inevitably led to self-mortification, which in its turn led to Paul. Cal's self-hatred was a beacon, whether to the expanse of his subconscious or to the great waste without he did not know, and Paul never ignored its light.

Cal watched the figure on the wall and imagined the two faces to be his own, imagined them to twist and writhe against each other, to resolve into a featureless chaos, a sculpture washed by a thousand years of whirling sand, to reform into the profiles of two young girls, to again disassemble and settle back into a Romanesque monster. Then he watched the wall itself. The simple, white-washed concrete. He thought about what it meant. What lay beyond it. What lay down the corridor. Hell on this side, hell on that, he told himself.

What's this, now? Paul said, his features condensing against the opposite wall.

Cal turned slowly. Paul had long ago ceased to startle him.

"Art, I think," Cal answered. He turned back and again traced a finger around Janus.

Art? Art should never be so consciously symbolic, you know that. This is didactic. This is trash.

Paul's features were sharply defined today, his form solid, that of a young man with long black hair and a brooding face, similar to Cal's own. So often Paul chose a shifting form, presenting a chimera of pieces assembled from Cal's memories—warm smiles, sly winks, the rosy hands of a grandparent, his father's work pants, his mother's favorite flowered blouse that she wore too often on Sundays—always mismatched, disharmonious in a horrid way. Sometimes Paul would appear as a normal young man, like today, except that his head would oscillate fast enough to blur the features of his face. Sometimes he was only a dark mist, a man-sized disruption in the air. Always, however, he spoke in the same high, androgynous voice.

"It's been days. Where've you been?"

Wandering the earth, love. Circumnavigating the existential void. Giving you time for your thoughts. I know how much you value quality time alone.

"A comedian to the last."

Paul gave a bow and smiled. *That's not all. I've been to see* him. *Been to see old man McKaskell. Thought perhaps you'd enjoy a report.*

"Stop," said Cal, surprised at the harshness of his voice and regretting having spoken. Such commands only encouraged Paul.

I have information. Sweet, delicious, naughty, vital information. News to make us squirm in our undies and play the rosary with remorse.

"Please, stop this. Please."

He's antsy. Unbelievably anxious. He's taken a leave from the firm because of his condition. He's good for nothing except pacing and muttering and crying. He's doing that a lot again—crying. My sources tell me that it's not happened much in the last six years. Now it's coming in bursts, little intense snotty red-eyed bursts. And that vein. You remember the vein? It moves like a snake through his face.

Cal lay on his back, pressing the heels of his hands to his eyes. Small violet dots came to the edges of his vision and were replaced by bursts of memory: his arrest, faces with names and faces without names, the dreamlike quality of the plea hearing, the sight of a man named Norman McKaskell who did not seem to be grieving or angry but simply bewildered. Nausea rose inside him at the sound of Paul's voice, which was warm and playful, singsong.

He's masturbating a lot. A whole hell of a lot. Does it on the bathroom floor, sitting against the tub. Doesn't even clean up after himself, he's that far gone.

"You're a goddamn liar."

A liar? Sometimes. Damned of God? Most assuredly always. But even He of the Glowing Bronze Bod with the Face Shining as the Sun knows what that small little man is doing with those twitching arthritic hands. And, Christ, Cal, what he thinks while he does it! Can you guess? He thinks of doing to you just the thing you did to his girls! Cries these angry tears all the while. Grits his teeth. Snake in temple, snake in hand, throbbing together. Just splendid.

Cal sighed. He had long ago resolved to stop resisting Paul's presence, yet every so often he was startled into a fresh rebellion.

The best part—Cal, are you listening?

He felt a pressure on his belly. He removed his hands from his eyes and found Paul kneeling in an attitude of prayer, using his torso as an altar.

The best part is that when he finishes, he prays, actually prays! Paul closed his eyes and screwed up his face in mock-reverence. *'Lord God, what am I doing? By whose compulsion is this happening? How can these be my thoughts? Oh, forgive me.' Yada yada yada. Reminded me of you all those years ago, sweating over that smut and then hiding with your rosary until you'd convinced yourself you felt clean.*

You know, McKaskell prays for your soul. Weird, right? Fantasizes about desecrating your body, yet prays for your soul! What a dear little hypocrite.

"Leave it alone, Paul. Leave him alone."

Paul smiled and rose to his feet. *Maybe we'll pick it back up when we see him tomorrow? He believes he needs this. Speaking of* this, *how will you be spending this last day? Hell, how have you spent the last few days, aside from the obvious?* Paul gestured to Cal's mutilated left thumb.

"I'd rather not talk about it." Cal thought of something warm and gentle that he wished to hide from Paul, and then he despaired over having allowed the memory to surface. No thought was safe in Paul's presence.

What have we here? Paul leaned forward, nostrils flaring. He pressed a finger to Cal's temple and it sank in up to the first knuckle.

The sensation was not unpleasant, a distant, cold tingling that pulsed through his mind. Paul did not need to do this, Cal knew. He had complete access to his mind however and whenever he desired. Paul simply loved theatrics.

Callie, he said gently. *You've been holding out on me.*

THE PREVIOUS day, he had been startled awake by pounding on the cell's door.

"What?" he called.

There was a brief silence, followed by a distant buzz and the mechanical sound of the door's bolts moving. In a moment a guard was silhouetted before him, looking suspiciously at the cell. Then he was gone. Dr. Thurman entered slowly, with an air of willful detachment. He ventured a smile and Cal did as well.

"As usual, we'll be recording," said Dr. Thurman. He showed Cal the small digital recorder, then returned it to his breast pocket.

"One last before the end?" said Cal. He sat up on his bunk. He was only a little surprised to see Dr. Thurman in his cell. Most of their meetings had taken place in the dayroom adjacent to death row. A visitor in his old cell would have been highly unusual. A visitor in his current cell would have been unthinkable were it not for the strange autonomy Dr. Thurman had been granted. He had explained to Cal three years ago that he was there collecting research on the emotional well-being of death row inmates, to eventually aid in certain discussions that would be taking place in the legislature.

"Only if you're willing."

"I don't have much to say."

Dr. Thurman waited.

"I try not to think about it. Let my mind rest on other things. I've been projecting scenarios for years. Nothing new. It will be whatever it will be."

"So you're accepting fate?"

"I thought we were past the fatalism discussion."

Dr. Thurman smiled. "I mean that, in this moment, you're in a state of acceptance. Is that peaceful?"

Cal thought for a moment before answering. "No. It really doesn't have a quality. Not peaceful, not troubling. It's just a feeling of absence. Like there's something missing in me that was there before."

"Can you provide a name for that something, Cal?"

"I don't know. And that's not an evasion. Humanity, I guess. Like something fundamental to my humanity is gone. But this is different. In a way, it's like I've already died."

"Is this what you think I want to hear? The sort of thing the state's opponents are after?"

"You know I don't care about that. This–" Cal stopped and looked at his knees, chewing the insides of his cheeks.

"This . . ." said Dr. Thurman, gesturing for him to continue.

"This is tiresome. This is becoming tiresome."

Cal lay back on his bed and for a while they were at a stalemate. He believed that ultimately these sessions were valueless, that his situation must be irrelevant to Thurman's professed research interest. He never had anything interesting to say and always suspected Dr. Thurman of being dissatisfied with him. This was particularly irksome as there were things about the man–a pastoral manner of speech, an air of private intelligence–that reminded Cal of his father. (Paul never failed to exploit this: *See how cautious he is? How he always seems to be struggling to hold the world at arm's distance? He only does this with you. Only you. Just like good ol' Pops. Keeping Johnny close but never too close. He knew what his boy was from the beginning. Turned his God-fearing guts to touch you!*) But the similarities in manner only highlighted other differences. His father was tall and thin, whereas Dr. Thurman was a short, sturdy mesomorph. His father had rich, dark hair; Dr. Thurman was bald. They both wore glasses, but his father's were cheap, thick, plastic, whereas Dr. Thurman's were rimless, round, and clearly expensive.

The most profound difference was in their self-regard. Thurman possessed a sort of quiet pride, a consciously unself-conscious dignity. Cal's father was simply humble, and since his son's conviction forced him to resign his pastorate, simply humiliated. In the beginning, Dr. Thurman had shown great interest in Cal's relationship with his father the pastor and in Cal's religious beliefs in general; particularly, they had long discussions about the personal implications of his Reformed theology—his confident despair over his own foreordination. Cal knew it was somehow significant to him by how willfully nonchalant he seemed in his inquiries. But in time the questions had stopped.

"Would you like to go to the yard for a few minutes?"

"How is that possible? I was told—"

"I'm given certain liberties here, as you well know. But we haven't much time. Come."

They passed out of the cell and down a length of hall, past the execution chamber itself, the guards a few paces behind them, and began working their way through the compressed maze that was Unit III. It was several minutes before they were outside.

It was a pristine, crisp November day. The sky could not have been more perfect, for the stark relief between the blue void and the sparse dappled clouds. For once the sight of contrast in nature did not bring to Cal's mind the chiaroscuro of the self, that liminal emptiness between the free, true, and ideal self that exists exclusively before God—an idea he had lifted from a prison-worn copy of *Kierkegaard: Selected Writings*—and the bleak and sullied terror that was the actual. He ignored the dried brown grass of the yard, the empty basketball court, the unused free weights, the empty aluminum bleacher, the blunt ochre of the prison walls, and in that confined and vacated space, looking up, only up, he felt weightless and free.

"Thank you for beauty," he said quietly after several minutes.

"Yes?" said Dr. Thurman, seeming startled.

"Nothing," said Cal. "Let's go back inside."

Paul removed his finger from Cal's head and began caressing his hair. The skin of Paul's face began to ripple. In a moment Cal was looking into the bespectacled eyes of his father, feeling the man's warm, rough hand resting on his brow.

Ander Cavanaugh wore a ragged woolen sweater. The threads were worn at the cuffs and neck, and a coffee stain darkened the lower fringe. The pastel stripes had faded like sidewalk chalkings after a light rain. A birthday gift from Cal, it had been hideous, but Cal knew that it was his favorite. Cal had picked it out himself (with the help of his mother); he had been eight years old. The sight of it brought a rush of memories to Cal and a tightening in his chest.

Paul did not do this often. Cal knew it for what it was, an exquisite torture, a small piece of wonder to enhance the horror of everything else Paul did, yet he could never resist seeing and touching the man who, unlike his mother, had not once visited or written since his confession. He knew the pain of his abandonment would be even greater once the illusion was over. But he did not care.

"Dad," Cal whispered. His eyes filled with tears.

His father smiled down at him, the skin creasing near his sagacious eyes.

John. Johnny, said his father. *How I've missed you.*

The guards had no trouble looking him in the eye as they escorted him to his death. This surprised him and he wondered whether he would do the same in their shoes. Perhaps not the first time or the first few times, but later, when the act had become a commonplace in his life. Maybe eyes told much on days like this. What did his eyes tell? He could, it turned out, discern nothing in the eyes of the guards. He hoped there was something in his eyes, something to tell them that he was more than his circumstances let on.

They led him down the short corridor. The prison superintendent stood outside the death chamber, his face white and empty. Cal could hear a hum of subdued conversation down the hall from what must be the viewing room. Earlier that evening he had been provided a large dose of Valium and now felt quite warm. The air was heavy and he felt as if he were gliding across the polished concrete floor.

The death chamber was an irregular hexagon, a curve-less semicircle with aseptic white walls and a gray tiled floor. A dark blue curtain obscured one of the walls. In the center of the opposite wall was a small window. Cords snaked through two portals beneath the window and curled at the head of a lime green gurney shaped like a fat crucifix. Two men and a woman stood near it, dressed in blue medical scrubs. Even clouded with Valium, Cal could see they held their arms rigidly, struggling to appear calm and patient.

Paul was waiting for him in the chamber, leaning against the far wall, one knee bent, his foot flat against the wall, a classic James Dean pose. He was sweating profusely and dressed in the regalia and armor of a Roman centurion. He looked like an actor taking a break on the wrong set. A burning cigarette dangled from his bottom lip. It was about half an hour to midnight and Cal hadn't seen him since midday. But *seen* wasn't quite right; he hadn't seen him, but he'd heard him. There had been no words, just an incessant dark laughter that filled the room for over an hour before abruptly ceasing.

As Cal entered, Paul flicked his cigarette at him. Cal tried to bat it out of the air, but was constricted by his chains. One of the execution operators flinched at his sudden movement. The others watched him silently.

Paul looked delighted.

Here we are at last, your big moment. I'm so proud of you, Johnny. Look at that poise, that proud stature. Meeting your fate with dignity. They must have doped you up something incredible!

Cal was startled to realize that he was standing quite erect, with his shoulders back and his chin out. But he did not feel proud or dignified. He felt little but the Valium.

The guards led him to the gurney and removed his chains. He lay down and they secured leather straps to his wrists, forearms, ankles, thighs, and chest. The female operator stood next to him, opening a sealed bag containing more IV lines, a deflated transparent balloon, and a strange cylindrical object. The woman was absurdly gorgeous, even in her baggy scrubs, and seemed as out of place in an execution chamber as a centurion. Cal received her beauty as a small mercy.

"What are those?" he asked. His voice sounded deeper than usual and distant.

The woman, whose badge identified her as Judith Bream, RPN, said, "Those are the catheter and anal plug."

Cal thought he must have looked confused or indignant because she continued, explaining matter-of-factly, "Upon death the bowels will sometimes void themselves. This is just a precaution."

Paul heehawed with laughter. His outrageously plumed helmet nearly fell off.

Well, shit, *Cal,* he said. *And you'd made it all this way through prison without getting sodomized! I guess what goes around* does *come around.*

One of the men came and hooked his fingers into the waistband of Cal's orange uniform and pulled his pants and briefs down to his knees. Judith put on a pair of latex gloves before squirting petroleum jelly onto the anal plug and rubbing it along its length. She turned to Cal and said, "You'll want to brace yourself."

Get ready for it, Callie! said Paul, yanking his sword from its scabbard. Extending from the round iron hilt, instead of a blade, was an enormous brown penis, mottled with pink spots. *Hira-cha!* Paul swung the absurd thing through the air.

Cal looked from Paul back to Judy. She lifted his scrotum, which, though shrunken by the coolness of the room, had been blocking the way. Cal inhaled sharply at her touch. With her other hand she rested the plug's tip against his anus and began slowly to push it in.

Paul brought his face right up to the action. *Oh, you like* that, *don't you? Mother Mary, look at that ragged asshole!* Paul, gaping, twirled his penis-sword over his head like a rally towel.

While they prepared the catheter, Paul sheathed his sword and walked behind the gurney and stood between Cal and the wall. *I understand you won't talk to me. No one wants to look crazy, right? Be that as it may, I have a dilemma. I want to write something here on the wall, but I haven't got a pen. So, if you would, please tell me how you took that fingernail off. It must be plain to a rather ingenious mind such as yours, but I just can't seem to do it.* Paul leaned forward, holding his hands above Cal's face, tugging at a fingernail. *It's no use!*

Cal felt a burning sensation as they fed the catheter into him. It hurt like pissing with a urinary tract infection.

Pulling is just no good, said Paul. *How else can it be done? Ah, I have it. Lift up, up and out! You tear it back!* Blood squirted from under Paul's fingernail and dripped onto Cal's face. *Yes! There it is!*

Paul started writing something on the wall with his mutilated finger. Cal struggled to watch. It was difficult, but he could just make out the words when Paul finished:

J.C.C.
King of the Pederasts

It's from the Red Letter Edition, said Paul. *Get it? Ha! The Greek might have been more fun.* Ioannis, ho Basileus ton Paiderasteon. *Something like that, anyway. It's been so long.*

Cal snorted and stared at Paul. His mood was shifting rapidly and he wondered if the Valium was wearing off. His heart beat faster and, after the male attendant pulled his pants back up, his sides and legs began to itch.

They wiped his arm with alcohol and kneaded his flesh to make a vein appear. Judith Bream inserted a needle and then fastened it with medical tape. She connected one of the lines protruding from the wall to the needle, and made a few adjustments.

Cal felt saline enter him. The coldness of it washed through his body, chasing away the remaining warmth of the Valium. He was then covered with a white sheet, and he could see nothing until the top was folded back against his chest.

Clothe me in white, Paul sang, his gauntleted arms uplifted, mocking a song Cal used to sing at his father's church, *so I won't be ashamed.*

"Fuck you," Cal mouthed.

Paul dropped his arms and stared at him in feigned abhorrence. *I'd wash that mouth with soap, young man, if it weren't about to be filled with maggots!*

The room seemed to have frosted over and the white sheet was a scrim of snow covering his body. Cal shivered. His mind darkened. So many emotions welled up inside that he could barely discern one from another. He pressed himself to focus, to pick out one from the mess. He thought that if he could isolate and name them he could remove them and return to placidity. A part of him wanted that, to drift into his fate calmly, without a trace of fear. A part of him wanted to die clinging to at least some private sense of dignity, to enter hell with stoic courage. But he deserved no dignity. What dignity had he left them? What small scrap of honor had he not torn away? No, this was right. He could feel the fear moving through him virally from cell to cell. He would die in fearful agony of his moral failure and of the coming judgment. This was how it was to be. Hell seeping up from the ground, the tongues of its flame licking and probing.

Jeez, Cal, said Paul. *Getting pretty grim, aren't we? Let's lighten the mood. I'd offer you a cigarette, but I don't think these fellows would approve. How about a joke then? Three men walk into a bar. 'Ouch!' they say, all at once. No, but seriously, three men walk into a bar: a priest, Michael Jackson, and a high school art teacher. 'What can I get you gentlemen?' says the bartender. 'Two tall-boys for us,' say Michael and the priest. (Get it, tall-*boys*?) *'What about you, sir?' the bartender asks the art teacher. He says,*

'I'll have two prepubescent girls in an abandoned shack off State Road Twenty-Seven! On the rocks!'

Just then the superintendent entered the chamber, carrying a clipboard. He was dressed in a blue suit and sported a red herringbone tie. He questioned the three operators and Judith Bream said that they were ready to begin.

What a fox! Paul said. He strode across the room and began looking her over. *It's not too late, Cal. Just ask her. She'll do it. Never mind the catheter. She'll manage. A real pro, this Judy. I can tell.*

Cal's shivering became more vigorous and the sheet rippled on top of him. He caught Judith's attention with his movement and she looked at him with what seemed to be despair and sympathy. She came to his side and smoothed some hair from his forehead. "It'll be over soon," she said. "I promise." She let her hand rest on his head.

How endearing! Paul smiled brightly and took off his helmet. *Go ahead, now's your chance. Just say it. Ask her for just one more touch.* He moved next to Cal, opposite Judith, and began rubbing the feathered plumes of his helmet against the sheet, just above Cal's crotch. *Look at her hands. God they must be soft!*

Paul produced a folded piece of paper from his girdle. *I've composed a little poem to celebrate the occasion,* he said. He tapped a leather thong against the floor, fidgeting like an amateur writer at an open-mic night. *Forgive me if it's a little stilted. Unlike you,* I *am not an* artiste. *Here goes:*

Hell's Cocktail Waitress

Oh Lord, that lush minx Judy Bream
The naughtiest piece that you've seen
She's firm and she's tight
And she can pour all night
The fuel for a young pervert's dreams
Come now, Cal, and tell me I'm crass

You know I'm a moral morass
But I'd be ly'n
If you're not cry'n
For sight of her tits and her ass

You lust to get naked and wrestle
To pitch your woo, cream in her vessel
Just like any fool
you pull up a stool

Paul giggled and glanced up from his paper. *Get it? Stool?* Paul shot his hand forward and pinched Cal's ass. Cal's body jerked under the sheet. Judy snatched her hand away from him and stepped back. Paul smiled and puckered his lips before continuing.

you pull up a stool
And beg her to serve something special

You flatter with words, so charming and gentle
Beguiler and smiler, sweet and sentimental
Ignoring your banter
She lifts the decanter
To measure the sodium thiopental

A twist of lemon and a hint of lime hide
The bitterness of pancuronium bromide
"Here's to Belial,"
She says with a smile
And tops you with potassium chloride

Finished, Paul rounded the gurney and bent over next to Judith. He ran his nose up her thigh, sniffing loudly, and buried it between her ass cheeks. He moaned dramatically, looked upward with a glowing face and said in Cal's own voice, *Thank you for beauty!*

Cal felt tears coming. He shut his eyes.

Really, Cal? You're crying? The poem wasn't that *moving. In fact, I think I rather muddled it. Tricky little bastards, those limericks. But I appreciate your sentiment nonetheless.*

The curtain was open now. Cal had lost track of the proceedings. The superintendent was reading the death warrant. Cal lifted his head and began scanning the witnesses in the viewing room. They were difficult to see because the viewing room lights were dim and the death chamber fluorescents reflected in the window. He had held out some hope that his mother might be there, even though she hadn't visited or called in over a year. There was no chance of his father coming, but he thought if she were there, if he could just glimpse her smile, he might die knowing he was still loved.

She had not come.

There he is, Cal baby, said Paul, pointing to Norman McKaskell.

"John Cavanaugh," said the superintendent. "Do you have anything you would like to say before the drugs are administered?"

Cal strained to look through the window at McKaskell. He sought his eyes, but he couldn't quite make them for the glare.

"I know that nothing I say or do can make any difference," he said. "I know there is no forgiveness for me. Your daughters—" Cal let his head fall back and closed his eyes. "I'm sorry."

You think anything you say will mean anything to that man? said Paul. *His wife committed suicide because of what you did. You took everything there was to take. He only wants the satisfaction of watching you die, but even that will mean nothing. Why speak at all?*

It was happening. Cal heard voices in the room behind him along with the sound of a machine clicking. He felt movement in the saline line. Fear thundered in his mind and blackened every nerve in his system. He moved his lips quietly. He was trying to say the Lord's Prayer. He did not understand why. For some reason he could not get the words out, could manage only a choked whisper. "God, God, my God."

His mother stood over him now, his mother as he remembered her when they would go to the city park when he was a little boy and watch the geese swim with their trains of goslings. She was smiling adoringly.

She said, *Oh my silly caboose, there is no God.*

HE HAD his rosary. He sat in his closet, his knees pressed to his chest, running his fingers in the darkness over each wooden bead. It had been given to him, just over two years ago on his tenth birthday, by his maternal grandmother, Carla, a dreamy, walleyed woman who had never reconciled to the beliefs of her Protestant son-in-law. She had tried to teach Cal the prayers—in spite of the mild consternation of Cal's mother—but they never took. Perhaps he had been too young to value Marys and Mysteries, too young to hold it all in his mind. So he had personalized the ritual. Each bead was a sin. He would sit in the darkness of his own confessional and turn the rosary until he had named fifty-nine transgressions. Sometimes this was easy. Sometimes he had to rename sins he had already confessed on other days to fill the space. When he came to the large beads which divided each decade ("The 'Our Father' beads," his grandmother had called them) he often felt it necessary to offer a larger confession, rid himself of a heavier burden. His father had assured him that God made no distinctions between venial and mortal sins, that if the law was broken at one point it was broken at all points, and he believed his father. However, it was always mortal sin he thought of when he touched an Our Father bead. He had a vague understanding of the distinction and was confident he had not committed one, though perhaps he had come close. Now, as he neared the end of his confessional cycle, he thought of the major event of the day—he often did this, saved important sins for last, built an order of severity—the sin that had left the seeds for so many smaller sins in its wake. He had gone to the pool at the civic center with his mother, his two cousins, Mattie and Anthony, and their mother, his Aunt Sarah. As was often the case because of age differences (Mattie was ten, two years younger than Cal, and Anthony was six), he and Mattie had gone off on their own. They were playing roughly, dunking and splashing each other, which was how they usually played because Mattie was nearly Cal's height and an exuberant tomboy, until she suggested that they team-up and chicken-fight someone. Cal had agreed, even though there hadn't been anyone around to fight. He squatted in the water while she climbed over him and sat on his shoulders. He remembered clearly how slippery her legs were and how startled he was to find that they were covered in tiny, almost invisible hairs. She had wriggled a lot and seemed uncomfortable; he remembered feeling her make adjustments to the bathing suit where it wrapped under her. The sensation had brought with it the sudden awareness that she was a girl and that he was a boy and that their bodies were very close. Distracted and excited, he had lost his balance. As they fell together, she brushed against his erection, and, in her surprise, her hand shot through the water, right to it. Her expression went from startled to curious. "Dare you to do it again," Cal said. She did. The thrill was enhanced by his terror that she would tell his Aunt Sarah, that his mother would find out and have a talk with him about the thing in his pants. But nothing of the sort happened. They merely froze for a few moments and then drifted apart, each feeling, Cal had thought, conspiratorial. This was not a mortal sin, Cal was sure. But it touched on one. While it frightened him, what frightened him more was that he could not stop revisiting, even relishing, the experience. He saw then the disparity of sin, of a hated thing that was also a cherished thing, and he felt he did not know his own mind.

Finished with his prayers, he sat forward on his knees, held before him the rosary's crucifix, and kissed it. Warm light spilled from under the door and for a time he allowed his eyes to drink it in. He stood and opened the closet door, intending to find his bed and snuff the light, to go to sleep.

But there was no bed, no lamp on its stand, no room at all. There was nothing save for the terror of looking upon a vast, black emptiness.

Then things changed.

The air was unnaturally cold and he could feel dirt beneath his bare feet. He called out ("Hello?!") into the darkness and was answered by a distant multitude of sounds, the cries of things dying and the howls of the things killing them. There was a breeze and he heard tree limbs swaying and scratching against one another. His eyes were adjusting to the dark and he saw that he was in an immense, moonlit forest. The breeze stopped all of a sudden and yet the movement of the gnarled trees did not. It was as if they were animate and wanted only to fill the world with their creaking. He imagined all the terrible things such a forest might hold for a twelve-year-old boy: pitfalls, wolves and leopards, drifters, dark men with darker tastes; other things, nameless things.

In the distance a run-down shack was visible through the trees. He heard voices whispering in the blackness beyond its open door. The sound of the trees grew louder, their branches gesticulating like the legs of spiders, silhouetted against the moon. The twitching branches began to reach for him as the whispering consolidated into a single sibilant voice: *I see you!*

Cal choked down a scream, turned heel, and fled back into the closet.

His mind shook with confusion. He had evaded something, but what? He had just been somewhere that was not his room, not his world, that's what his emotions, his slamming heart, told him. But no, he was in his closet, huddled in the corner, his knees to his chest, the rosary wrapped about his hands, his toes digging against the itchy carpet, seeking his daily absolution. Why did he feel so strange, so uprooted? Had he been hallucinating in the darkness? He was sixteen years old, rapidly approaching adulthood, too old for such nonsense, too old to fear the dark. He forced his mind to return to the confession, to a posture of contrition. He began to work his way from bead to bead, straining to remember the day's misdeeds. It had been a mild day—crude jokes at school, an awkward brush against a cute girl that wasn't exactly unintended, anger at his mother when she was late to pick him up, other sins, absentminded and quotidian—until that night, after his parents had gone to bed and he was left alone to fiddle with the computer. The glowing humming thing sat there every day, beckoning like the open gate of an amusement park. "Come inside and take a ride!" it seemed to say. "If you're nervous, just watch others do it!" It was becoming irresistible. Tonight he had strayed from the familiar stables of airbrushed T-and-A and ventured into the darker, seedier hovels of the Internet. He hadn't gone too far, no, just extended a leg over the edge and toed the murky waters: images of women tied and gagged, suspended by chains, even flagellated. It was shamefully thrilling. He had felt powerful. He could tell that the water ran deep there, fathoms deep. He'd felt an urge to go further, but the urge had been fleeting. It was an accident, really, an exceptional trespass, and had he not felt a strange heaviness all the while, something bearing down on him? That sensation alone was deterrent enough. This would not happen again.

When it inevitably did happen again, over and over, Cal felt the heat of shame cooling. He knew something was changing inside of him. He was "searing his conscience," as his father would put it, threading scar tissue through that delicate organ. A part of him mourned the loss of innocence. But a more assertive part mourned the loss of shame that had become so pivotal to his rites of self-pleasure. The hotter the shame burned, the harder he came. And the harder he came, the more fervent his self-recrimination. That ebb and flow of sin and repentance offered its own pleasure. So he found himself chasing ever more shameful content, anything that might awaken fire in his nerves.

He was in the closet again, a year and a half later, hunched over his Bible, searching frantically for a passage in Romans. The pages seemed to burn his come-damp fingers. "Why can't I stop, Lord?" he said, eyes brimming with tears. He had managed to string together two porn-free months before tonight, but that was all over now. "I hate this. Why do I keep going back?" He held the Bible nearer the light coming in under the door and read aloud, "I do not understand my own actions. For I do not do what I want, but I do the very thing I hate."

Tonight, the very thing he hated was a video titled "Barely legal teen throated unconscious." Cal had watched similar fare before, but he would always pull back at the end, switch videos and finish himself to something less dehumanizing. If he didn't come to it, he reasoned, it didn't define his sexuality. But the sight of the girl's oxygen-starved body going limp had undone him. He imagined that it was his member swelling her throat. Then, in his post-climax lucidity, he discovered something that made him retch. While conscious, the girl had looked as young as the girls in his 11th grade class. But now, her face slack, she looked much younger. He paused the video and zoomed in on the tattoo circling her forearm like a bracelet. It read in cursive: "R.I.P. Percy ~ 3/2/1994 - 9/21/2008 ~ Forever my Hero, my Big Brother." The video had been up for two years. He did the math: She couldn't have been older than fourteen when it was shot.

The feeling of damnation that swept over him was so great that he had fled to his prayer closet without even bothering to clean himself. Now he was reading Romans 7 over and over, trying to calm his racing mind. "Never again," he said.

Then, a voice like the sizzle of roasting meat whispered in his ear, *We're just getting started, love.* He jerked in surprise and then dismissed the voice as an epiphenomenon of his self-loathing. He dug his knuckles into the carpet, clenching the rosary. Where was God? he thought. Where was His grace? How—

His ruminating ceased abruptly. The closet was typically stuffy, but when had it ever been this hot? He moved away from the wall, which had begun to burn his back, and stood in the middle of the closet. Smoke was leaking from under the door. He pressed his hands to it and felt it bowing toward him. He tried the knob but it was searing hot and he could not hold on long enough to twist it. He realized that the house must be on fire, that his parents were still sleeping and in danger, and he quickly pulled a shirt from a hanger and wrapped it around his hand. The smoke stung his eyes as he flung open the door and lurched into his room.

It was now much larger than his childhood bedroom, and the off-white walls were covered in vintage posters of foreign horror films. Dario Argento. Jean Rollins. Jesus Franco. These names were suddenly familiar. He had begun watching their films obsessively a couple of years back when he was a freshman in college. College? he thought. No, I'm seventeen, I don't even like horror, it turns my stomach, I . . . something's burning, somewhere something is burning. But he wasn't seventeen, he could see that now. He was twenty-one, standing in the bedroom of his off-campus apartment, scratching his shaggy head. It was the start of Christmas break and he'd not yet left for home.

He was waiting for someone.

He heard the sound of ice filling a glass in the kitchen. A few moments later the door of his room opened, and Valery trudged in, seeming to wade through something viscous and unseen. She sat on Cal's twin bed, which creaked under her bulk, put her ice water on the nightstand, and lit a cigarette. She took a drag and gazed at him, spreading her lips in a wanton smile.

Cal was attracted to her in a way he couldn't quite parse. She was several years older than him and had a pretty face, but this only exaggerated her corpulence, her sallow cave-dweller's skin.

She revolted him, certainly, but that revulsion itself inspired a brutal lust. He had met her in an online forum. They were both seeking an outlet to satisfy certain curiosities. They had been meeting for about a month.

"What's that?" she asked, looking at Cal's right hand.

He realized that he was clutching his rosary and for one blinding instant the thing seemed to sink like molten metal into his flesh. He quickly shoved it into the pocket of his jeans.

"Let me see," she said.

He felt outside of himself. A voice rang in his mind, a voice similar to his own, yet foreign, as if someone had fashioned from the substratum of his thought an idea that could never have originated within him. It said, *Yes, let her see it. Shove it into her mouth.*

In the end he didn't know why he obeyed. Maybe he didn't do so consciously. He had often felt at certain moments throughout his life that he was acting out a script written for someone else, that his thoughts and actions were proceeding from some other consciousness, that there was a course, a set of rails, on which he rolled inexorably forward. He did not feel that he was being coerced; rather, some other mind seemed to stand before him, blending its desires unrecognizably into his own volition.

Valery grunted painfully through teeth gnashing against his grandmother's rosary, her body quivering beneath him. She managed to cry through her gag, "Again!" and he obliged, striking her naked, vinegar scented flab, feeling her jerk and tighten and then go loose, the spark flooding in and out of her muscles.

Finished, he could not look at her. He felt himself growing hollow inside. He was overcome by a sudden glimpse of the pale shuffling thing his soul was becoming. He rolled off the bed and then slid underneath, hiding himself in the dust and darkness, holding the saliva-wet rosary in his hands, shivering in disgust.

THE MEMORIES unfurled, haunting and obliterating, the leering ghosts of dead sins, an endless cavalcade of corruption. Each scene increased his desolation, nibbled away at the substance of his faith, leaving it nearer and nearer to an empty form. Sometimes he could displace himself, retain enough lucidity to watch the proceedings as a film, a sort of waking dream. But when he did so he could feel another horror burning against his back: a sheer drop, a black void across whose infinite expanse he sensed the writhing of other souls. Mostly he gave himself to the memories.

It was the end of the school day and he was entering grades into the computer when Valery messaged him.

"Ever hear of sex magick?" she said. "It's weird but I like it. Feels crazy taboo. Anyway, I know these people who want to try it out together. As a group."

"I'm imagining *The Craft* as a porno now," he responded. "Thanks."

"Light as a feather, stiff as a [eggplant emoji]."

"Careful. You might lose all your hair."

"Seriously though," she wrote. "Come with me tomorrow night. I don't want to go alone."

"Let me think about it. Occult shit makes me nervous."

"If you don't come, you won't meet my friend Kate. And that would be a tragedy. You'd never get over it. Just look at her."

A nude image of Valery's friend appeared on the screen. He enlarged it and felt himself stiffening.

"Mister Cavanaugh?"

He jumped up from his chair, nearly dropping his phone. He hadn't heard the door to the art room open. One of his students stood a few paces into the room, surely too far away to see what was on the screen. Still, he pocketed the phone in embarrassment.

"Sorry, Tim," said Cal. "I'd completely forgotten it was Thursday. Go set up while I finish with these grades."

Cal powered down his computer and joined Timothy as the boy removed the wet paper towels covering his sculpture to keep the clay moist. The figure was of a hydra. Timothy lay out a set of sculpting tools and sprayed the hydra with a water bottle. "What do the judges tend to like?" he asked.

"This is only my third year teaching in this district. Well, in any district. But the first place in sculpture the last couple of years went to *clever* projects."

"Clever?"

"Good enough in terms of technique, but with a clear meaning," said Cal, resisting the temptation to answer the phone buzzing in his pocket. "Too clear, in my opinion. I distrust art that wants to teach me something."

"So it might help if I have a message in mind while I'm working."

"It might. It also might make your work mediocre."

"I have no idea what my message is," said Timothy.

"I think that's a good thing. But thinking it through can also be a good thing. What made you want to sculpt a hydra?"

"I've always loved Greek mythology. Especially the Twelve Labors of Hercules."

"What about the stories moves you?"

"Well, I think about how I'd feel if I was forced to kill my family and then given all these quests to make up for it. I think I'd hope I'd fail. That one of the quests would finally finish me off."

Cal worked alongside Timothy for an hour, sketching concepts for a self-portrait he intended to paint, before he packed up his bag and led him out of the building. Timothy's mother was idling at the curb in a Volvo SUV, his little sisters, twins, sitting in the backseat. Mrs. McKaskell waved at Cal and he waved back. As she drove away, Cal pulled out his phone and messaged Valery, "I'm in."

CAL WALKED with Valery up the front steps of the house, a craftsman set well back from the canopied street. In the four years he had known her, Valery had lost ninety pounds and undergone at least three cosmetic surgeries. He enjoyed her new body, which he had watched slowly take shape, but a part of him missed indulging in the sheer physical nastiness of her former self.

The door opened to reveal a curvaceous woman in a silk nightgown. He recognized Kate from the photo. "Welcome," she said, and pulled them each in for a kiss.

The living room was decked out in New Age paraphernalia, some tasteful, some trite. But his attention was immediately seized by the raven-haired woman who sat on the sofa, flipping through a *Mother Jones* magazine. He thought she might be the most beautiful woman he had seen in the flesh.

"Tatiana, this is Valery and Cal," said Kate.

"A pleasure," said Tatiana, rising from the sofa. Her dark eyes lingered on Cal's.

Kate's partner, Paolo, entered, carrying cocktails.

"I thought we're supposed to keep our bodies clean for the ritual?" said Valery.

"We've never done this with so many new people," said Kate. "We figured alcohol will make things easier as we, um, get acquainted."

Three more people arrived and soon they were all sitting naked, bathed in candlelight, in a circle on the floor.

"Sex magick works best when all our wills are directed toward the same object," said Paolo. "Tonight our goal is to access our soul bodies, the highest plane of our existence, the most energetic. The part of us that is God. Our goal is to see clearly the divine in ourselves."

Kate began passing out tarot cards to everyone, leaving them face down on the carpet. They all turned over their cards together. Cal's was The Devil: a crude baphomet seated on a throne, attended by a boy and a girl, chained together at the neck.

"Study the image on your card," said Kate. "Hold it in your mind. Tonight, your soul body has a special connection to your card. The image, whatever it means to you, will lead you to see more clearly what is divine in you. When you climax, when we all climax together, visualize your card and what it represents."

They began to have sex, swapping partners every few minutes. As the agreed-upon time approached, Cal found himself with Tatiana. "I was hoping we'd get to finish together," she said, as he penetrated her for the second time that evening. "I want to feel you come inside me."

Once everyone signaled that they were at the brink, Kate exclaimed, "See your soul! Behold!"

Cal didn't let himself come until he felt Tatiana contract around him. Her body shook as she added her throaty cries to the climactic clamor. Cal stared down at the tarot card lying face up next to him. The baphomet returned his gaze with dull goat eyes the color of feces.

HE WAS sitting at his desk the next night, drawing a self-portrait in charcoal: naked and satyr-legged in the same position as the Devil from the tarot card. For the two human figures standing before the throne, he used older versions of the McKaskell twins. As he filled in the shadows, the sound of charcoal to page transmuted into a dark, scuffing voice.

Lovely work, Johnnie Boy. How about you give him a nice big juicy cock to match those hooves.

The voice grew louder at the end and Cal realized it was not merely in his head, but that someone was in the apartment with him. He spun on his stool.

The voice spoke from behind him, right next to his ear.

Settle down, sweetness.

Cal jumped off the stool and turned. But he saw no one. A high laughter filled the room.

"Who's there?" he said, afraid he was losing his mind.

An old friend.

He searched the bedroom and bathroom, to no avail. "Show yourself," he demanded.

I'm right here.

Cal turned to see a slender man sitting on the stool by his desk.

"Who are you?" he said. "Why do you look like me? Am I hallucinating?"

You're welcome to believe so, if you'd like. But that'll make things less fun.

"Fun?"

I've been watching you for a long time. You've been a sheep without a shepherd. So much wandering. So much fumbling. I've offered the occasional whisper, of course, the occasional nudge in the right direction. But now, at last, you have ears to see and eyes to hear.

"What are you?"

I'm your shepherd. Stick with me, kid, and I'll keep you on the straight and narrow. We're going to make such beautiful messes together.

He lost himself in the torrent of memories. Some were nightmarish, others titillating. Often they were both. Always they moved with a rapidity that kept him from preserving a continuity of self, kept him from standing apart from the phantasmagoria. One moment he and Valery were in his apartment, piercing each other with needles through their cheeks, ear lobes, under their fingernails. The next moment he would find himself bound on his stomach to a slanted table, his mouth held open by a metal dental retractor as anonymous men and women took turns spitting into a funnel meant for his throat. Sometimes the memories were not memories at all, but nightmares or panic dreams woven into the unfurling tapestry. The memories flowed chronologically, until suddenly their sequence was shattered by illogic. He would be gazing up at an unknown woman as she rode him, her eyes wild behind a black leather mask, blood gumming the zipper that hid her lips. Then he would find himself alone, months earlier, weeping at the bathroom sink, unable to look at the mirror without being confronted by his own face oscillating in a featureless blur.

As the memories raged on, Paul appeared more and more as a bold physical entity, manifesting myriad appalling forms, urging sin at every opportunity. Through all his rendezvous with other lost souls he found drifting through cyber wastelands; through all the tentative approaches in underground bars and the subsequent self-reproaches in the small hours of the morning; through every foul experience in or behind highway rest stops; through all the periods of dissatisfaction when he had attempted *normal* relationships; through every reunion with Valery where they chased each other through empty mazes of sexualized suffering; all his searching through his heart, through many books, for a resonate meaning to a life that no longer felt his own; through everything there had been Paul, always Paul, the echo of his high laughing voice earning the name Cal had given him, mocking in all the authority of his unholy apostolate: *I do not do the good I want, but the evil I do not want is what I keep on doing! Wretched man that I am! Who will deliver me from this body of death? No one, no one, no one. It's sin, Cal baby, alive in the flesh. Alive and wriggling!*

He was wandering through a night club for bondage fetishists, drinking, trading provocations with women. He paused to watch a performance of naked rope bunnies being trussed up and suspended in aesthetic poses. A tall woman with narrow-set eyes and a sly smile approached him and ran a finger down his chest, hooking his waistband, and pulled him willingly from the stage. Once she had him away from the crowd, she placed a dog-collar around his neck and began to pull him along behind her with a chain. She led him down a winding flight of stairs, filled with carousers, and into a deeper, more sexually explicit, level of the club.

Strange artwork hung from the ceiling, living people wrapped in wire. A fog machine filled the room with a gray mist, illuminated by lights pulsing in time with the industrial music. The people down there were stranger. Obese men and women, amputees, transsexuals, and people with monstrous deformities.

The woman leading him through the horde seemed to grow taller, thinner. Soon her clothes were ripping, falling off in tatters, as her spine stretched and stretched, vertebrae jutting like the serrated edge of a knife. A naked towering creature, it cast a wanton glance over its shoulder, and he saw that it was Paul. The strange people began petting Cal as he passed. One of them was his grandmother.

Paul led him into a hallway filled with more groping people. Doorways opened at each side onto horrifying tableaux: humans sensually mutilated on tables; bodies writhing in orgiastic tangles, skin fused to skin as if by crazy glue; enormous fleshy demons reclining on sofas, drinking from IV lines that dangled from the veins of men and women fastened to the ceiling in cages.

He was brought to a room at the far end of the hallway, where Paul pushed him against the wall. His grandmother followed them in, her fat, wrinkled skin bound in leather fetish gear. She shackled his wrists and ankles with chains.

"Grandma?"

She smiled at him and pinched his cheek.

"What are you doing?"

She kissed Paul obscenely and walked across the room to where a large crank rose from the floor. An assortment of torture instruments hung on the wall behind her. She began turning the crank and the chains tightened, spreading Cal's arms and legs. He cried out as his joints began to give. Paul clasped his hands together with glee.

When Cal looked back to his grandmother, her head had grown and her lower jaw was so distended that it hung halfway to the floor. Her eyes were black, seeping tar, which also gurgled from her mouth.

The chains tightened, pulling Cal's shoulders and hips out of socket and lengthening his limbs. Paul vanished.

His grandmother locked the crank in place, walked to the door, and grunted. Cal's mother and father entered.

"Mom, Dad," he said. "Please help me."

"You hear that, Trace?" said his father. "He wants us to help him."

"Help him?" his mother said. "Help him?"

"Please. I'm so scared. I don't understand what's happening to me. Please, help me."

"Please! Please!" his father said.

"It never ends with these millennial brats," said his mother. "You give and you give and you give and they take and they take and they take."

"You didn't come," said Cal. "Why didn't you come? You let me die alone."

"You're unworthy," said his father.

"Don't you know what happened to us after what you did?" said his mother. "Your poor father lost his pastorate. The church fell apart. No one would hire him. You took everything from us."

"We can't bear the shame," said his father.

"Those poor girls," said his mother. "That poor family. I should have smothered you in the crib."

"Why are you here?" asked Cal, weeping.

"We're here to tie up our loose ends," said his father.

His mother walked to the opposite wall and scrutinized the instruments.

"Grab something that'll make it quick," said his father. "I don't want to listen to him bitch."

She chose an ax from the wall and handed it to her husband. He unceremoniously hefted the ax and chopped off Cal's head, which tumbled to the floor with a thud.

Ander Cavanaugh picked up his son's head and carried it through a doorway at the back of the chamber. The adjoining room was dark and quiet. Paintings hung on the walls, their features indiscernible. He set Cal's head on a display pedestal as if it were a sculpture. Then he walked away, whistling.

Cal sputtered from bloody lips as the whistling faded.

Lights came on in the gallery, smarting his eyes. He became aware of the sound of people milling about and conversing. Classical music began to play.

He discovered that he was fully intact, bent forward with his chin resting on a gallery stand, and stood up straight. He touched his neck, his face, his body, and found himself clean and well-dressed.

He wandered through the gallery show, looking at various student projects. He found Timothy's and studied it, the familiar hydra. A dead Hercules now lay beneath one of the monster's feet, his lion skin half-torn from his body. The piece was called, *Wish Fulfillment.*

In an adjacent room, the awards were being announced. After the announcements, Cal entered the gathering room, where he learned that Timothy had won top prize for sculpting. He congratulated him, clapping a hand on his shoulder.

"I'm proud of you, Tim," he said. "Although I'm not surprised. It's very fine work."

"Thank you," said Timothy. "I was nervous. I thought that girl from Northridge was going to beat me."

They were joined by Timothy's parents, Norman and Susan McKaskell. Cal shook both of their hands as Timothy introduced them.

"We've heard such lovely things about you from Tim," said Susan. "Thanks for the time you've put in with him."

"It's been my pleasure," said Cal. "You'd be surprised how rare it is to have a student who's genuinely interested and talented. A breath of fresh air, really."

Timothy looked embarrassed. His twin sisters joined them, each holding a plastic cup.

"Girls, this is Mr. Cavanaugh, your brother's art teacher," said Norman. "These are our young'ns, Cal. Jessie and Kimmie."

Cal leaned forward, resting his hands on his knees, bringing his head nearer to their level. "It's a pleasure to meet you both."

"Nice to meet you," they said in unison.

He straightened up and saw Paul standing a few paces behind the McKaskell family. Paul flicked his tongue obscenely. Cal pulled out his phone and checked the time.

"You'll have to excuse me," he said. "I'm due to meet some friends."

"Or course," said Norman.

"It was lovely meeting you all."

"Likewise," said Susan. "Would you let us have you over for a home-cooked meal sometime soon? As a thank you for all you've done."

"Absolutely," said Cal. He smiled and made for the front door of the gallery, ignoring Paul, who continued to stare at him lasciviously.

Cal left through the glass double-doors. He was in the dark forest. The branches creaked and scratched in the breeze. He turned around, looking for the gallery, but he only saw more forest. The abandoned shack loomed in the distance and he began to walk toward it. Above him the tree limbs moved like spider legs, trailing strings of silk. One stuck to his elbow and he had to fight himself free.

The tree trunks were alive as well. Naiads and dryads living in the flesh of the trees were entwined with one another, copulating in a mess of bark and sap. Light poured from their eyes. He moved closer and peered down at them. Pornographic films were playing inside their heads, spilling flesh-colored light and sighs of pleasure into the night.

Cal walked on through the forest toward the shack. Soon he heard footsteps following him, stopping whenever he stopped. He quickened his pace and then spun around to see what was pursuing him. He glimpsed something fleshy and bony disappearing behind a tree, trailing a phallic tail.

All of the naiads and dryads were suddenly staring at him. He looked at them, horror-stricken. Tree limbs descended and attached silken strings to him, fixing him in place. He fought against his restraints as the creature approached. The naiads and dryads began to scream.

At the last moment, he tore free from the spider silk and ran to the shack, slamming the door behind him.

DELIRIOUS, HE found he was back in his apartment. It took him a few minutes to catch his breath. He went to the bathroom to splash water on his face.

"What are you doing?" Tatiana said, looking up from the sink in lingerie.

Cal took a step back. Dread still gummed his veins, although fascination and lust were beginning to replace it. He was appalled and provoked by the sharp beauty of her Slavic features.

"If you wanted to watch, you should have just said so. It's not my thing, but I'm flexible."

She dried her hands. She pulled a thick strand of spider silk from his hair and ate it, licking her fingers. She crossed the room and removed a coil of rough rope from a tote bag.

"Were you ever a Boy Scout?" she asked.

"No," he said. "My Dad was always suspicious of them. Said their outfits look like Hitler Youth uniforms.

"But you know how to tie knots?"

"Sure."

"I mean good knots," said Tatiana. "Knots I can't get out of on my own."

"This isn't my first rodeo."

"I hate that expression," she said. "Rodeos are barbaric. I should tie a rope around your balls just for good measure, see how hard *you* kick."

He soon had her hog-tied and gagged on his bed, fucking her brutally. Eyeliner streamed down her face, a rivulet of blood from her nose. "Make me ugly," she had said.

The wall above the head of the bed began to bubble outward. Paul's face, enormous, burst through the wood paneling and grinned down on Cal and Tatiana.

Cal was startled and pulled out of her until she grumbled. He stared at Paul while he brought himself off. He slumped against her, breathing heavily.

Feed her to me, said Paul. His lower jaw unhinged like a snake's as his head protruded farther from the wall. Saliva dripped onto the headboard.

He lifted Tatiana by the ropes and put her inside Paul's mouth. She screamed through the gag, her eyes wild. Paul began to chew. Soon the screaming stopped.

Sometime after the contest, he was sitting at the McKaskell family's dining room table, between Norman and Timothy, across from the twins. Dinner had just been served. Norman laid his hand open on the table, meaning for Cal to take it. The rest of the family held hands as well.

"We're a praying family, Cal," said Norman.

Cal took Norman's and Timothy's hands and bowed his head as Norman prayed a blessing over the food.

"I hope we didn't make you uncomfortable," said Susan, fixing plates for the girls.

"Uncomfortable?"

"The prayer. You seemed a bit uncomfortable."

"I'm just out of practice."

"When was the last time you were in church?" asked Norman.

"Christmas. I always go with my parents when I visit home. My father pastors a Presbyterian church."

"So you're still close with them?" asked Susan.

Timothy gave his mother a sharp glance.

"Not exactly," said Cal. "We love one another. But things have been a bit strained for a few years."

"I hear that's normal for kids in their twenties. How old are you, Cal?"

"Twenty-five."

"Well, if you're ever open to it, you're welcome to come to church with us," said Norman. "I know how easy it is to drift when you're young. It helps to have consistent ground to stand on."

"I'll keep that in mind." He took a few bites of pot roast and a sip of water. "This is very good, Susan. I so rarely get to have a home-cooked meal."

"Why, thank you."

"So, I'm curious. Where does Tim get his artistic talent from? Mom? Dad? Both?"

"I'm afraid that's all Susan. I couldn't draw a straight line if my life depended on it."

"Mom taught me acrylics and oils when I was younger," said Timothy. "She did those paintings in the living room."

"That's wonderful," said Cal.

"He's been such a quick learner," said Susan. "Sometimes I think the only reason the Lord blessed me with the talent and interest was so I could pass it on to Tim."

"How about these two?" he said, looking at the twins.

"We're beginning to get more serious about the arts," said Susan. "Aren't we, girls?"

The girls rolled their eyes.

"They're more interested in music and dance right now," said Timothy.

"What instruments do you play?"

"Clarinet," said Kimmie.

"Violin," said Jessie.

"They also play a little piano," said Norman. "Again, this is all Susan's doing. All I can do is balance a checkbook."

"What kind of accounting do you do?" said Cal. "CPA?"

"Forensic."

"Interesting."

"It sounds more interesting than it is," said Norman. "It's just consulting work, reconstructing lost financial records, making statistical best guesses. That sort of thing."

"You should see him in his little green visor," said Susan.

"You really wear a visor?"

"Only when Susan wears her nursing uniform," said Norman.

"Jesus," said Tim.

"No blasphemy at the table," said Susan.

Blasphemy? Did someone say blasphemy? It was Paul.

Cal went rigid and then forced himself to relax. Only he could hear Paul.

What a lovely little domestic scene. You should have invited me, Cal. Look at that spread. My mouth is already watering.

"Tim, you were saying earlier that you and Cal have been chatting about colleges," said Norman.

"He's been warning me against going to an arts-exclusive school. Like Savannah."

"I thought Savannah was a great school?" said Susan.

"Oh, it is," he said. "It's just that, in my opinion, going to a school like Savannah can narrow your career options if you don't want to teach. It's so hard to make a living selling your work."

That's not the only thing that's hard, said Paul. *How long have you been sportin' wood? It must be those giblets.*

"So what's your recommendation?" Norman asked.

"I think taking a non-arts major is a wiser move, and maybe doing visual arts as a minor or second major. There's always an opportunity to go back to grad school and get a Master of Fine Arts. That's something I keep considering for myself."

Paul was staring at the twins.

What else are you considering, Callie? Maybe a little ménage à tween*?*

"But what bigger schools have really strong arts programs?"

"Michigan. New York. Columbia. All of the Ivies. Most top academic schools have strong art programs. What's important, I think, is that some schools seem to be a better fit for double-majoring than others."

If I were a man in my prime I'd be aiming young, too. Clean as a whistle. Best of all, no chance of knocking them up.

Cal battled his disgust and frustration. Paul whispered in his ear, *Look at those slender necks. That supple flesh. Such fine, silken hair. Imagine it whispering against your skin. Imagine those tiny hands–*

Cal slid his chair back and stood up. "Would you mind pointing me toward your bathroom?" he asked.

"Down the hall, on the right," said Timothy.

In the bathroom, Cal splashed water on his face. Behind him, Paul stood naked in the shower, its plexiglass door translucent up to his chest. Two small human figures moved on each side of him. Paul threw his head back and moaned loudly. Cal wiped his face off with a hand towel and returned to the dining room.

Susan was setting out dessert.

"So, is there a Lady Cavanaugh on the horizon?" asked Norman.

Cal forced himself to laugh. "If there is, she's far enough away that I can't see her yet."

"All the more reason to come give our church a try. We have a really active singles ministry."

"*Dad*," said Timothy.

Norman raised his hands in surrender. A vein pulsed in his temple.

"I appreciate the sentiment," said Cal.

I bet you do. Go ahead. Ask him for the hook-up with one of these little ladies. They're quite single. These are humble religious folk, after all, they'll be game for an arranged marriage.

Paul walked around the table and began sniffing the McKaskells.

Are they Mormon? he said. *They smell Mormon. And don't worry about age. What's good for that goose-stepping Joseph Smith is good for the groveling gander. Hell, even that old camel-mounted Casanova Muhammed married a six-year-old!*

Cal tried to focus on his dessert, a brownie covered in ice cream, garnished with a cherry.

"What's the future hold?" asked Susan.

He looked up. Her head lolled to the side, a greenish pallor marring her face, her unseeing eyes filmed over with death. Dried vomit caked her mouth and chin.

And then the vision passed. She was asking, "Do you like Xavier Prep enough to stay here long-term?"

"Possibly," said Cal. "I had reservations at first. But this is my third year and it's growing on me."

"Reservations?"

"I always imagined myself in the northeast, or out west."

"Where out west? Norm's from Oregon, you know."

"LA or Seattle," said Cal. "Both have huge art scenes."

Paul was standing between the twins, holding a cherry between thumb and forefinger. He sized up both girls and licked his lips. Then he squeezed the cherry until it burst.

RETURNING HOME that night, Cal shut his door and leaned against it. He slapped his cheeks as if to wake himself up. The slaps became more and more violent. He couldn't tell whether he was fighting his arousal or revving it up.

He sat on the edge of his bed and masturbated. The objects of his room began to fade into darkness, but he hardly noticed. As he climaxed, silken threads descended from overhead, fastening to his elbows and hands. He wept.

"What is wrong with me?" he said.

More silken threads fell from above, attaching to his knees, shoulders, and head.

"What have I done?"

Exactly what you were bidden. You've given yourself to me.

The line affixed to Cal's head jerked upward. Other lines forced his arms out to the sides. He was yanked to his feet and made to look at the black sky. A giant Paul loomed over him, holding a marionette's control bar, to which the silken lines were attached. Paul's hand gesticulated like an enormous white spider working the threads of its web.

Dance, monkey! Dance!

Paul brayed laughter.

God, I love owning shit.

Cal wept as his body was forced to march in place, his right arm outstretched in a Nazi salute. "What are you doing to me?"

I'm frog-marching your pale ass to its destiny!

HE STOOD alone outside of the abandoned cabin, smoking to calm his nerves. Finished, he butted the cigarette and walked to his car. He removed from the trunk a box of garbage bags, clear plastic sheeting, a long knife, a hacksaw, rope, duct tape, a gas can, and bottles of bleach and ammonia and took them to the cabin.

He didn't need to drive far, but the trip seemed to take forever, like clicking up the track of a rollercoaster. He parked on the side of a back road and removed a cloth and a bottle of ether from the glove compartment. He unplugged the burner phone from its charger and turned it on.

He walked quietly through the sunlit woods until he reached a clearing. From the edge of the woods he watched the McKaskell twins playing in their large backyard. Susan sat near the house on the patio, reading a book. He dialed a number on the burner phone and the landline in the house began to ring. Susan rose from her chair and went inside the house. Cal stepped out of the woods. Even though a year had passed since he was in their home for dinner, the twins recognized him and smiled.

HE SHUT the car trunk carefully. Using the ether cloth, he wiped down the burner phone, broke it in half, and threw it into the woods. He had imagined he would feel that he was off the rollercoaster track by this point. Instead he found another track at the top of the first, waiting for him to begin his clicking ascent.

It was getting dark when Cal carried the wildly kicking twins into the cabin. He laid them in the middle of the floor, their hands and feet bound with zip ties, duct tape wrapped around their heads, sealing their mouths against screaming.

He finished one last cigarette outside the cabin and stood, fingers interlaced behind his head, and exhaled forcefully. He looked at the forest. The tops of the trees moved gently in the breeze. He could discern in the distance the sounds of cars moving along the highway. His anticipation was so overwhelming it seemed to drip like sweat from his pores.

He approached the shack slowly, forcing himself to savor each step. It was small and decrepit, the walls worn by the years to the same gray-brown as the barren earth on which it sat. It seemed one bad storm away from collapsing entirely. Standing at the door, he envisioned himself inside, moving over their bodies, losing himself in forbidden intimacy, filling up the void inside him, and sating the voice within the void that called out and seemed to lead him by the nose. He opened the door with a trembling hand and entered the shack.

The twins were beautiful, eleven years old and wrapped in white-blonde hair. Their four green shimmering eyes should have been staring up at him from the floor of the shack. But they weren't. The room was empty. There was no trace of them.

He stood dumbfounded, staring at the floor.

Laughter erupted from behind a door set into the back wall of the shack and he started violently. Door? There had been no second door. The shack only had one room. And yet the door opened on a stone staircase descending into unknown depths. Somewhere in the darkness below the girls were laughing at him. He pulled a small flashlight from his pocket and descended the stairs.

THE VOICES had seemed so near when he first started running. Now they led him deeper and deeper into a twilight of stone and mold, down a tunnel that descended far into the earth. An odor like decaying flesh and charcoal became more apparent the deeper he went, and he pulled his shirt up over his mouth and nose. The deeper he went the stranger the walls became. At first they were only streaked with blood, but then he saw bits of flesh caught between the stones. Farther on the flesh seemed to be growing on the stone itself. Soon the walls were covered entirely in quivering flesh. He felt like he was inside an intestine. Cal pressed onward past pulsing polyps embedded in the walls. The ground seemed slicked with feces.

He became disoriented. The beam of his flashlight fell spastically everywhere. One moment the voices would seem so close he thought he could smell the girls' skin and hear the soft whispering of their hair; the next moment their footfalls were so distant as to be indiscernible from his own.

Exhausted, but mesmerized, he feared the chase would go on forever.

Then he saw them.

They were running toward him now. Only that wasn't right, it seemed they weren't running at all. He could see only their heads floating on empty air. That is, at first. Cal stopped, steadying his flashlight, forcing himself to register what he was seeing. It was tall, bony and wraithlike, its neck long and drooping out and down below the line of the shoulders like the neck of a dragon, its twin heads screaming, the four eyes pursuing him with a sexual hunger. And then the thing was on all fours, a lizard with human flesh running to consume him. Its hydra neck was now completely bifurcated and Cal could see the notches of its spine winding down its naked back. In the crevice where the necks met hung obscene curtains of labia.

"This is eternity, Johnny!" the heads screamed in unison.

The voices twined like hot wires into his mind and echoed down the endless tunnel.

Cal clutched at his temples, crying out, his voice wasting into a rasp of sand. The flashlight fell and rolled away. He crumpled to the ground and crawled after it. When he seized hold of it, the bulb began to flicker on and off. He hit the flashlight hard against his palm. Everything went dark.

Then, on his hands and knees, he discovered that the ground was not stone but glass. Smooth glass, like the surface of a mirror.

He could feel the damned thing hanging over him now. A double blast of roasting sulfur washed over his head. He heard the chattering of teeth. Then the snake-like hiss of their voices, "Play with us, Callie. Aren't we still sexy?"

He smacked the flashlight against his hand again and the light flickered back on. The creature was bearing down on him, the girls' faces looming, their jaws monstrously distended.

Paul's face emerged from the vaginal fissure between their necks, birthed in a gush of veiny gore. He opened his mouth impossibly wide as it filled with row after row of shark teeth.

"Jesus," Cal sputtered. The word burned his mouth.

Not here.

"Not in Hell," said the twins.

"Jesus!" he said again, and the word was a gleaming coal on his tongue. But he forced himself to continue, each repetition producing the same effect, until his face was a black, swollen furnace.

When he felt hands like tremendous spiders fasten onto his shoulders, Cal cried, "Christ save me!" and the burning exploded down his neck into his chest. Yet again he bellowed, "Christ save me!" And then softer, "Forgive me. Oh, my God. Forgive me."

His entire body was burning. Every nerve-ending sang of holocaust.

THEN IT was over.

He was cool and alone in the vast darkness of an unfamiliar place. He repeated the name of the empty shape at the center of his universe and, slowly, the shape seemed to become less hollow.

He began to weep.

THE SKY was too blue to be real. He had always distrusted the word "azure"—it was too poetic and thus seemed somehow false—but this sky was nothing if not azure; it had the quality of an untainted abstract, the way Cal imagined the sky must have looked before there were people. It seemed so unreal and yet Cal could smell the rain inside the clouds when he moved through them. He was naked, drifting like a spirit, and felt fresh, very much alive. He hoped the experience would never end.

But it did. Lines appeared in every direction, twelve lines that became edges. The purity of the vision fled and Cal found himself in a large room whose every surface was painted in blue and white. Then the blue disappeared and Cal was left blinking in a luminous whiteout.

As he became increasingly aware of his own physical reality he discovered several things: He was not naked but wore an almost weightless pale-gray jumpsuit of fine cotton. He was standing on something cold and smooth like glass, his groin ached where a catheter had been, and he was hungry. New edges defined themselves in the center of one wall, and a door appeared. A thick, velvety darkness shone from behind the opening door, throwing its tendrils into the white room.

Then Cal was on his knees with vertigo. All at once the glowing walls became dead black, while the darkness behind the door became a bright light.

He stood and surveyed the room. The ceiling, floor, and every wall had the look of dark mirrors but gave back no reflections. They seemed to drink in the light coming from the door.

He took a few steps toward the door but made no progress. He bent to the floor and swept his fingers over it. The surface was not glass, as he had thought. Rather, it consisted of billions of frictionless black beads finer than grains of sand.

The floor began to hum. He felt the beads move beneath his fingers, clumping together like iron filings in a child's magnetic art board. Friction had been restored.

The men outside the door were dressed in white uniforms and looked more like hospital orderlies than guards. Over their ears they wore covers of white plastic that, as Cal discovered, canceled out all sound. Entirely unresponsive to his questions, they may as well have been moving statues. They led him away from the room, and Cal had just enough time to see that it wasn't a room at all but an autonomous structure, overgrown with cables and wires, within a much larger building.

He saw that he was in something like a warehouse or hangar. They passed row after row of smaller buildings, some of which were interconnected. A few were fronted by glass walls and contained what Cal thought were called "clean rooms." Others were blunt cinder block cubes. The guards brought him to one of these.

The room within the cinder block cube contained three folding chairs, a polished metal table, and a large, thin LCD monitor fixed to one wall. A slight man in a dark suit coat motioned for him to sit at the table, across from him.

"Welcome, Mr. Cavanaugh," said the stranger. "I'm Dr. Runqvist."

The man smiled nervously. He had dark hair and eyes and a bloodless, angular face. His hands, folded neatly on the table, were pale as bone. He appeared uncertain how to begin.

Cal did not respond. He crossed his arms and stared at Dr. Runqvist.

"I expect you'll have many questions," Dr. Runqvist said at last. "But first, please—"

"How am I not dead?" Cal asked.

Dr. Runqvist looked down at his hands. He exhaled slowly. "You must forgive me. I'd no time to prepare a speech. They've never had me do this part before. Typically, Dr. Thurman—"

"Dr. Thurman?" exclaimed Cal. "Dr. Thurman? Where is he? Is he here?" His heart beat furiously. Tears played at the corners of his eyes.

"You must settle yourself," said Dr. Runqvist. "Settle yourself and I will tell you."

Cal cupped his face in his hands and leaned forward, forcing himself to breathe deeply. A minute later he was in control again.

"As I was going to say, Thurman handles debriefing, among other things. I'm an operator. The lead designer, actually. Thurman, he has a way with people, as I'm sure you're aware. You were meant to come out an hour later than you did. Thurman has been indisposed."

"But—" Cal was silenced by Dr. Runqvist's raised palm.

"You were never administered the drugs," he continued. "At least not the lethal cocktail. There were other drugs, certainly. To make you appear as if you had died. We maintained a rigorous control of the situation. You were declared legally dead by the medical examiner and then brought to our facility. That was three days ago. We maintained your coma until this morning."

"Won't someone expect my body?" Cal asked. "My mother, she'll be coming for the remains. She—"

"Has them already."

"What are you saying?"

"Come now, Mr. Cavanaugh. Ash is easy enough to come by. Had you made other arrangements, things would have been trickier. Luckily, you're a practical man."

Cal did his best to determine whether anything this man said could be trusted. Nothing made sense. It seemed he had woken from the longest, most vivid nightmare of his life only to find he was still dreaming. He felt powerless.

"Why?" he asked. "Why do all this?"

"Research, Mr. Cavanaugh," said Dr. Runqvist. "Necessary research."

"This is legal?"

"Very. This has been, you could say, sanctioned."

"Is this government? Military? Who are you?"

Dr. Runqvist laughed. "*I* am privately contracted. And I am paid a great deal of money not to answer these sorts of questions."

Now it was Cal's turn to laugh. He began to giggle uncontrollably. His voice became high and frantic. He forced himself to stop laughing. "And just what is the nature of this 'sanctioned' research? Or are you paid an even greater deal of money not to answer this question?"

"I can provide a partial answer," he said, smiling faintly, "one I believe will satisfy you."

He rose and turned on the monitor. It was a minute in warming up. Then the screen came to life. Dr. Runqvist pressed a finger to the screen and slid it to the left, scrolling through a series of still-frames until finding one that satisfied him. "Believe me that I've not chosen this to embarrass you. So much of what we recorded is very dark. Viewable, yes, but not in such weak resolution as we have here." He tapped the screen twice and the still came to life.

Cal watched the screen in horror. The image bowed inward, like a reflection in a curved mirror. "This is impossible," he whispered. It was a memory, his memory, rendered in frightening detail, as if his very eyes had been cameras recording the episode for just this moment. He watched—through the watching eyes of his past self—as Valery undressed on his bed. This Valery was much skinnier than the one he had known in college, which meant that this was several years after their first meeting, time enough for her lifestyle to have eaten away most of her bulk, and for surgery to refine the rest. He wanted to tell Dr. Runqvist to stop playing the video, but he could not. He was transfixed, reliving for the second time today a vile, yet titillating, experience. He sensed his video-self moving closer to the bed. The view panned from Valery's naked body to the nightstand, where an old car battery sat. In a flash Valery had put on rubber gloves and was playing with the leads.

There was a quick knock at the door. Dr. Thurman entered without waiting for a reply.

"For shit's sake, Reginald," he said. "What are you thinking?"

"The contrast! I needed a scene with more light—"

"Shut it off. Now."

Dr. Runqvist tapped the screen again and the video paused. His pale skin flushed. "He came out early. We thought it best—"

"You should have waited," Dr. Thurman said, staring at the blur of flesh on the screen. He walked past Dr. Runqvist and powered down the monitor himself.

Dr. Runqvist left quietly and Dr. Thurman took his seat. He was dressed in a green sweater-vest and khaki pants. Despite the neatness of his clothes he appeared ragged. Cal discerned about two days' growth of hair horseshoeing the crown of his head and a corresponding crop on his face. His eyes looked as if they had been open for a very long time. "I'm sorry about this, Cal," he said. "They should have waited."

"It's nothing I haven't seen already," said Cal. He tried to master the lust, anger, confusion, and hunger feuding within him.

Dr. Thurman sighed.

"How long was I in that room?"

"Eleven hours. Another thirty minutes if you want to count the time at the beginning when you were unconscious."

"What is it, Dr. Thurman? What is that place? What is *this* place?" he asked, gesturing to encompass the entire facility.

"This," said Dr. Thurman, repeating Cal's gesture, "is the life's work of a great many people. A multitude of collaborative, international projects are housed here under one roof. My research is just a drop in the bucket of the whole. There are other facilities like this, but this one is, to my knowledge, the largest on the continent. Beyond that I'm afraid I can't tell you much. Information here is curtailed to function. I'm allowed to see what is necessary for me to do my work, and nothing else. Suffice to say that you are a long ways from North Carolina. Now the *room*, on the other hand—" he paused, looking thoughtful. "Have you ever heard the expression 'a prisoner's cinema'?"

Cal had, but could not quite match the phrase to a meaning.

"The concept has been around for a long time. It's based on a fairly common phenomenon. When a person is exposed to complete darkness for a long enough period, hallucinations often occur, ranging from simple visual noise to more complex projections. That series of images, seen over a screen of darkness, that is the prisoner's cinema. What you experienced was an elaborate, finely tuned prisoner's cinema. That room is special, Cal.

It's the only one of its kind in the world. Dr. Runqvist is a very gifted man. Whatever his personal quirks and indiscretions," at this he glanced at the monitor, "he has helped to give us something very important."

"So all that nightmare was because of a dark room?" Cal thought suddenly of Paul. He had dreamt of him before, generated him with his own imagination, and he had also *encountered* Paul, a real Paul, in his dreams. He understood the difference. He knew his experience in the room had been a mix of both.

"Fundamentally, yes. However, the room provides certain enhancements. It's all rather complex, but the idea is that it utilizes certain methods for modulating brainwaves to frequencies that correspond to different stages of sleep. It's called brainwave entrainment. When you expose the brain to a certain frequency for a period of time, the brain will begin to mimic that frequency. The most useful frequencies are alpha waves. These correspond to the onset of sleep. You know, that strange period where you're not awake but not yet sleeping?"

Cal nodded.

"The state is often called hypnagogia. The room functions to help induce this state, to allow more readily for conscious and subconscious projection."

"Conscious?"

"Yes. It's much like hypnosis, where there must be some level of complicity between the mesmerist and the subject. You have to *choose* to be hypnotized."

Cal was in no way surprised by this. Given the opportunity for extreme masochism, why would his mind, of all minds, refuse?

"Much of what you experienced was self-directed. You plotted your own course through your memories, even created a background. You expected Hell. So you consigned yourself to a phantasmagorical experience."

Cal was quiet for a long time. He picked at the bandage over his left thumb. He was emotionally exhausted and his desire for answers was flagging. He wanted food. "I guess you'll need to run tests, or something? Evaluate me?"

"We already have. The most remarkable feature of the room you were in is that it records everything. There is a certain energy that accompanies thought. The room records this energy and is able to render it with great precision." He gestured again to the monitor. "We can see—have seen—everything you saw. In addition, we performed extensive imaging of your brain. The correlation between the imaging, the inner workings of your brain, and your imaginative projections is what our research is all about. It allows us to get at the mechanics of the subconscious mind. And in your case, as someone whose mind was entirely convinced it had died, we were able to study the way belief, as a brain-state, delimits other neurological functions."

"You look tired, Dr. Thurman."

Dr. Thurman smiled. "These periods are very exciting. But also very draining. So much must be done in so little time, and performed so precisely. I imagine you must be tired yourself."

"And hungry," said Cal.

"I suppose we can take care of that." Dr. Thurman stood and led Cal out of the little room. The white-clad guards were waiting outside. "Gentlemen," he said, laughing a little.

They were unresponsive. They followed Cal and Dr. Thurman at a small distance.

Curious, Cal asked about their imposed deafness.

"Precautions," said Dr. Thurman. "It seems rather arbitrary. I mean, they can *see* this place, after all, and the researchers are eternally cautious. But I suppose a subject such as yourself could disclose something of importance if given the opportunity."

They crossed back through the ranks of inscrutable buildings and made their way to the front. There they had to pass through a complex series of checkpoints, manned by more white-suited men with ear caps.

Outside it was hot and dry. The sun beat down on everything with a conscious fury. Cal was in a long courtyard enclosed by many interconnected white and gray buildings. Behind him was the warehouse. It was the size of an airplane hangar, but more rounded, and gave the startling impression of the white crest of a skull poking through sand.

Without any preamble, Dr. Thurman asked, "Who is Paul?"

Cal was startled by this question, though he had expected it. After watching eleven hours of that hellish schlock how could Thurman not be curious?

"Someone I hope to forget."

"You're being evasive. Why toy with half-answers when you know what I've seen? Now tell me: Who is Paul?"

He stood motionless, silent, smelling the air with its hint of sage, and studying the vastness of the courtyard. The place looked nothing like the penitentiary—no grass, no ochre-colored bricks, no guard towers—but it was clearly designed to *contain*. Beyond the immediate ring of tall buildings he expected there would surely be another ring, a formidable wall. "I'm a lunatic and a killer, remember? What does it matter what I say Paul is?" He realized that he had said *what* instead of *who*.

"As I've explained, the room you were in is very special. I've experienced it myself—there's not an operator on my team who hasn't. It records everything that your mind projects. What you saw is what we saw. However, there were instances when your 'Paul' seemed to be present to you when we couldn't see him. You responded to something, at times even *obeyed* something, which for us simply was not there. Do you remember acting out in terror because of something in a long, dark corridor? You were terrified of something, something very real to you. What was it? Was it Paul?" Dr. Thurman sighed. "Do not fear my judgment. Whatever it was, it did not originate in your mind."

Three human figures appeared at the western end of the courtyard, standing by a narrow bed of cultivated desert shrubs.

Cal was surprised that Paul had taken so long to show up. He held the McKaskell twins to his sides, his fingers enmeshed in their platinum hair. They were all three naked and their pale skin flashed like glass in the sunlight. Paul was wounded in each side, deep jagged tears from which bends of intestine spilled. The girls pulled at the exposed organs with their teeth, and Cal thought of robins wrenching earthworms from the soil. Dark blood caked their mouths and streamed down their white necks. Paul was not looking at Cal. He was not looking at anything. He had no eyes. The sockets were empty as if they had been fashioned that way—smooth, shadowed recesses in a luminous face. Cal concentrated on those empty holes and willed that Paul disappear. And, to Cal's amazement, he did. He vanished like a vapor in the wind.

"Cal?" said Dr. Thurman.

"I can't do this. Not now. I'm sorry."

"That's quite alright. We have plenty of time."

"What's going to happen to me?"

"I can't fully answer that question. But it would be best if you began to think of this place as home. You were very expensive. Those who run this facility will want full use of you. But you needn't fear. We have good people here and you'll be well cared for. And let's not forget that you've already 'died.' You've already been to 'Hell.' What worse could there be?"

Dr. Thurman led Cal inside a new building, through more checkpoints. The place looked like a top-of-the-line, maximum security mental asylum. Dr. Thurman handed Cal off to a couple of white-smocked, ear-capped orderlies.

"These men will take you to your room. I've arranged a little surprise for you there. I hope it's to your liking."

The orderlies walked Cal down a series of corridors to his room. Inside were simple furnishings: a bed, desk, and chair. Everything was crafted so as to exclude sharp edges and moveable parts that could be used for self-injury. A camera was encased in a plexiglass orb in a ceiling corner.

The orderlies left, shutting and locking the door. Cal approached the desk, where a wrapped gift sat. He opened the wrapping carefully and discovered a stack of canvas paper and an elaborate set of charcoals. Tears filled his eyes, but he was too tired to weep.

NEVER FIND US HERE

There is a man who lives in my chest. Or, rather, *lived*. He is exactly one foot, seven inches tall, but will insist that he is one-nine. He is slender and pale, hairless, and I think he enjoys the warmth behind my ribs. He won't tell me his name as he holds the occult belief that to name something is to have power over it. I've been trying for some weeks now to evict him and it was not until just this evening, here at the end of a season of naming (diagnosing), that I've had any luck. A few minutes ago he left, having torn a rather nasty hole just below my sternum, and walked stark naked through the coffee house, past oblivious patrons, out into the night. And the strange thing is, I'm already regretting this. I've grown so accustomed to his presence. I'm not even sure he hasn't always been there, nestled like an overripe fetus, clutching my lungs like pillows. I'm tempted to venture a hand into the chasm of my chest, feel around for what may be growing there in his absence.

I ask myself, speaking to the wobbly wooden table before me, *What's next?*

The answer comes from somewhere down and to the left: "Strangeness. Consuming strangeness."

I turn and search out the voice's source and find it amidst the brick and mortar and profuse graffiti of the coffee house wall. It is a cartoon caricature of me, drawn in what looks to be crayon. The head is oversized and the eyes are too blue, like a self-portrait I might have drawn when I was five. My little self is staring at me, blinking his yellow eyelids, waiting for me to say something. I glance around the room and see that no one is looking at me and so I turn back to the wall, lean forward and whisper, "Yes, small one, it is strange."

He smiles and points a ballooned finger at my chest and asks, "Where has it gone?"

"Through the door," I say, "into the night."

My caricature situates himself, sitting on one rose-colored brick and letting his disproportionate legs dangle in the gray grid of mortar. His elbow rests on his knee and his chin on his knuckles; he is Auguste Rodin's *Thinking Man*, as remade by a caffeinated kindergartner. "You would do well to take caution," he says. "You may wake tomorrow and find that he has clawed his way back home."

I look down at my chest, at the dark, meaty hole there, and see that it is healing. I think about the strangeness of it all, the strangeness of all beginnings, of transformations, and know this nipping of prodigal emotions will pass.

"How does it feel?" asks my caricature.

"Warm," I say, "like animal fur rubbing against my skin."

"As it should. You are changing, reforming, being made anew, at long last. You are awakening to things you've not felt since you were a child and innocent. Somewhere and everywhere, in that infinite, infinitesimal, white-burning ethereal place, someone quite large and important is smiling at you. And out there, in the night-darkness, *he* is shivering. He cannot bear his own glacial intensity. He longs to return home, to bore deep, to blow his breath into your heart."

Rubbing my fingers against the precipice of the hole in my chest, I think about what happened earlier. I remember the sensation—that blue-cold, electric pulsing—when that pale hyperborean man first tore through my ribcage and emerged, in a shower of flesh and sinew, into the evening. The memory makes me shudder.

The door chimes and I look up to see Emily. She walks to the counter and places her order, speaking the words *plain* and *dark* loudly enough that I can hear them across the room. She is underdressed for the weather: a T-shirt advertising a local fund-raiser, tight jeans, flip-flops. The barista hands her the drink, and she smiles and pays him. We've spoken a few times, Emily and I, but it is not until just now, as she sets down her satchel and coffee two tables away, that I discover she is beautiful. I watch as she talks with the man sitting at the table between us, another regular, a familiar stranger. He is Muslim and a Saudi, but looks European on account of his plaid sport coat and beret. I've never learned his name. Emily sits at her table and turns toward him. She sets her hand on his table and I see that her nails are unpainted and neat. She glances at me and, meeting my eyes, smiles. I smile, too. Then she returns to her conversation.

"What is it, what are you looking at?" asks my caricature.

"Can't you see?"

"No, not from this angle. I'm two-dimensional, remember?"

"It is a woman."

"Perhaps I should have a look. Give me a hand."

I offer my left. With a pained squeak, he breaks through the dimensional boundary and lands in a quivering ball on my palm. He unfolds his limbs and stands up awkwardly to his full height of six inches. His bare feet feel oily against my skin, like melting crayons. I set him on the table and he immediately falls to his knees and vomits burnt-sienna goulash.

"Are you okay?" I ask.

"Sure," he says, regaining his composure and standing up. "Never better. Where is this woman?"

I tell him and he ventures out to the far end of the table and peeks around the Saudi. He studies the woman for a moment and then returns. “She is quite lovely.”

“Yes,” I say. “I feel odd when I look at her.”

“Good,” he says. “Look at her more.”

She is still talking with the Saudi and does not notice me studying her. She has a sharp face, the sort of face that sells makeup on television commercials, only she does not wear makeup. She is utterly unadorned. Her face is framed by woolly hair that is blonde and auburn and peach. She is a dusky manifestation of autumn. Her eyes are coffee-brown, but from this distance they appear obsidian. Looking at them makes me feel as though I’ve never once in all my life been in love.

“Why have I never studied her so closely before?” I look down at my little friend. “Tell me how to guard against *his* return.”

“Resolve and remembrance,” he says. “You must think about that thing that drove him away, let it sit well and deep and resonate within you. Once you know it through and through, you will need to do it again, serve again.”

“How do I make it resonate?”

“Tell it to me. The telling will make it all the more real to you.” My caricature sits down a few inches from his bright waxen vomit and crosses his legs into a lotus. He looks much less silly now that he is in three dimensions.

“I don’t know where to begin. Should I–”

“Don’t speak it,” he interrupts, “write it, there, on the wall. Bleed it out atop the other graffiti.”

“I have nothing to write with.”

My caricature looks first annoyed, then thoughtful. With his right hand he takes hold of his left arm and rends it free from its socket, tearing it clean off. Magenta droplets trickle from the hole, like hot wax down the shaft of a candle, and quickly harden into chunks about his waist. “Use this,” he says, handing me the arm.

I take it and move the tip to the wall. It is a bleeding yellow crayon with fingers. I press the fingers into the brick and watch them crumple, then I drag until the hand is gone to the wrist. I look back down at my caricature with mingled awe and confusion.

He looks up at me and says, "Write your story. It begins: *It was a fine autumn afternoon . . .*"

It was a fine autumn afternoon. Michael stood outside of 234 S. Eighth Street, the local Salvation Army building, and looked at his watch. He was late. He wondered whether he was too late to be of any use. The glass door before him was tinted and Michael could barely see a man on the other side of it, wiping a cloth back and forth. Michael opened the door and the man eyed him with suspicion. "I'm here to volunteer. I signed up with Mrs. Hansom last week." The man was tall and heavy and African American. He wore a horn necklace and his left eye flitted about, as if there were unseen dangers whirring through the air. "Sir?" asked Michael.

"You want the other door, there," he pointed.

Michael looked and saw several people forming a line outside the other entrance. "No, I'm not here for a basket," he said, turning back to the man, "I'm here to help register people." But the man ignored him, shut the door, and returned to his wiping. Michael looked at the ground and sighed.

The people in line gave him angry looks when he walked to the front and tried the door. It was locked, so he found a place at the end of the line and waited. He looked around at the people in line and then closed his eyes, trying desperately not to judge them. That was why he was here though, judging. Michael was a young man, intelligent and educated and handsome, or so he was told many times over the years. Recently, during a lengthy bout of self-analysis, Michael took to reading the Diagnostic and Statistical Manual of Mental Disorders, *and, having arrived somewhere near the middle, discovered that, unquestionably, he suffered from Narcissistic Personality Disorder. This came as no surprise; it merely provided an official explanation for why all the relationships in his life were crumbling into animal dung. Michael's narcissism, however, was atypical in two respects: He had in no way been abused as a child and he was always willing, even eager, to accept his faults and seek to repair them. Perhaps in this he was the ultimate narcissist: In accepting reproof and enacting change and self-improvement he stood only to move nearer perfection. Chief among Michael's shortcomings was his inability to empathize with others. This had caused near irreparable damage to his friendships and in some instances had resulted even in ostracism. Now Michael meant to fix this, and the clearest course (according to his therapist) involved serving others and understanding their various plights. That was why Michael had volunteered to help register poor people for free Thanksgiving and Christmas food baskets.*

Those poor people were all around him now, waiting outside the Salvation Army building for the social workers to unlock the door. The man in front of Michael was resting his chin on the shoulder of a woman who must be his wife. They were both overweight and had holes in their clothes. Michael could see the man's pallid skin through what he took to be the Mother Hole, the large hole near the man's left armpit all the other holes seemed to be trying to escape. Michael expected the man smelled awful and tried very hard not to lean forward and confirm his suspicion. Then he checked his thoughts. He was judging, elevating himself above the people around him, people whom he did not know, people who could be in their current straits for almost any reason. Why did he presume it was their own fault, that their own laziness or ineptitude had brought them here?

"Michael?"

The austere beauty is leaning over my table, her hands planted for support mere inches from my coffee. She is unaware that a small creature composed principally of wax and pigment is cowering on the other side of the cup, his teeth chattering, his eyes bugged loose and horrified, fixed on the giant's hand that nearly ended his absurd existence.

"Hey, Emily."

"I hope I'm not prying," she says. "It's not every day you find someone journaling on a coffee house wall."

"It is strange, I suppose. Do you think I should stop?" I look down and my caricature is shaking his head back and forth, all but screaming.

"I don't know," she says, looking ponderous. "It certainly is bizarre."

"I haven't even reached the climax," I say.

"Will it be a good climax?" asks Emily.

"I hope so."

"Then you should continue. And if it is a good climax, I'll let you walk me home." Emily turns her head to the side and smiles a wondrous, lipstick-free smile.

I smile, too. I look at my caricature and he is fist-pumping in the air. I begin writing with his severed arm on the wall again.

In line at the Salvation Army, Michael tried to choke back his bitterness and, in his distraction, leaned forward and was readying to sniff the man in front of him when the door suddenly unlocked from the inside and opened. Michael left the line and approached the white-haired woman who stood in the doorway.

"Hello," he said, "I'm here to volunteer. I registered with Mrs. Hansom."

"Ah," said the woman. She took Michael inside and handed him off to another white-haired lady who took him down a hall, through a meeting room, and into a dining commons where several tables were arranged about the edges of the room. Behind the tables were more old women. They were thumbing the forms that littered the tables. Mrs. Hansom sat at the nearest table with another, slightly younger, woman. Mrs. Hansom caught Michael's eye and he went and sat next to her.

"You're here, excellent," she said. "Michael, this is Brenda."

Michael shook Brenda's hand and appraised her. She was middle-aged with dyed blonde hair and too much makeup. She wore golden hoop earrings that moved a lot when she talked.

When Michael looked back at Mrs. Hansom, she began to explain the registration process and showed him the various forms he would have to fill out for each person. Finished with her explanation, Mrs. Hansom wrote down her phone number and then grabbed her purse and left. Michael and Brenda were left alone at their table until the first of the people were ushered in and led clockwise around the room. Each table performed a different function. The first verified the identity and indigence of each applicant. The second recorded their contact information for the Salvation Army's records. The third registered the people for Christmas baskets. Michael did not know what the fourth table did, only that it was manned by a grouchy-looking woman with blue hair. He and Brenda sat at the fifth table and registered people for the Thanksgiving baskets, which were to be distributed the Tuesday before.

People came and went, always leaving with the little orange identification card that Brenda or Michael had given them. Michael's psychologist, who was used only for advisory purposes (certainly, Michael did not need *counseling, especially from someone skeptical of his attempts at self-diagnosis)–*

"OH, NO," I say, and turn to Emily, who has pulled up a chair to watch me write. "I've run out of crayon." I look over to the caricature and find that he has moved behind the table lamp near the wall to hide. He looks at me and I show him the little diminished nub of his arm—it is only a yellow smudge on the tip of my finger now. My caricature looks at his right arm, which is resting against the lamp, and frowns.

"Here," says Emily. She fishes a sharpie from her pocket and hands it to me. I look back at my caricature and see little beads of sea-blue sweat break out on his forehead.

–HAD ADVISED him to try to engage everyone he encountered while serving at the Salvation Army, to listen to them and share in their struggles. Michael, however, said very little apart from perfunctory

"Hello"s. The few people he did try to talk with did not seem to want to share their struggles.

At one point, a rather large man with a gray mustache sat down in front of Michael. He was clearly drunk (at two in the afternoon, no less), and the smell of booze was noxious. Michael attempted to engage him, but the man only laughed. Once he had his orange card in hand, he shambled back out the way he came, and Michael had to count prime numbers in order not to think unfair, judgmental thoughts.

During a lull where there were few applicants, Brenda asked, "So, what led you to volunteer?"

"Well," replied Michael, "to be brutally honest, I have very little love for people naturally. I believe performing acts of service is about the only way to change that."

"It certainly will, you can take my word on it. I've been volunteering four years now, and I can tell you I'm a different person for it."

"That's encouraging."

Brenda smiled and shuffled some papers absently. Michael looked across the room to the first table. A large woman sat next to her bespectacled child on the applicant side. The little boy was fidgeting and now and again getting off the chair and then climbing back on. He was very young and wore a green turtleneck and dark gray flannel pants.

Michael's mind began to drift and he wondered whether all the hassle was worth his while. Was it working? He did not know and figured he would not until he had been at it for some weeks. He began to rub the center of his chest and tried to think empathetic thoughts about the people he had encountered. It was not easy. He remembered being in middle school and being told by his father that his family was poor. That had been irritating, not at all the sort of thing you want to hear from your father. Michael imagined that most of the people he had encountered must be pretty damned irritated.

Michael looked up again and found that the woman and child had arrived at his table. She sat down in front of Brenda, and the metal folding chair squealed beneath her bulk. Brenda took her information and began to fill out the necessary forms. The little boy leaned against the table and tried to see what she was writing. Brenda paused and looked at the child and said, "Well hello there! What's your name, little man?"

"Girl," said the large woman, "She's a little girl." Her voice sounded to Michael like the bleating of a goat.

Fearing the girl might experience the beginnings of gender confusion, Michael injected, "Of course she's a girl! Didn't you see her pretty fingernails?" The child held up her hands in triumph and Brenda exclaimed over how cute her pink nails were. Michael studied the child he now knew to be a girl and saw that she was not so boyish after all. Her face was a near perfect oval with a sharp little chin and subtle cheekbones. Her eyes were gray and knowing. It was her short hair that had confused him.

"So what is your name?" Brenda asked again.

The girl did not speak her name, but spelled it, "L-A-U-R-A." She smiled brightly and then leaned forward and divulged in a whisper that she was five years old.

"Is she your only child?" Brenda asked the woman.

"No, I have four," she said. "The younger two are with me here in town."

Brenda's eyes narrowed ever so slightly.

"Max and Sue, they're in Texas," Laura chimed. "With her ex."

"Oh?" said Brenda. Michael watched the little girl.

"Yeah," said Laura. "One time, he picked me up, like this—" she held her hands to her neck, "and he put me in the water."

Michael looked at the mother, expecting her to say or do something, anything. But she just stared vacantly at the wall.

"Were you in a pool?" asked Brenda. "Were you playing?"

"No," whispered Laura. She looked back up at Brenda and, after a moment, said, "He'll never find us here. Not in Terre Haute."

The mother continued looking at the wall.

Brenda finished the remainder of the form and handed the woman an orange card. The woman walked away with her card in one hand, her child's wrist in the other. The little girl kept looking back over her shoulder, smiling. Brenda watched them go, shaking her head. Once they were out of sight, she riffled through a few papers and then traced down a page with her index finger. When the finger stopped, she said in a dark voice, "My God, October 4th, 1984."

"What?" asked Michael.

"The mother's date of birth. She's only twenty-four and she has four kids."

"Wow," said Michael, "I'm only twenty-four." He tried imagining himself with four children, broke, running from abuse. It would be more than an alien life. He feared that in such circumstances his sense of self would diffuse like vapor.

Brenda stared at the page for a full minute. "You know why the little girl's hair was cut so short?"

"No," said Michael.

"I think they're staying over at the Lighthouse Mission. Children who stay at those places have to have their hair cut close. On account of the lice."

"Oh."

No one else came to register after the mother and daughter. When it was three o'clock Michael said goodbye to Brenda and walked outside. Standing by his car, he looked around Eighth Street and smelled the air. It still smelled like autumn, with not even a hint of the cold to come. He tried to think about things like love and compassion and empathy. Instead, he thought about that mother standing at his table like a dead tree—all bark, the inside rotted away. He thought about her eyes: empty and sepulchral.

I FINISH and put the cap on the marker and stare at the wall. The change from sloppy yellow chicken-scratch to neat black script is jarring. I look over at my caricature and he is smiling approvingly. Then I look at Emily, expecting a pronouncement as to whether I have written a compelling climax. But she doesn't say anything. She is looking at me, though, and there is something somber in her eyes. She opens her mouth, and closes it. Then I feel her fingers playing lightly over the tops of mine.

"Let's go for a walk," she says.

I smile and nod.

We walk past the Saudi and he smiles at Emily, and she smiles back and grabs her satchel off a chair. Somewhere behind me I hear a little mouse-voice calling my name and the frantic slapping of crayon feet on hardwood. As I reach for the door I feel my caricature grasp hold of the cuff of my jeans. He climbs up my leg and slips into the front right pocket of my pants. I look down and see him there, buried to his chest, his little arm riding the rim of the pocket. He is looking out into the world, out into the dark night, knowing that a small, pale man is nestled in some black alley, quivering and plotting and waiting.

COMMAND THESE STONES
(A Briefer Epic, Part I)

TIME AND SCENE: *A pathless desert, dusk with horrid shades. A dead juniper tree dominates at stage-left.*

MICHAEL *emerges from the gloom and summons* PAUL *from the throng of his apostasy.* PAUL *appears in a flash of silent lightning, dressed in the garb of a first century Palestinian rustic.*

PAUL:
This isn't how it's supposed to go.

MICHAEL:
No?

PAUL:
You're supposed to have been here forty days, fasting and fucked-up on faith. I'm to seek you out in a ruse of rural weeds and slyly simper my solicitude.

MICHAEL:
There is no "way this is supposed to go." It simply goes and we shape it as we can.

PAUL:
Wresting order from chaos, eh? Marduks slaying our Tiamats, painting pretty pictures with the blood of Leviathan? Apolloing Dionysius into a headlock?

MICHAEL:
That's rather cute, making a verb of Apollo. But please scrap the alliteration. It's making me seasick.

PAUL:
You must forgive me. What with you plundering Milton, Sophocles, the Bible, I thought you'd allow me some literary license.

MICHAEL:
There you go again.

PAUL:
"Going" is all any of us do, unless I misheard you a moment ago. Tell me: What shape will you impose on this "going," this startlingly awful attempt at dramatic dialogue?

MICHAEL:
I haven't decided yet.

PAUL:
Let me help. Okay, let's see . . . Mano a mano spiritual melee, a tête-à-tête of temptation. Dueling dialectic, building toward synthesis, arcing toward climax. Aha! There it is. That's what we want: climax. There's your narrative shape: a nice ruddy phallus spewing its load!

Transforms into an enormous cock and balls.

Let's do this thing!

MICHAEL:
Oh, please. You're not even ruddy. Or erect.

PAUL:
Give it time, love. I'm stage-shy. Haha! Get it? Stage-shy? You meta-dramatist menstrual pad.

MICHAEL:
Sure enough I get it, and it's all—

Motions to PAUL*'s form.*

much too on the nose.

PAUL:
How's this for "on the nose"?

Fires a dollop of jism that lands squarely on MICHAEL*'s nose.*

MICHAEL:
Gaaaah!

Recoils and paws at his face.

PAUL:
This is no more on the nose than any of the pedantic bullshit you've filled these pages with. Seriously. "Each new love requires rebirth"? What didactic nonsense. Those are your words, not "Lara's." You're so clumsy—

MICHAEL:
Hold up. Did you just try to make air-quotes by bouncing your testicles?

PAUL:
I don't have arms!

MICHAEL:
And whose fault is that?

PAUL:
You're making me one despondent dick.

Becomes extra flaccid.

MICHAEL:
Enough.

PAUL:
Is this better?

Falls into a puddle of gelatinous flesh and rises transformed into MICHAEL, *naked.*

God! How can you stand to live in this body? The neurons fire soooo slowly and I can literally feel your heart-murmur. Worst of all, you've really let yourself go.

Bounces his paunch.

Look at this shit! And the micro-penis! Holy Mother of Mass Crackers! This is the worst junk in history. It's like a clitoris with testicles!

MICHAEL:
Very funny.

PAUL, *doubled over laughing, holds up his index finger, gesturing for patience.*

PAUL:
I slay me. Okay, okay. I gotta fix this thing or I'll just keep giggling.

Penis enlarges dramatically. PAUL *grips the base and brandishes it like a cudgel.*

There it is. Something to put the fear of God in the fairer sex!

MICHAEL *snorts and walks to the juniper tree and rests his arm against the withered trunk.*

MICHAEL:
I suppose you have a point to make in all this?

PAUL:
Of course. See how uncomfortable you are? You won't look at me. Won't look at your own naked form. You do it often enough in the mirror, alone, vainly examining, exulting in the swell of your own flesh. Why not now? I'll tell you why: Because it arouses you. It's all well and safe when you're alone. No one's the wiser, and even if they were, none would begrudge you a little concupiscent self-idolatry. But your lust over an autonomous male form terrifies you. Am I wrong?

MICHAEL:
Not about my discomfort, just about my arousal. But you already know that.

PAUL:
What I know is that you've left a trail of breadcrumbs all through these pages, all leading to one rather obvious, rather dull conclusion. . . .

MICHAEL:
Which is?

PAUL:
That you're a latent homosexual.

MICHAEL:
You'd think that after all these years I would have figured that out.

PAUL:
"Latent" is the operative word here.

MICHAEL:
Let me guess, I've yet to uncover and give reign to the "Real Me," the divine spark squirreled away in this cage of a body?

PAUL:
Follow the trail, the Breadcrumbs of Buggery! Just turn any midwit psychoanalyst loose on these stories and see what they dig up. Shit, kid. This trash reads like a Lacanian wet dream. Let me see. We've got a man—a theorist, no less—embodying primal femininity by giving birth to himself. Then there's Drazen's Oedipal terror of his mother's feminine embrace, a nice complement

to my beloved John Calvin's hatred of female beauty. And what could better manifest the male homosexual's disgust at the naked female form than your symbolic annihilation of Jillian's body? And don't get me started on those phallic, shit-covered tails in "Faintly Falling."

Penis lengthens absurdly, grows bulging vertebrae, and coils on the ground.

Or that blisteringly obvious gay subtext in "Lovecraft." Colin literally jizzes his shorts while staring at a male body. This stuff is just bubbling out of your subconscious like the sweet, putrid juice that pools beneath dumpsters. Admit it, Mikey. The jig is up. Buy some condoms and find the nearest rainbow-garnished poofter palace and unburden yourself.

MICHAEL:
Let me know when you're finished "performing" your text-critical naiveté.

Sighs and sits under the juniper tree, leaning his back against it.

PAUL:
It's all perfectly plain. If only you had eyes to see.

MICHAEL:
It's all perfectly lazy. I have no patience for psychologizing critique or any other form of criticism that attempts to force a text into the narrow purview of an extrinsic "lens." Eisegesis is the domain of the inept and cowardly.

PAUL:
Cowardly?

MICHAEL:
Yes. Most of us seem willing to do most anything to escape acknowledging the claims a text makes on our lives. Such contortions are transparently acts of cowardice.

PAUL
I see what you're doing–trying to preempt criticism of your own work. Do you really think you can force your readers into the "lens" of your choosing? And don't give me any Romantic bullshit about being a vessel of gods or muses. Know this, you moralistic hack: They will all see through you.

MICHAEL:
Tell me, oh blind Tiresias, what will they see?

PAUL:
Good for you! Stand up for yourself! Let the sarcasm roll! Embrace irony! As for the unfortunate souls who read you, they will see past these pages to a spiritually exhausted, lonely, possibly suicidal man desperate to abuse art in order to save himself. You cannot honestly expect anyone to take you seriously about "psychologizing." You command such reading even as you condemn it. You might as well have simply transcribed your therapy sessions. It would have saved time and energy.

MICHAEL:
And it would have been a joyless exercise. Self-knowledge requires fictionalization as much as careful reflection.

PAUL:
You think that by defamiliarizing your own experience you can learn about yourself? You fool, there is no self and there is no author. All is just a din of words.

MICHAEL:
Nabokov once said—

PAUL:
Pah! There you go again, dropping names, as if by allusive sorcery you can elevate yourself to even the barest significance. As if someone might be dunderheaded enough to read this and say, "Ah, now here's a man who matters." Do you deny it?

MICHAEL:
No, I do not. You know the terror that's in me. My greed for approval. But none of it matters if the allusions actually serve the text.

PAUL:
And do they?

MICHAEL:
I hope so.

PAUL:
Perhaps I should force you to revisit the tedium of your own words. No, no, that would be too—tedious. Better to give the pedant his pedestal and watch him swan-dive into concrete. Please, continue with whatever asinine grab at credibility you were about to make. Nabokov. . . .

Motions for MICHAEL
to continue.

MICHAEL:
He once said something to the effect that the pathos achieved in Gogol and Kafka results from a kind of double estrangement. Both world and character are rendered unreal. The absurd character, belonging to an absurd world, tries desperately—absurdly—to climb his way out into some place saner.

PAUL:
He also said such characters are doomed to die in despair.

MICHAEL:
But the way truth is accessed in his stories—

PAUL:
Tell the truth but tell it slant, huh? That's a pile of horseshit. And don't give me this "but Kafka" twaddle. You're no Kafka. You haven't suffered enough. Your soul hasn't accumulated the scars necessary for second-sight. But let's, for shits and giggles, entertain the absurdity that you were indeed possessed of his vision. What good did it do him? For all his fabulistic self-expression he was miserable. He died despised of God, despised of men, his self-loathing eye fixed forever inward. It was introspection that killed him.

MICHAEL:
You mean tuberculosis.

PAUL:
Introspection! Consumptive introspection! The gravity of self-hatred attracts the germs like flies to rotten meat. I would know. I am such a fly!

MICHAEL:
And yet truth—

PAUL:
Oh, Jesus, here we go. . . .

MICHAEL:
In the freedom of all that emotional honesty he was able to transcend his own experience. There is more truth in Kafka than the truth of his despair.

PAUL:
Perhaps. But is there more truth in you? And if so, who the fuck cares? You're just one more straight white male in an endless whitejizzy stream of them fishing publicly for self-knowledge, for affirmation.

MICHAEL:
I thought I was a latent homosexual?

PAUL:
You are what you will.

MICHAEL:
And the dance of sophistry continues.

PAUL:
You might as well be a latent homosexual, or else a eunuch, for the way you pussyfoot around pussy. Take Emily, for example. She didn't simply "let" you walk her home, she wanted you enough to ask. Did you notice the way she kept bumping into you and grazing your arm as you walked? Of course you did. You were hard as a corked baseball bat. You could literally feel the

heat coming off her. And that conversation on her front steps. Why in almighty fuck didn't you kiss her? She was talking about the universe. The universe!

Transforms into a flush, naked EMILY.

EMILY:
It means one thing, only one thing, when you're alone with a woman and she starts talking New Age-y nonsense about the cosmic oneness of all things and the universe speaking through our desires. I literally rubbed my face against yours. And you just sit there all "Gee golly, I wonder what this means?" And what do I say when you refuse to do what any sane hot-blooded male should do? "You need to learn to listen to the universe."

Flesh becomes a pale, arctic blue.

God help the man who would rather make worlds than make love.

Face ripples and is replaced by MICHAEL*'s own.* PAUL *begins to tweak the nipples of his still quite feminine body.*

Shit, son! She wanted you to launch your Sputnik, probe her interstellar space. Girl was down to get astronaughty!

MICHAEL:
And what would it have gained me? What did it gain me with Greta? With all the women after her? Experience? Pleasure? Knowledge of the world? Perhaps. And pain. Confusion. Estrangement from myself. Loneliness deeper than I'd thought possible. Shame.

PAUL:
Such exquisite shame.

MICHAEL:
Spiritual delirium.

PAUL:
There are no lessons to be learned here, Mikey. Better to let the past extinguish itself. There is only the present moment and its exuberance. Yet you persist in the belief that reworking life in strange forms and colors will somehow reveal it all to have been meaningful.

Begins to fade away, his body disappearing from the feet up.

And is it? Is it meaningful?

Teeth glimmer in the air before PAUL *vanishes completely.*

MICHAEL:
God, I hope so.

Wanders silently into the desert night.

LOVECRAFT

Oh, Meredith. Mer. Christ. Where are the right words?

A rapist is a multitude of things, but he is foremost a thief. He even takes away one's powers of articulation. The experience is inside, jellied to the victim's guts, yet out of reach.

In that first month after it happened she told me that fruit, any fruit, tasted like ashes. But that was a lie. The truth, she told me later, is that she only wished fruit tasted like ashes. She felt unfit for sweet things.

He stole her joy, her almost preternatural ability to receive the world with wonder. He stole that from me as well. It's perverse to write or speak about what I have lost in all this when she has lost so much: dignity, peace of mind, the familiarity of her own body, sweet and settled sleep. It is perverse, but Meredith is right. I can't go on leaving it unattended. We suffer when those we love suffer. Darren stole her wholeness, made her into a furtive, shattered thing, and in consequence stole from me the illusion that I am a protector, a healer. It's not for me to piece her together. I can only watch as she struggles to do it herself.

I described my experience to my friend (and landlord) Mr. Garrett, like this: Imagine no longer being able to feel wonder at the sheer fortuity of existence. Imagine feeling hollow in the face of the absurd fact that there is *something* rather than *nothing*. I shared with Mr. Garrett a recurring dream that has become something of a guiding metaphor for how I want to see the world. In the dream, I'm floating alone on a skiff in the middle of a placid ocean, no land in sight. It is night and the surface of the deep is lit by alien constellations. I am terrified by the water's depth and the idea that *anything* could be moving beneath me. But it is a joyful terror, the thrill of hugging the rind of infinite possibility. Darren Pederson ripped away that joy. He made the world less mysterious.

But that sense of mystery has returned, thanks to Mr. Garrett. That's what Meredith wants to know about. The envelope was sealed when he brought it to me, but I assume she had already spoken to him about it, because he asked, "Do you trust her? With your whole heart, do you trust her?" I said I did, not understanding until I read the letter.

She has begun writing. Tracing the experience in detail, what came before and what has come in its wake. She believes that if she narrates the event just right, she will redeem it. The past is fixed, she says, Darren's shadow is there, but she refuses to believe it can't be diminished through a proper perspective, a proper *telling*.

I have a part in this, too, she says. My own story to tell. "Decide how what happened will shape you, the story of you," she writes. "Decide how it will shape *our* story."

But it's not so simple. Mine is more than a narrative of trauma, of self-assessment, more than a means to catharsis and healing. Mutual friends have brought Darren's two-month absence to Meredith's attention, and now she's concerned. "Tell me what you did to him," she writes. "I've imagined terrible things and I don't care if the truth surpasses the worst of them. Tell me so that I can know and move on and love you for and in spite of it." She's asking less for a story than a confession. And it's so damned difficult. Will she love me for this thing I've done? Should she?

Sisyphus eternally rolls a boulder up a mountain, only to lose control before reaching the top. My love of the unknown has always been a near-desperate affair. I stand with my boulder at the edge of an abyss, ceaselessly hoping, ceaselessly fearing, that it will fall. This is potentiality. Exquisite torture. I have a neuroticism of wanting to press as close to forbidden knowledge as possible without accessing it. Such wonder is hidden in the cooling shade of indeterminacy. When anything could live in the waters below, fear quickens the imagination, and the experience becomes aesthetic. Beauty may lurk in those depths, too.

Though I have since drifted in the aimless ambiguity of a faithless adulthood, in my youth I was decidedly religious. My metaphorical ocean first presented itself to me at church, on a Sunday afternoon when I was eight years old. Having stayed after the service with my father, who was helping run fresh wiring through the walls of the church office, I hid myself in the sanctuary, under the grand piano. I was reading the Psalter and came to Psalm 42. I couldn't help but linger over the seventh verse:

> Deep calls to deep,
> in the roar of your waterfalls;
> all your waves and breakers have swept over me.

Such beauty, such mystery, is contained in that verse. The voice of God calling from the depths as the waves crash about my head. The deep love of God speaking to the deep nature of man. I remember that the idea of God residing beneath me in the depths of the ocean began to take on a certain terrifying quality. To a child, things in the ocean are often either beautiful or menacing–and menacing in the way of jagged teeth and broad gullets. The idea that God should somehow be among them seemed to me unnatural, incomprehensible.

I was lost in thought when my father, having finished his work, crept up to the piano and pounded a minor chord. I lurched in fright and almost knocked myself unconscious against the wooden base. I have fixed on the ocean as a source of mystery, terror, and beauty ever since.

My parents, together, introduced me to faith when I was too young to have any recollection of the experience. But, when I was ten years old, it was my father alone who introduced me to H. P. Lovecraft. The first story he read to me, "The Picture in the House," caused me to wet the bed for the first time in five years. I remember hiding the soiled sheets early the next morning. My mother, had she found out, would have more than disapproved. Books would have been burned, crosses signed, door frames anointed with oil.

To my great pleasure, the writings of the Dark Lord of the Macabre remained a secret between my father and me, until his death when I was fifteen. (It's worth mentioning that we also busied ourselves with some of the lesser lords, such as August Derleth, Robert E. Howard, Arthur Machen, Ambrose Bierce, and, of course, a goodly portion of Poe.) He would read them to me late at night, before crawling into bed with my mother and making noise. Surely he knew the stories were keeping me awake long enough to hear them shake the house like a couple of poltergeists.

When I was thirteen, he noticed my embarrassment at still receiving bedtime stories as "a teenager." He told me not to be a bitch (though he more likely said "little cur") and that, "Horror stories at bedtime are the only thing guaranteed to keep you straight." *Words to live by*, I used to think, until discovering Clive Barker.

He even encouraged me to write my own stories. None of them were ever any good and yet he would listen patiently as I rehashed dying tropes, stole from Lovecraft's lexicon, made allusions to fictional arcana I'd not created, and, with the nail-bitten fingers of an ungainly teenager, reduced an entire system of unholy mythology to an October evening in a corn maze. He would gently encourage me to let mystery do its good work, to never show my hand unless forced. But I've always been a lousy bluffer and easily enamored by shitty cards. The encouragement never took.

And now *this*—what Meredith is calling "narrative therapy." Maybe she's right. Maybe shaping the events of the past five months into an identifiable form will help us understand them, help us move on. Oh, to be good at storytelling. I can see the dark shape of my father's ghost, shaking his head, *tsk-tsk*ing me, perhaps saying the words "too much" and "exposition," biting off the -ion, as if his mouth were too dry to continue.

My father contracted a flesh-eating virus while serving on a short-term missions project in Port au Prince. I was only fifteen. I hadn't known such things existed. He died a miserable death. I have no doubt that this is why I left the church. One of the many terrors lurking in my ocean around this time had been the possibility that God was a monster. Serendipity had left a Sharpie wedged in the cushion of the front pew at my father's memorial service. *Fuck you, Cthulhu.* The words are still written on the stall door of a men's restroom in my parents' church in Chattanooga.

Everyone articulates emotion in their own way. It's beautiful how private associations are formed and slowly work themselves into a system, a language, of feeling. This happens organically for most. In my case, however, I chose another man's language, Lovecraft's, as a living memorial to my father. Give me a Myers-Briggs Type Indicator assessment and I'll deface it with the name of whichever of the *Great Old Ones* I feel most threatened by at the moment. The Crawling Chaos is a common culprit. Beautiful things are always being eaten.

It is a wonder I ever found a woman willing to endure my particular brand of crazy. But Meredith is a poet. A real poet. She comes from a land just as absurd as mine.

We met in undergrad and, fearing the economy and the idea of "real life" (such boring, nameable beasts), stuck around for grad school to suck every last drop of rancid milk from the withering tit of American academe. Last August when Meredith was raped, we were both starting our fourth year. We were PhD candidates, she in English Literature, I in Clinical Psychology. We had nice fellowships. We tried living together for the first year of grad school—what my mother called "testing the merchandise"—and it almost killed our relationship. I moved into the loft above Mr. Garrett's butcher shop. That was about two and a half years ago. How I hated my mother for predicting our failure. Perhaps I treated her words as prophecy and thus guaranteed their fulfillment. My mother despises the sexual pluralism of my generation. Cohabitation, to her, is purely economic—a trial period to determine compatibility. Granted, all too often it becomes just that. But Mer and I loved each other. Deeply. We couldn't bear to be apart. It seemed a perfectly natural decision. But once my mother had spoken that word it began to color my vision. *Merchandise*. Every day it felt as if the whole of my future was in the balance. Every peccadillo of Meredith's I extrapolated categorically. Her startling incursions into my writing space. Her incessant, off-tune humming. Her erratic housekeeping. Poets are damned dirty people.

Wait. There it is. I was waiting for it to come out. I didn't know how to come directly to it, so I waited, knowing it would come to me of its own. *Disgust*. "Poets are damned dirty people." Oh, Mer. God, I love you. You disgust me. You've done nothing to warrant this, but you disgust me. Jesus. I'm not ready for this, it's not time yet. No.

Poets are damned dirty people. Meredith could not, *would not,* keep house. I was not a particularly clean person myself—I always adjust my level of cleanliness to that of whomever I'm living with—but I did not attract roaches. I did not let my private receptacle overflow onto the bathroom floor. I did not have a private receptacle. I did not cook chicken tikka and leave it in the closet for weeks. If I shut myself in a closet with food, I ate the food in the closet and, at the very least, ran water over the dish when I left it in the sink. Shit. This is pointless. Why am I doing this again? Remind yourself. Remind yourself now, Colin, you shit. You fuck. You goddamned arrogant son of a dead father and an estranged mother. You coward. You would-be murderer. Why are you doing this? Stop. STOP.

Oh, Mer. I'm sorry. I'm so sorry. You wanted me to do this and not stop. I tried. I tried so hard to be measured, to hold my composure and write this for you, for me. I had it, I had that storyteller's voice in my head. But this is where I'm at. This is for you. I don't know if you've been able to keep a distance in your own story, to maintain at least the pretense of objectivity. But I expect so. You write so beautifully. You are so beautiful, so hauntingly beautiful. You're a walking, breathing elegy to every man who sees you and will never have you. I pity them. All but one of them.

This isn't about saying nasty things to each other. But I've said and felt such nasty things. You asked that I not erase anything, and I haven't. I won't. I love you, my precious girl. God, reading about the revulsion, knowing it in theory, just didn't prepare me. It's common for secondary victims to feel an inexplicable disgust for the primary victim. This is especially true of romantic partners. It's unclear to me whether this is more a result of biological wiring or of socialization. All I know is that it has been happening and I'm freaked out by it. The revulsion steals into me when I least expect it and I become rigid and short-tempered. It's as if deep down, in the sub-basement of my mind, I've taken the anger and revulsion justly directed toward the violation itself and transposed it unjustly onto you. It's wretched and irrational.

Oh, Mer. You are not disgusting. But I feel disgust for you. He made you disgusting. Darren fucking Pederson's goddamn vile fucking come made you disgusting to me. You did nothing to deserve any of this. There is nothing about you that could ever merit my feeling this way even in passing. My disgust simply does not cohere with reality. I'm losing my mind. You are pure and kind and giving, so giving. He took advantage of your solicitude for others; you never would have been alone with him at Blythe's party if you didn't believe he was hurting, that he needed someone to listen. I believe you saw my own pain in him, how could you not? Even if his father didn't die, disappearance may as well be the same thing. And we must have been about the same age. It's terrifying to have even the smallest thing in common with such a person. Wait. Do you see that? My soulless, bullshit insinuation that you somehow invited this to happen because of your goodness? Oh, fuck me. I want to scream. Forgive me. What you must have experienced. I play it through my mind incessantly, imagining every detail. The drug he slipped you working its sluggish way into your cells. Him working up crocodile tears over his daddy issues, getting you to follow him upstairs. A bedroom door closing. His hand clasped over your mouth and his monstrous weight bearing down on you. Your vision dimming to static and moving shadows. Him piercing you like a parasite. Your terror as you regained lucidity in that dark, lonely room.

God, Mer. I envy the goodness of your heart. I want so much to hold you, to swallow your hurt. But I don't want to feel any of this mess. I feel so impotent, Mer. I let you be raped. Oh, Jesus, I let you be raped. I know it's not true. I know. I know it's not my fault. But it is. How could it ever not be?

Why was I not there?

I'm so lost, Mer. I don't know how to tell this story. How can I write about what I did? I know, I know, that's the whole point. Christ, why does this have to be as much for my sake as yours?

Continue.

Colin.

You. Must. Continue.

Poets are goddamned filthy people.

No. There is a better way.

Do you remember the night I made you cry twice? Shit. I'm sorry. That fucker Azathoth is kicking in his sleep, shaking the universe. Or it's the influence of cosmic rays, I swear. Alright, story. She wants you to tell it as a *story*. Let's try this again.

WHEN I was first getting to know Meredith, I tried to read important books to impress her. I read this book by John Ashbery called *Self-Portrait in a Convex Mirror*. She said she loved those poems. So, of course, I loved them too, for a while. Then I broke down one night and confessed that I thought the book was an overrated ass-cloth. "Who starts a poem with, 'I let a guy blow me once?'" I said.

She laughed and confessed that she hated it, too, but wanted so much to fool herself into loving it (it was quite in vogue at the time, having won a triple-crown of American book awards). "Behavior training cognition," she said. (Weeks earlier I had lost myself in an arrogant, flashy monologue about cognitive therapy—a demonstration of my *intelligence*. She would occasionally loop things back to that conversation to embarrass me. It was not long before she began cultivating my embarrassment like a fetishist.)

Once it was on the table that I was only reading to impress, I surprised myself by continuing. I began ransacking her bookshelves, taking only those volumes that were well-worn or had been honored with her marginalia, even works on theory. I fell in love with literature as I fell in love with her. It was a crash-course in understanding her spirit, in accessing her world of private symbols. And it opened the door for me to share about my father and my own world of symbols, about Lovecraft.

She read him rabidly, even though she claimed to have qualms about his style, which, if I'm to be quite honest, is rather purple. I recall Mer once saying, "I enjoy Lovecraft. But I don't love his craft." Quite a chestnut.

Inevitably, I tried my hand at a few poems. I didn't dare show them to her. What I did end up showing her was not exactly a poem, but a long, exuberant description of her person, which I titled "A Consideration." I had just read *Lolita* and, by some fluke, Poe's "Ligeia" and contrived to combine the voices. I keep a copy of it in my wallet as a talisman against idealizing women. (I don't believe it's working.)

I can still see her, in her apartment on Center Street, on the floor in front of the couch, feet curled under her, a plume of hair fallen in her face, concealing her eyes. She read the title aloud but the rest silently.

"A Consideration"
by Humbert Humbert

And how shall I describe Meredith? There is an air of mystery to her, but that is, perhaps, a cheap, overused expression (favored by lazy authors and foolish men incapable of defending their rabid, irrational romances). There exist explanations for every character and trait—even for this thing that seems to be a 'mystery'—except with regard to the worst, most interesting of villains. But Meredith—though villainous at times—is no villain. She is distinctively beautiful. She has full, sleek brown hair, which finds a fair match in her nether regions, though of course those nightshades have not been blessed by the chroma-variegating influence of the sun. Her skin is pale, her summer tan fading, soon her luscious slick exterior will approach alabaster—Oh, how you should see this girl, this lithe lady of lucid wit and laughter, whose very touch is the seraphic caress of the unfallen lolling, lusting, looming toward the pit of Apollyon, how you should see her in moonlight! Her skin aglow in ghostly ambience, every pore giving forth moisture that this ethereal Eve might scintillate in nacreous sympathy with the watching stars, her great and gracious face a hallowed hanging upon the ink of night. Her forehead is high but by no means mongoloid; rather, it bestows the appearance of immemorial youth, of a timeless and unconquerable girleen beauty. Her body, however, is a different matter, the stuff of Jovian myth. Lean and taut yet buxom and soft enough to make a mystery of why whatever grand spirit underpins this universe has not crept like an imp into her bed and filled her with Titans. One cannot imagine her breaking the seal of ocean astride a yawning clam, opalescent jewel though she is, as nothing so bitingly banal should ever be ascribed to her, and, equally so, because her beauty finds fullness at night. Her breasts are weighty in the way of grapefruits, and nearly as firm and orbicular, with cinnamon nipples like haughty eyes placed in a perfection of anatomical symmetry. Lower, faint lines of ribs can be discerned through lush, diaphanous skin, and lower still, a production of precision umbilical pruning, the small dark pit of navel, beneath which lies a Dionysian paradise unrivaled in all the dreamiest harems of the most depraved sultans, the hair dark and crisp and of a precise, revelatory profusion, the nub and lips nestled like an oriental delicacy. If Poe truly believed with Bacon that there is no exquisite beauty without some strangeness in the proportion, upon seeing Meredith he would surely recant his folly (or else declare her utter perfection in itself a strangeness). I could go on—I have yet to cover her thighs, knees, calves, ankles, toes (by Zeus! delicate and long, attached to arched perfection, perfection!), her arms, hands, fingers, the inner workings of her viscera, the square pearls of her teeth, that rosy bud of tongue, et cetera and et cetera and et cetera—but I will say only this last thing: Her eyes are a blue to make the

> *whole world colorless, but whenever she is melancholy or frightened they become gray. And the mystery I mentioned so long ago, it rests not in that she is unknowable, but in that such a creature has never before been known.*

When she had finished reading and looked up at me, brushing her hair back, I saw that there were tears in her eyes. I did not understand. I had meant the piece to flatter and amuse her. I sank to the floor and held her and she pressed her forehead to my neck.

That night, I would learn that Meredith had been trifled with by her teacher when in the fourth grade. It wasn't physically aggressive, but it's something that stuck with her—the first time she glimpsed how utterly alien the world can be. He never touched her, but lured her into bringing him her soiled underwear in exchange for As. He was eventually discovered and dismissed from the school. There had been a year of therapy for Meredith. Then it was only an impotent memory, a fact among facts. But for some reason the thrill and revulsion of the experience had revisited her as she read my words. She blamed Humbert.

I tried to take the page from her and tear it to pieces, but she resisted. I grabbed her wrist and struggled to pry the paper away. We wrestled a bit and I let her pin me. She was straddling my abdomen and leaning forward, smiling at me, her elbows digging into my chest. "You're such a dunce," she said.

She took the crumpled page and laid it against me, smoothed out the wrinkles. She read it aloud, only she replaced the name of Nabokov's pedophile with "*Colin Harris*," saying my name as emphatically as she could. When she finished she gave me a loud kiss that sucked the air from my mouth, and then lay on top of me. After a few minutes I could feel my shirt getting wet with her fresh tears, but these were better tears. She kept the page, secured it to a frame of smoky-blue construction paper. It's currently in a drawer in her nightstand.

What a strange thing to have written. So sadly prophetic: . . . *the great spirit that underpins the universe . . . crept like an imp into her bed and filled her with Titans.*

This would mean nothing if Darren Pederson, her rapist, had not had a dark complexion. Let me explain. In Lovecraft's Cthulhu Mythos there is a creator deity, only he's not like "God" in the Christian sense. He's more of a malign Gnostic demiurge, a conscious node from where the other gods and materiality were budded. This is Azathoth and he has been sleeping since before there was time, floating in the center of the universe, entwined in its fabric, which he created. He is encircled by the Outer Gods, who in-their-own-being are indescribable, yet have manifested before on our world and yearn to return. They have startling, often unpronounceable, names suggestive of alien languages: Cxaxukluth, D'endrrah, Huitloxopeti, Lu-Kthu, Yog-Sothoth. Somewhere, a flute is playing. It is what keeps Azathoth from waking. If the flute ever stops, the demiurge will rise, and then all that exists will be unmade. While Azathoth sleeps bodily, his essence, his spirit, will at times embody an Outer God by the name of Nyarlathotep. While this avatar has many manifestations (the strangest of which is The Crawling Chaos), his favorite form is that of a tall, swarthy Egyptian with the divine bearing of a pharaoh. He is a harbinger of black destruction, mindless chaos, the end of worlds, a haunter of dreams.

Meredith has such awful nightmares. She'll wake up stricken, her skin aflame, the trauma a flesh-memory that awakens only when she sleeps. She might as well be the boarder from "Dreams in the Witch House," harried by the malevolent "Black Man" and his servants. Darren Pederson was hardly Egyptian, but he was darker than most Caucasians, and he moved about with an arrogance that refused to be ignored. And he tore our world apart.

Meredith was the first to make a connection to Nyarlathotep. She first used that name last November, two months ago, on the Saturday night before I did the thing I'm having such a hard time coming to. I've been hiding. Avoiding. I know this. I have a duty here, a story to tell, a very specific story, only I don't want to tell it. It's so much to face. And I'm afraid I won't have the words I need to properly communicate it.

Or maybe I'm afraid I do have the words. Maybe I'm afraid of the shape it will take, afraid of my place in it. But that's foolish.

Romance. Tragedy. Comedy. Satire. I want to scoff at the idea that I could fit within such a simple typology. At this point I do not fit; my story is incomplete. Everything depends on what comes next, after this is written, when Meredith and I share our stories. But what comes next could turn on this, on my honesty, here and now. Nix satire. Nix romance—there is too much nihilism in this story; there are no dragons; I am no knight; the princess may already be lost for good. Comedy? Perhaps in its broadest sense of a fall from, followed by a return to, grace. Dante's *Inferno* is part of the *Divine Comedy*, but only because Dante finds grace. I'm certainly in a form of hell. (Is there grace for me, Mer?) Or is this a tragedy? Having committed the irrecoverable act, will I simply play out my fall?

I indicated near the beginning that this story is not merely about what was stolen from me, but about how I got it back. This is it now, this is what I recovered. I am on my skiff, bobbing above the unknown. There is a shape in the water, but I cannot make it out. Something beautiful or something hideous. During those months after her rape, before that Sunday morning in late November, there were only hellish possibilities, the unknown, devoid of beauty.

God bless you, Mr. Garrett, you fucking lunatic!

Ahhh! Christ and Cthulhu!

"SHE SAYS the world has become thin."

Mr. Garrett sipped carefully from his basalt mug, the twin of mine, inhaling the coffee steam through his nose. He stood on the opposite side of the long cutting table at the room's center.

He smiled and, with a playfulness I'd have found offensive in anyone else, said, "And what is the world like when it's thin?"

"I suppose it's the world as it really is."

I thought about how fine it was to be drinking a hot beverage from a cup made of volcanic rock. Then I thought about the smell of coffee, how it fused with the butcher shop's base-scent of raw meat and disinfectant. The result was a vile sweetness. Like the juice that seeps from beneath a dumpster.

"She's always felt protected," I said. "As if there were an invisible barrier between her and all the shit we see on the news. She had this trust that nothing could ever go wrong. I mean *really* wrong. Wrong like this. And now that barrier's been ripped apart and her old world, the good world, is gone. She says what's left feels gray, without substance. Thin."

"Naiveté," said Mr. Garrett. He was tapping his thumb on the edge of the table. On the chopping block were the flayed, piecemeal remains of a sow. A large cleaver lodged in the shank.

"No. It's hard to think of her in that way. She's just good, you know? She's the most generous person I've known. She's never put much stock in Eastern philosophies, but she used to believe implicitly in some karmic principle, that if she's noble, she'll experience the world's nobility. She had so much joy."

Mr. Garrett stood silently for several moments, holding his mug against his apron, not minding that the blood was rubbing off onto its smooth surface. "*Be not overly righteous*," he said, "*neither make yourself overly wise: Why should you destroy yourself?*" Whenever Mr. Garrett recited scripture, his voice—normally a low tenor—acquired a deeper resonance.

"Proverbs?"

"Ecclesiastes. You should read it, both of you. It'll speak to you."

I gave him my best shit-eating grin.

"I know, I know. Not your thing, right?"

"Not my thing," I said. "Not since I was a kid."

"Well, I don't give three shits from Wednesday what your *thing* is, Colin. The book's about someone trying to push through all the inconsistent, unjust hell of life, and yearning for integrity and value. It's probably the most empathetic thing ever written." He walked across the room and poured himself more coffee, pausing to scratch some dried blood off the glass pot with his thumbnail. "You millennial brats still believe in empathy?"

I had lived in the loft above Mr. Garrett's butcher shop for over two years now, ever since my failed attempt at domesticity with Meredith. In the early mornings I would awaken to the metallic scream of the shop's alley door. Within my first month I had made a habit of stopping by for coffee before heading off to teach. Even from the beginning Mr. Garrett served as something of a surrogate father to me. He had been divorced for twelve years. There had been no kids. A miasma of loneliness hung about him. I liked to think that I was serving a purpose for him as well.

"I don't need empathy," I said. "I . . ."

"Yes?"

"I need this all to resolve. If only she were willing to go to the police. Christ, Mr. Garrett. *I want to kill the man*. I sincerely want to kill him." I sighed. "I need that out of my system."

"Remind me of his name."

"Darren Pederson."

Mr. Garrett coughed. "I've never liked the name Darren. It feels pretentious, a politician's name."

"He is pretentious," I said. I balled a fist behind my back. Somehow, my elbow popped. "Everything about him is a production. He's always wearing these jeweled rings on his right hand. Sports rings or something."

"Sounds like a champion."

"He's a fucking mass-produced dago without the Italian blood."

"My ex-wife is Sicilian."

"Sorry. You know what I'm trying to say. I'm not trying to offend."

"Colin, my ex-wife's a whore," he said. "I'm just ribbing you."

Mr. Garrett set down his coffee and then pulled an actual rib off of the sow. He held it up until I caught his pun.

"Anyway. You want to kill a man. So let's kill a man." He walked into the adjoining room. He returned carrying a clean apron. "When I found out Connie had slept with that lawyer, I spent a lot of time in here, just venting my emotions." He handed me the apron.

I put it on and secured the laces in the back. I looked at Mr. Garrett and held my arms out as if requesting a tailor's opinion on a fitted suit.

He pulled the huge cleaver out of the sow and handed it to me. It was wicked and heavy.

"You need to vent," Mr. Garrett said. "So vent. I've got most of the good meat off her anyway."

I looked down at what had been the sow's face. It was a snarl of candy-striped sinew. I imagined that it was smiling and this made me laugh.

"It may seem silly," said Mr. Garrett, "but trust me, it's fantastic stress-relief. Just pretend its name is Darren."

And I did, Mer. I chopped the hell out of that pig and made a mess of my clothes. I had to change again before coming to see you that night. God, what a night. I left your apartment so frustrated. Not at you, not really. It wasn't your fault. I knew you couldn't be ready yet, even if you said you were, but I had convinced myself that I needed it. *I.* How utterly selfish. Forgive me, Mer. When you began kissing my neck, I thought Christmas had come early. I began to do what I've always done, what you've always wanted me to do. But then you were white and shaking. The change happened so suddenly that it frightened me. I didn't know I could shed tears over sexual frustration.

If I'd just stayed. If I'd just slept on your couch, guarding you in your sleep as I had done so many times since that night in August.

That night, I took the long way home and walked through the park. I gave myself too much time to stew. I think I came undone there. That was when I crossed the line. I remember this: standing amidst the trees, as the lust and revulsion burned away in my chest, watching the dim flicker of stars through the bare branches, feeling the crunch of winter-hardened dirt beneath my feet, the shattering of grass that was not just dead but petrified. I had that feeling again that there is something behind the stars. Something utterly indifferent to my existence, but whose least exhalation from the remotest corner of the universe could extinguish my sun like a useless votive. I imagined Azathoth, *blind idiot god,* rolling in a black sleep, dreaming the unnameable dreams of a demiurge, lolled by the sweet atonal sound of a cosmic flute, watched by a thousand Old Ones as they drift impassively around his nebulous bulk.

I remember pressing my cell phone to my ear, hearing a ring, another ring, then a voice.

"Yeah?" Darren's voice was much deeper than I'd remembered. It could have been the voice of a god. Of Nyarlathotep.

"Is this Darren Pederson?"

"The one, the only," said The Crawling Chaos.

For weeks I had rehearsed hateful words to drill into his head like incantations from the *Necronomicon*. But I found none of them.

"Who is this?" he said.

"Me? I'm just someone very much in love with a person whom you have hurt deeply. Now you listen to—"

"Who the fuck're you?" There was some distant thudding in the background.

I was silent.

"Look, some prick's knocking on my door. I don't have time for this mystery shit, so go fuck yourself."

The line went dead. I walked home forcing myself not to think about calling again.

When I made it to the stairs in the alley, even from a story below I could tell there was something strange about my apartment door. I reached the landing and found that a small, folded piece of paper had been wedged between the door and frame in the slim space above the lock. It was a handwritten note, but it was too dark to read the words.

So I went inside. I turned on the table lamp and sat down in my broken leather BarcaLounger. The note was written on an old receipt.

Colin,

I just wanted to drop you a note of encouragement. Things happen in this life that make absolutely no sense. Hell, sometimes it seems that the wicked are always prospering. I just wanted to let you know that, in my experience, people such as Darren never cash in their chips before the house comes down on them. Don't fret long over it, son. I hate adultery with all that I am, and I expect God does, too. This champ will get what's his.

Come by this week and let me know what's happening with Meredith. You're a good young man, Colin. I am confident you will do well by her.

—Mr. Garrett

Adultery, he'd written. It startled me and I sat awake for a while puzzling over it. I thought that somehow Mr. Garrett had conflated his own hurt with mine, or gotten confused. I wondered if perhaps he had written it in a rush. But the hand was not hurried; rather, it was neat, precise.

Adultery.

It occurs to me now that these wretched emotions I've felt for Meredith would be better suited to a cuckold. I've felt—hell, I've written—that something was taken from me. Some*thing*. Do I really see her that way, as an object, as something capable of being polluted? My beloved as mere chattel? Is my soul that Marxian?

I thought none of this, of course, the night I found the note. But maybe it was there, a seedling in my cerebrum. Whatever the case, I mulled over that word until I fell asleep in the BarcaLounger.

I awoke early the next morning, my back and neck stiff. The light from the windows was gray and cold. I heard a faint shuffling sound coming from the shop below. After a few minutes, I began to hear, at irregular intervals, the distinct sound of a cleaver on hardwood. Mr. Garrett was in, which was strange, because he rarely worked on Sundays. But I was glad. My mind was cutting the previous evening into pieces, trying to understand what had possessed me to call Darren Pederson. I needed a sounding board.

I left my apartment without bothering to bathe or change my clothes, and I walked quickly to the front of the store. A CLOSED sign hung in the window but a weak light glowed around the edges of the preparation room door. So I went back around to the alley. The metal door was shut firmly; however, as was often the case, the deadbolt was not properly set. Maintaining my custom, and Mr. Garrett's general expectation, I forewent knocking and jerked open the door with both hands. There was a high-pitched grinding sound as the top of the door slid against the frame.

Mer, do you remember reading Machen's story *The Great God Pan*? The story that inspired Lovecraft? I need you to remember it if you are to understand what I saw, and why I didn't run. Early in the story, Clarke, a principal character, is asleep in a chair in the home of a fellow scientist as a dreadful experiment is taking place. The nature of the experiment is of no importance, except that it involves not Clarke but a young woman; he is merely an observer. While asleep he dreams that he is in a familiar wood near his family home and that he has come upon a strange clearing he has never seen before. There is a horrifying presence in the clearing, something that is neither man nor beast, neither living nor dead, but somehow all things at once and yet nothing at all, something that should not be and yet is.

What I saw from the alley door was not supernatural. I could see the entire room, but there was something there I wouldn't let myself recognize. My eyes slid over it, as if it were a hollow space where nothing could exist. I remember everything of that moment, save for that roiling absence; it was all singularly vivid. I remember the way the pale morning light yielded to the bright fluorescents of the preparation room, how the white tiles shined like snow on a sunny day, how all the knives and instruments lining the walls seemed polished and brand new. I remember Mr. Garrett's face, the sweat dripping down from his bald head, his flush cheeks, and the light in his eyes, how they reminded me of a great moment of horror from my childhood, where I burst into my parents' room because I thought I had heard a shriek, and discovered my mother bent over like an animal, clutching the sheets with white fists, pressing her face into the mattress, and my father above her, gripping her hips, his brow bunched and his mouth silently open. His eyes noticed me, expressing at once surprise, shame, anger, and a strange delight in having been caught.

Such were Mr. Garrett's eyes as he stood before the chopping block wearing nothing but an apron, covered in a thin mist of red, his naked flesh tight, puckered with goosebumps.

"*Colin*?" said Mr. Garrett. "*What are you doing here*?"

I was speechless, for a moment, as I tried both to look and not to look at that strange void. "I came to talk," I said. "Last night—last night I did something."

"Come in, quickly," he said.

I did. He rushed past me and pulled the door shut.

"Coffee?" he asked, the pale weathered skin of his bare ass shaking loosely.

"Yes, please." I didn't know what I was saying. A naked man had offered me coffee.

Mr. Garrett brought me a basalt mug, full and steaming. "It's fresh," he said. "Just ground this morning. It's Ethiopian."

"Thank you."

I took two sips and then fell to my knees and vomited a heavy, citrine broth all over the white floor. The basalt mug fell and shattered.

"Now, Colin, is that *really* necessary?"

I coughed, dry-heaved twice, coughed again. I crawled away from the vomit and sat with my head between my knees.

"Are you alright, Colin?"

There was real concern in his voice. I raised my head and saw that he was at the sink, filling another mug with water.

"Here," he said, hunkering down and setting the mug beside me. "If you need it." He patted me on the knee and walked back to the other side of the cutting table.

As I followed him with my eyes, I noticed something on the floor. It was a blue blowtorch. I didn't know how I hadn't registered the smell—an undeniable mix of butane and burnt meat—earlier. Perhaps I had but wouldn't let myself recognize it, the way I still wouldn't let myself see what was on the table.

I hung my head and tried to think, to focus. There was a loud *chock* sound. But this meant nothing to me. I was numbing out. Then I felt a cold hand on my shoulder. I turned my head to see. Mr. Garrett was holding Darren's severed right hand, rubbing my shoulder with it.

Mr. Garrett sat down on the tile a few feet from me, his ruddy junk exposed. He was leaning against the cutting table. He still held the hand and began twisting the tawdry rings on its fingers. "These are really something, aren't they?" he said.

"What have you done?" I said.

"Nothing much, really. Just restored a bit of order, helped balance out my corner of the universe."

A thick drop of blood fell from the lip of the table and splashed the side of his bald head. Either he didn't notice or he just didn't mind.

I realized that he was waiting for me to speak. "What?"

"I'm waiting for a 'thank you,' but it's not all that important. Was never planning on receiving such a thing in the first place." He scratched the side of his head with Darren's hand and then looked at the blood on the fingertips. "I knew his father." He pointed the hand at me. "Twelve years ago, his sneaking, adulterous daddy put his sneaking, adulterous cock in my wife. Like father, like son. Always taking what's not theirs. I put that champion right here on this table, just where his son is now."

The strange void was gone. I got up and allowed myself to see what had become of Darren's body on the cutting table. The left leg was hacked into segments, and the right was flayed, the skin cut at the ankle and rolled up to the knee, leaving just a meat-sock. His genitals were missing entirely. Whatever remained after they were cut out had been thoroughly torched. There was nothing left but a flat blackened mass of gristle that leaked a cloudy fluid.

"The sins of the fathers visited on the sons of-bitches!" Mr. Garrett yelled.

He shook the body roughly and then grabbed its chin with his left hand. He pried open the dead mouth. Then he reached for something behind the table that I could not see and brought it up with his right hand. He carefully placed Darren's severed genitals into the open mouth and then closed it the best he could. Satisfied, Mr. Garrett lightly slapped Darren's chin. "Ball-gag," he said gleefully.

I no longer even felt nauseous.

"I suppose you should be going now, Colin," said Mr. Garrett. "Unless, of course, you could use some more stress-relief?"

Forgive me, Mer. This is not who I am.

I took my clothes off, all except for my briefs, and I took a long, serrated blade from the wall. Mr. Garret crossed his arms and stepped away from the table, smiling. When I was finished, what was left on the table was not recognizably human. I was not recognizably human.

Standing over his body, flecked in his blood, that sense of wonderful mystery began to return to me. Even in this, I thought, there is a tinge of the aesthetic. I looked down at my body, at the red sheen of my abdomen, the fresh patriotic stripes on my white briefs, the shades of spent life jellied in lines down my legs.

I am beautiful, I thought. I am a god.

NICODEMUS

Now there was a young man named Renato Buendía, a second-generation Spanish-American and doctoral candidate in comparative literature at a prestigious university in a more or less dignified city located somewhere in the drear of New England, who, sitting across from a fair-skinned, lucid-eyed rascal of a woman at a trendy downtown eatery (Café Nonchalance), arrived, rather elliptically, at an epiphany: He was in love.

Immediately, Renato Buendía distrusted this idea. What was love, anyway? Emotion? Commitment over a lengthy course? A transcendent spiritual connectedness? Just this thump in his chest? He thought of his father sermonizing to him on the subject when he was sixteen, skinny, and rather ugly. They were alone on the back porch of the family home in Georgia, sharing a cold Coors in the heat. "Never over-glorify it, son. The emotion comes and goes. Mostly it goes. In the end love is nothing more than an action." José Arcadio was a sturdy pragmatist (oblivious to the irony of his name, though his son was not), a no-nonsense sort of man full of wisdom and bullshit in equal measure. Renato expected this advice was something of both. Certainly the emotion was there, and had been for the bulk of his seven-month relationship with Lara. The action was there, too, presenting itself in gestures large and small—repainting her house and cleaning the gutters; the time-sacrifices he made to accommodate her nursing schedule; the notes of encouragement he secreted about her home whenever he sensed she was melancholy or exhausted. But was seven months long enough? He suspected not, but had a strange urge to scream otherwise.

Lara was staring at him, challenging him through the chromatic dissonance of her eyes, waiting for him to say something, probably reading his mind. She spoke.

"Stop it."

"What?"

"Shifting your glance. First you stare at my green eye, then at my blue eye. Then back again. Just pick one. You know it makes me self-conscious."

"I'm sorry. I really can't help it. *You* know that. It's what people normally do in conversation. They look at one eye, then the other. It's not like I called you Blugra."

Lara narrowed her eyes. The sobriquet *Blugra*, an uninspired contraction of "blue-green," had followed her from the second grade through the end of middle school, in permutations ranging from *Blago* to *Beluga*. Lara hated it. She sipped her water and then spat a fine mist at Renato.

He swatted the air, cursed, and wiped his face. "I love you," he said, and sat rigid. He had startled the hell out of himself.

"Are you sure?" Lara asked.

"What? God. Of course I'm sure." He thought maybe he was losing his mind.

"Well, I'm not so sure. You look like you just pissed yourself."

"I—" A heat crept into his ears. "I caught myself off guard. It's not something I thought I'd say for a while."

"If it's true, then why shouldn't you say it?"

Renato sighed and leaned forward. "There's no reason. Actually, I think it just now occurred to me that I am, that I do, that—" He lost it again. "Hell, you know what I mean?"

"Nope. But I love you, too."

She leaned forward, grinning like a succubus, and grabbed him by the collar and pulled him across the table. The kiss was quick and fearsome, her tongue slashing through his mouth like an orthodontic instrument. Renato flailed his arms. Somehow, all of it was delightful.

When they unfastened, she wiped the saliva from his lips with the blade of her hand and sat back in her chair. "You know, women expect more from Spaniards. We want to be conquered and swept away. Or at least I do. I want a Conquistador. I expect a Conquistador. And you literally just flailed your arms when I kissed you. *Conquistadors don't flail.* If we're going to be in love now, you need to get your shit together."

Renato's neck went flush. He never knew what to expect of her. Even though she was clearly teasing, he felt ashamed. He longed to be suave, self-assured, debonair. He longed to dash around on a white horse, brandishing a gilt rapier, rushing into danger. Longed to brush aside his tired, scholarly husk, to dive out the lone window of his ivory tower. For a moment he stared at Lara, imagining her in a glittering white gown, tied to her chair, at the mercy of some murderous rogue (the Rogue Barista of Nonchalance, perhaps). Suddenly, he was aware of men looking in their direction, or at least thought he was aware of them—scores of them, hundreds of them, thousands, hell, all of the men in New England seemed to have materialized within the walls of Café Nonchalance, or perhaps it was just their essences, or one single essence, the essence of the *other man*, the usurper, the scourge. He stood abruptly, absurdly. An ancestral wildness flung itself upon him, unearthed blood-memories, images of savagery, of brilliance, of men in round-ridged helmets with long spears and iron breastplates, of men dressed in flamboyant gold capes, of the deaths of bulls and the silver-throated cheers of dusty crowds. Without a word, without a clue as to what in holy hell he was doing, he strode around the table, lifted Lara over his shoulder and rushed out of the café.

THEY MADE their way to a nearby park and lay down under an oak tree, wanting desperately to touch each other, worried about the impropriety of doing so in public on a Sunday afternoon while still wearing their church clothes. Lara settled for laying her head on Renato's shoulder.

A lovely silence ensued for half an hour.

Then, "Do you feel reborn?"

Lara spoke with her cheek against Renato's clavicle. It felt as though his own body had produced the sound.

"I've been thinking—" she began.

"Oh, honey, don't do *that*." As soon as he said it, Renato felt the pinch of Lara's teeth on his pectoral. "You bit me!"

"You interrupted me," she said. "I was being serious."

"Then be serious." Renato rubbed his chest.

"What did you mean when you said you loved me?"

Renato froze. He became aware of an acorn digging into his back. "How am I supposed to answer that? I meant, I mean, that I love you."

"But what is love? What does 'love' mean to you?"

"It means what it means to everyone—"

"Stop parrying."

Renato sighed. He reached beneath him and removed the offending acorn. He looked at it.

"I don't want you to love me with some non-specific, off-brand love. I want juicy, idiosyncratic, weird-ass Renato love. Come on, tell me what that love is."

Renato squeezed a fist around the acorn and sat up. He thought for the second time that day about his father. Jose

Arcadio rarely said the word "love," but Renato could always feel it—in his attentiveness, his patience with his wife and son.

"It isn't non-specific," he said. "It's just new. Even right now I'm discovering what it means."

"That's better, but it still feels like a dodge."

"Earlier, when I carried you, that was absurd. But it was right. It was like all of sudden I was jealous. But it was an abstract jealousy. Being around you, I want to conjure up enemies to contend with. I want someone to try and mug us so I can throw myself at the guy to protect you." He was silent for a moment. "That's it," he said. "The certainty I'll act for your good."

Lara smiled. She took Renato's hand and pried the acorn from his fingers.

"Your turn," Renato said.

"I asked you earlier if you feel reborn," she said.

"Reborn?"

"Into water and the spirit?"

He had retained only vagaries from that morning's sermon—God's love, spiritual rebirth, light bursting into the world and all that jazz. He had spent most of his time at church entertaining the horrific image of old Nicodemus clawing his way back inside his mother. "Yeah, I do. Of course I do."

She rocked her head on his chest for a moment and then sat up. She looked at him and said, "I've been thinking that it's more than that."

"More than what?"

"More than spiritual. That it's here and now, and messy. God's love demands that we die and be reborn. I want all love to be that way. To force me to let go of things. Be a better me. I want your love for me to do that. And I want my love to do that for you."

Renato leaned forward and kissed her once.

She smiled. "Now that we love each other, what are we leaving behind? What part of the old self is falling off?"

"You go first," he said.

She laid out for him all the emotional baggage of her past relationships, all her insecurities, her dissatisfactions with past lovers, her expectations of future dissatisfaction. She told him about her distant father, the way she felt like a stereotype every time she chased a man's approval, how she had never learned to simply be alone with herself. She told him she would leave it all behind and be reborn through their romance.

"Now you go," she said.

Renato searched his mind. His self-inspection tended to be a passive affair, a search for self-knowledge for its own sake, rarely for application. He knew this in itself was something that had to go, and he told her as much. He also shared the full extent of his loneliness. Renato was almost thirty years old and Lara was his first serious relationship. Because of her the loneliness had abated, but it was still there, waiting like a shadow under soft lights. He could not tell her about the specter of his shame, how he believed his long years of isolation to be a justice, that there was something within him that others could smell and knew to avoid.

As he spoke, he felt himself withdrawing from her into a half-honesty. He sensed Lara's mood cooling. *She knows I'm withholding*, he thought.

He ended their date with the excuse that he needed the rest of the evening to write. She kissed him unreservedly as they parted, but then held his gaze until he saw the curiosity and sadness mingling in her eyes.

He returned to his apartment feeling that he had stalemated things, knowing that something awful had its claws in him.

He could get no work done on his dissertation that night, only false starts and dead ends. He would write a brilliant paragraph and lick his lips with excitement, only to realize that it had absolutely nothing to do with his thesis (Kafka's influence on South American magical realism). He was about a fifth finished and his working title was *Awe of the Absurd: Kafka Through Borges and Garcia Marquez*. Tonight, for the first time, he realized how pretentious that title sounded and slammed his fist against the desk.

At one point he got cooking for about forty minutes and kicked out nearly three pages. He lifted his hands from the keyboard, rubbed his eyes and reviewed what he had written:

> It is no exaggeration to say that Borges not only esteemed Kafka, but also found in him an inspiration that surpassed even that of Dante. This, of course, is no small claim. We see in *La Infernos*, the first of Borges' *Seven Nights*, the renowned lecture series given in Buenos Aires during the week of the week of the week of the unspeakable the unspeakable the intractable the week of that thing which was done perpetrated exacted to and from you when your cosmic fool of a father took your blessed family to the gold and dusted land of your forebears and left you let alone you a poor babe alone with your uncle on that brown outskirt of Madrid in the gray room of that gray house left you to the foul unknown tastes of of of when he had left gone for sights and romance with mother touched you there in the grayness stole you there in the grayness voided you there held hands behind your back and slid jeans down twelve-year-old thighs placed ruddy laborer's thumb there in the sweet foulness licked salty tears from dirty cheeks stole made corrupt left chaff only chaff dry and salt and fuck and drained of innocence and this this this rips down all a blind white flat-headed worm sightless drinking darkness absorbing the blood the life the the Christ the the

The passage went on like this, folding back on itself, cyclic, inane, engorged with both nonsense and painful truth—a dark, solitary abreaction. Renato rose and walked steadily to the bathroom and began dry heaving over the sink. The image of a man's face sat dark and heavy over his mind. He felt very old. A long-buried self-hatred burned its way to the surface of his consciousness and Renato gripped the porcelain sink hard enough to pop his knuckles. He was breaking apart. Despair like a beast fell upon him.

He dropped to his knees and tried to cry out. But he spoke in a whisper, "*Forgive, forgive, oh. Burn it away.*"

He stood and lumbered his way to his bedroom. He collapsed onto his covers and was overcome by a black sleep.

WHAT DREAMS he had were dark and fleeting, the shapeless dreams of a fetus suspended in ether. When he awakened he blinked at the strange yellow light pouring through the window. He was in pain the likes of which he had never thought possible. He tried to move his toes but could not. He exhaled and the meat of his lungs rattled his ribcage. He touched his face and then looked at his hands. He screamed, but what came out was dust and rasping. During sleep he had undergone a transformation. He struggled to prop himself up and look at his twisted body, naked though he knew he had gone to sleep in his clothes. What he saw was monstrous: He was an old man, ancient and rotting. He smelled of dead things, of excrement. Renato let out a long moan and cried.

Suddenly, he felt an urge to leave his apartment. He tried to move his legs, but they were dead, useless logs. He pushed himself upright and let his own miserable weight tumble him out of bed. His head thudded against the floor and violet lightning struck in his periphery. When he felt his head, he discovered that it had split open and that it was hairless. He began to crawl forward, knowing that something like gelatin was sliding down his face.

He made it to the stairway and began pulling himself down using the rungs of the banister. The carpet tore at the flesh of his belly and he knew it was peeling off and rubbing away. He felt like a skinned rabbit dumped into a salt-bin. At the bottom of the stairs he twisted his neck and saw that he was trailing gore. One leg had detached from his hip and lay oozing three steps up. A brackish fluid gurgled from his mouth.

He arrived, miraculously, at his front door. Salvation lay beyond the threshold. He knew this, knew only this. All else was darkness. With all his strength he pushed forward and fumbled at the knob. He grasped it, organs falling out of his open chest, and turned.

The door fell ajar and the apartment was flooded with the crisp light of an October morning.

Renato slid forward over the slickness of his discharged viscera. He collapsed with his head just beyond the threshold, staring at the street, his mouth leering obscenely.

Something twisted in what remained of his chest, pushing itself upward. Soon it was in his neck, thick as a bowling ball and driving hard. It exploded out of his mouth in an excruciating splash of teeth and gums.

And then he was that something. He clawed his way forward, pushing away at the bloody lips constricted around his chest. Then he was free.

He stood up, naked, hot with youth, covered in black blood and unspeakable fluids, and looked back at the withered mess of old man that sat like a pool of placenta in his doorway. Its mouth was the size of a toilet bowl.

An irrepressible joy filled him, head to foot.

RENATO BUENDÍA tore down the street, wanting desperately to embrace Lara. It took him ten minutes of sprinting to reach her small, yellow house. He pounded on the front door, unaware that he was dripping afterbirth on the welcome mat. A rustling came from within the white-shuttered window. The venetian blinds were cracked and a green eye blinked out at him. Lara opened the door and stared wide-eyed at Renato. He stared right back.

She was stark naked, her body wrapped in the same bloody, gelatinous caul as his own, her long brown hair a dark curtain of mucous pasted to her back. Her breasts were slick, lidded with film like the eyes of bullfrogs. She reached out and picked a veiny tendril of gore from Renato's shoulder and looked at it before flicking it aside.

He opened his mouth to speak, but she pressed her index finger to his lips and shook her head. Smiling, she pulled him inside and shut the door.

FAINTLY FALLING

> And then Louder: "So now you know what else existed in the world outside of you, before you knew only about yourself! Yes, you were a truly innocent child, but you were even more truly an evil man!—And for that reason, I hereby sentence you to death by drowning!"
>
> —Franz Kafka, "The Judgment"

The string of bells jingled as the door opened and a cold draft worked through the bookstore's cafe and into Michael's skin. He rubbed his arms as he looked up and saw the girl from church ordering at the counter. He had seen her here before and had the impression that she lived nearby, as she was never quite dressed for the snow. Today she wore a thin navy cardigan over an oxford, tight, beat-to-hell jeans, and canvas sneakers with no socks. She smiled at the barista and fiddled with a few dollars as he poured her coffee. Seeing her, Michael's heart did not flutter, nor did it bounce, skip beats, or do anything even remotely romantic. Instead, it burned with a sudden shame. His subconscious broiled with the fear that she must know that he stared at her at church, entertaining preposterous fantasies about her to pass the time during services, and that she could smell him for what he was—a gutless, lustful, lonely man terrified of intimacy. The idea drifted up through the layers of his thought until he saw it clearly. Was he really any of those things? He chose to deny it as absurdity and the sensation of embarrassment slowly abated. But when she looked over her shoulder in Michael's direction he quickly plunged back into his book and would not allow himself to look at her for several minutes.

He was reading *The Dark Night of the Soul*—a quagmire of endless sentences, painful approximations of the original sixteenth-century Spanish, and unfamiliar mystical theology. It was only one-hundred-fifty pages but the more Michael read of it the more he thought it would never end, as if the book fed back on itself in some invisible textual Moebius. Though the book was rife with the aroma of near-heresy, Michael found succor in its honest treatment of human emotion. It was comforting to know that someone else (St. John of the Cross), in another time, had also felt abandoned by God, had felt his faith whittled down to splinters, and yet saw through the experience to a greater reality: All was purgation. His senses were being deprived of the divine presence, he was being subjected to pain and loneliness and isolation in life, all so that he might be rid of his dependency on himself and on mere emotional experience. He told himself that it was a temporary trial, that at the end would be genuine peace and a greater intimacy with his maker.

Michael closed the book and rubbed his eyes. He felt muddled. A few customers navigated the aisles of books that enclosed the cafe, but they were silent, as if they were in a library and not a bookstore. Michael usually enjoyed the quiet—it was why he often came here to write and study—but just then it felt oppressive. The cafe was empty save for himself, the barista, a pair of men speaking softly at a table near the front, and the beautiful stranger from his church, who had taken a seat facing him just two tables away. It occurred to him that it would be nothing to get up and introduce himself to her. Their eyes had met on more than a few occasions at church and she must certainly recognize him. He knew that once he rose, and she saw him approaching, the necessary words would come to him, that he would be friendly, charming enough to perhaps sustain her interest for a while. But it was that initial movement that caused him trouble. Fear, anxiety, the weight of shame—their sum was a powerful inertia. Michael leaned back in his chair and stared at the high, bare ceiling. It was nothing but row after row of I-beams and a smattering of pipes, all of it painted green. Above it were two floors of dusty, unused apartment space awaiting a remodeling that might never come. Michael sighed. He imagined the emptiness of those rooms as bearing actual weight, keeping him fixed in place.[1]

The girl answered her phone, which had begun vibrating on the table. Her lips curved in a smile that, for its brilliance, might have passed through the receiver and touched whoever was on the other end. Michael assumed it must be some arrogant frat boy with a predilection for popped collars and hemp anklets. But her emotion fled as quickly as it had come and her lips sagged in a weak pout. Someone had stood her up, Michael thought. She closed her phone, returned it to her pocket, and attended to her coffee. This was an opportunity. He could tell she intended to leave soon because she was fidgeting and drinking her coffee too fast. But he couldn't work up the nerve to approach her. He decided to seek a sign. He would return to his book for a few moments and then look directly at her until she met his gaze. If she held it and smiled, he would pull his head out of his ass and introduce himself. Michael tried to ignore the

1 These are not the words I want. I have always been easily ensnared by sentimentality, that singular weakness of introspection, and I do not know how to incorporate here a certain line of Pascal's without surrendering it to mawkishness. *The eternal silence of these infinite spaces fills me with dread.* Why, O sentence, can I not make you mine?

prickly sensation in his arms and returned to St. John of the Cross, pressing a finger beneath the heading, *Chapter IX—Of the signs by which it will be known that the spiritual person is walking along the way of this night and purgation of the sense—*

Foolish, he thought. *You're being foolish. Cowardly. Stand up. Just stand up. Go to her.*

He stood. She looked at him and he smiled. She returned the smile.

"Hey," he said.

"Hey," she said.

"Do you mind if I join you for a bit?" he said. "I've had my head buried in a book for a while and could use some human contact."

"Be my guest." She sat up straight and adjusted her long braided blonde hair so that it fell behind the backrest of her chair.

Michael collected his book and coffee and sat down across from her.

"You go to Trinity Fellowship, right?" she said, her words a bit too quick.

"Yes," he said. "I've gone there my whole life."

"Really?" she said. "I just started about a month ago. I'm Greta." She smiled, her lightly freckled cheeks dimpling, and extended her hand.

Michael took it and the spark of physical contact threatened to undo him. Greta's hand was soft, small, and contained a subtle hum of electricity. Michael fought the urge to linger on the sensation, managed a smile of his own, and told Greta his name.

"I enjoy it," she said. "It's already starting to feel like home. But I'm curious. What was the former pastor like? I noticed him last week but felt awkward about introducing myself. People talk about him like he's a saint."

"I don't know about saint, but he was an incredible teacher. He's much more cerebral than this new guy. He was a seminary professor before coming to Trinity. He'd always dip into the Greek and Hebrew if he thought he could get away with it. I miss his sermons."

"You're not a fan of Pastor Don, then?"

"Oh, it's not that.[2] He's much more personable than Pastor Kramer ever was. But I grew up listening to Kramer and, well, it's not that I'm averse to change," Michael paused, thoughtful. "Transitions are always awkward."

Greta smiled. "Tell me about it."

"What are you transitioning from, or to, for that matter?"

"I transferred to State at the end of last year, from a small school in North Carolina. Barton College. I'm still adjusting to being in a new place." It was then that Michael took note of her voice: It was deep and melodic, Southern, but not so Southern that he found it irritating.

"Can I ask why you transferred?"

"You just did."

"Hey," Michael said, raising his hands in mock-defense. "If you don't want to answer, don't answer."

"Sorry. It's not a matter of not wanting to answer. I don't know. I have a hard time gauging how open I should be when I first meet people. I've been known to run people off with too much information." Greta blushed and Michael thought her embarrassment so attractive that he also reddened.

"I consider candor a virtue." Michael tried to smile but managed only to squeeze his lips into a thin line. He shifted uncomfortably in his chair and worried that Greta would think him pedantic, or worse, insincere.

If she did, she gave no indication. Instead, she unraveled an account of the great emotional blight of her first twenty-one years of existence. She explained how she had been in love with a young man named Landon Gibbons since junior year of high school, how they had maintained their relationship through two

---

2 It was precisely that. Donnie Aberline is not just an asshole, but a poorly educated asshole. If you're standing behind a pulpit, you sure as shit better know Greek. Pastor Don, how little respect I have for you and your Independent Baptist heritage. Your High Calvinism. You split my church with your graceless theology, you shifty, fundamentalist fuck.

years of college and seven-hundred-and-forty-five miles of rolling Appalachian and Midwestern nothingness, how last spring Landon had proposed with a gleaming Buick-sized stone, paid for by an obscene, musty wad of Carolinian old money, how she had all but screamed her acceptance and began to arrange, at Landon's coaxing, her transfer the same week, only to discover six months later, after a blissful summer of ocean-side strolls and late-night lovemaking, her fiancé—the man who had quietly taken her virginity three years before, whose soul, she believed, had grown so enmeshed with her own as to allow for the silent transmission of thought and emotion—desperately fucking, with the reckless, bestial abandon of bonobo chimpanzees carousing within the bowels of Sodom, a buxom brunette of unquestionably mongrel parentage, whose name Greta hoped and, in more barbarous moments, prayed would be stricken from the Book of Life and found writhing and teeth-gnashing in the insatiable maw of Hell, and how the entire experience, the *transition*, far from dulling out with time, had managed to unfix itself from its place in history and tear at her heart with every lucid, nightmarish memory. She suspected it would never end.

Michael leaned back, at once startled by Greta's coarseness, by the power of the emotional miasma that she had flushed into the air, and resonating with the sentiment, this spontaneous willingness to vent and, hopefully, commiserate with a stranger.[3] He did not quite know how to respond. They watched each other for an uneasy moment, until Michael, tottering on the back legs of his chair, lost his balance and nearly tipped over. He recovered and the front legs crashed back into place, scuffing the floor. They both laughed until their laughter became coughing and the two men cast admonitory glances at them from their table at the front.

---

3 I learned later that it was Landon who had stood her up that afternoon, that she was so receptive to me because she needed an immediate distraction. She couldn't bear going to her apartment to be alone.

"I know. T-M-I, right?" She was still laughing or coughing or both, and struggled to get the words out.

"No, that was perfect. I suppose anything else would have been dishonest."

Greta smiled. She shifted in her seat to uncross her legs, and, in doing so, brushed against Michael's shin. The contact lasted only a moment but was powerful enough to send a cold thrill spiraling up Michael's thigh to his groin.

"So, what's this?" Greta lifted *The Dark Night of the Soul* and began to scan the back cover, which only vaguely revealed the book's contents.

"It's hard to explain. I guess you could say it's about spiritual transitions."

"You're transitioning, too?"

"Sort of. The word implies that there is a destination, something to move into. As of now, I have nothing. I graduated last May and was all set to begin seminary this past fall. Then finances fell through."

"What are you doing now?"

Michael grunted a weak laugh and let his eyes fall to the table. He wanted to be open with her as she had been with him, but something held him back. He wanted to explain why he was reading the book she held. He was searching for glimmers of truth and wisdom to preserve him through what had become a microcosmic hell, a fuddling, premortem limbo where he hung flaccidly between the end of college and the beginning of whatever came next. Graduation had been eight months before, and every day Michael felt more strongly that nothing was on the horizon, that he was one more rocket grounded on its launching pad by the recession. If asked, he would affirm that he had hope for the future, that he knew this was a temporary trial, that *life* would begin soon. But for Michael hope was an intellectual theorem that did not translate into emotional reality. Though free to do as he pleased, living under his parents' roof seemed an abortion of his independence. But he was unemployed, too poor to afford graduate school or move anywhere, and too abasing of his own maturity to allow himself to work for the church. He had no options. The one thing he did have was his writing, which was nothing if not stifled by his circumstances.[4] He had produced only five stories since graduating and only one—written in a caffeinated flurry after the first of a handful of attempts at charitable service—was worth its ink. Michael hated the town of his birth, hated his state. He longed to be somewhere mountainous, with open water, in a place that nurtured a sense of the aesthetic rather than smothering it with corn and beans.

Finally, he answered her. "I'm living in my parents' basement. Trying to find gainful employment. Discovering how unhirable I am."

"You really live in their basement?"

"No." The Catherwood basement was entirely unlivable. It served as a laundry room—or, rather, the place where a quarter century of Catherwood clothing had been dumped and mostly forgotten, left to fester in moldering mounds and generate an ever-changing, utterly rapacious odor—and habitat for mutant, inbred crickets. Michael told Greta as much, and she laughed.

"There's nothing wrong with living at home," she said. "Unless you're dating, or bringing back girls. I suppose that could be awkward." She took a sip of coffee. Then, almost as an afterthought, she said, "Do you have a girlfriend?"[5]

---

4 Overly familiar places—places stained with memory—stifle creativity. Too much psychic residuum and my brain starts chirping like a Geiger-counter. Even now, two years later and a thousand miles away, I've allowed a new place to become familiar, to accumulate resonances. The dry heat of Waco deadens my soul and I will abandon it soon.

5 It occurs to me that you may be wondering why Greta was so forward with me. The answer is easy: Though inexperienced with women and almost perpetually nervous, I was, nevertheless, remarkably attractive. Please, by all means, laugh at my hubris. I have included no physical description of Michael because it feels unnatural to describe my looks in the third person. I am, give or take, six feet tall with dirty-blonde hair and blue eyes—an Aryan specimen. My face is not as symmetrical as I would like it to be.

"Ha. No." Michael tried to force himself to act casual, but could not, for the life of him, decide what behavior qualified as casual.

"Really?" Her smile was quizzical and flirtatious. She drew a finger slowly around the rim of her mug, waiting for him to say something.

History flashed through Michael's mind, still-frames of all those moments he had fallen on his ass during dates, failed to make a girl laugh or smile, said something off-color or insensitive or, worst of all, been merely bland and unaffecting. An irrational notion found its way into his mind. He felt as if he were in an interrogation room, sweating under a boiling lamp, a powerful, darkly dressed woman sitting at the opposite end of a steel table, spitting questions he did not know how to answer at him.

"Really," he said.

"Can I ask why?"

"You just did."

Greta feigned indignation. "Did you just get out of a relationship, or something?"

Michael wanted to say that his singleness was merely a result of his being in flux, that finding someone here, at this time, would tie him down to his home, which would be terrible. But the half-truth didn't sit well with him. "I've never been in a relationship. Nothing with a label, anyway. I know. Pathetic, right?"

"No. It's not pathetic, it's—" she paused, seeming to search for something tactful. "I don't know what it is."

"Well, I don't know either."

Greta smiled, and Michael found the expression reassuring. "It's unusual," she said. "In a good way. Relationships inevitably mean baggage. Landon is the only guy I've ever been with. I really wish I could have those years back."

"But you now have access to wisdom that someone like me doesn't."

"Yeah. I don't know. That doesn't help wash the taste out of my mouth."

"Can anything?"

"Time. Maybe a few more failed relationships to put some space between me and the memory."

"Am I supposed to find that funny?"

"I don't."

Had Michael been a braver man, he would have taken her hand and squeezed it and said something adequately reassuring and romantic. Instead, he smiled and told her he needed to get going.[6] "Will I see you at church Sunday?" he said.

"Sure," she said. "It was good to meet you."

OUTSIDE, MICHAEL took a deep breath, letting the cold January air wash through him. It was early evening and the sun was setting beyond the Wabash River, casting swatches of gold and orange and light hints of violet into the clouds. Michael often thought that if anything could redeem Indiana, for all its flatness and philistinism, it would be its sunsets. They were miraculous, and, for their strange juxtaposition with such awful blandness, mysteriously dissonant. Save for a silver Lexus, the street before him was vacant, covered by a sluice of brown snow. A man sat in the driver's seat of the Lexus, scribbling on a legal pad and moving his chin to the beat of whatever music played from the stereo. Michael studied the clouds, their brilliant interlaced hues, struggling to achieve some spontaneous aeromantic insight into what lay ahead for him. He did not pray exactly; rather he cast his thoughts and inquiries skyward, not quite hoping and not quite doubting that they would be answered. He closed his eyes. A placid indifference settled upon him. He succeeded, for the moment, in shutting out all thought of Greta. His inclination was to evaluate the encounter, slice it into logical slivers, determine if he had made a solid impression and how best to

---

6 I recall having suddenly remembered an age-old relational chestnut advising guys to make sure they're the ones to end a phone call, date, etc. On *Seinfeld*, I believe George Costanza referred to this as maintaining "hand" in a relationship. This may be the only time I have put *Seinfeld* wisdom into practice.

approach his next interaction with her. But that would happen later in the night, when he would toss and fight to fall asleep. For the moment he was content to think of nothing.

Michael opened his eyes. Across the street a robin hopped along the edge of a second-story windowsill. He wondered why the robin had returned so early from the south. Its presence at this time of year was unnatural. The robin twisted its head left and right, studying the world before it, and then paused, seeming to look at Michael. The bird dropped from the ledge and flew down in a sweeping spiral to the street only a few feet from where Michael stood. It skittered around, fluttering its wings and puffing out his chest, and began to pick at the multitude of sunflower seeds that had spilled from a discarded bag. The bag lay partly beneath the parked Lexus, sunken in slush near the left front tire. When the engine turned over and grunted to life, the robin merely twisted its head and looked at it and then resumed picking at the seeds. Michael thought of shooing the bird away, but did nothing. If the robin was aware of his presence, it was indifferent. It was out of place, all alone in the cold north, and had found nourishment. And that was all that mattered.

The image of what happened next burned itself into Michael's mind. The robin snapped up several seeds and raised its head, seeming to savor them before swallowing. As far as a creature without lips can express emotion, the robin seemed to be in a state of rapture. Even in the shadow of the Lexus, the bird's dark eyes gleamed. Then, as the driver shifted the car into gear, the robin, standing amidst the seeds and slush, closed its eyes. The car thrust forward, over the robin. Its abdomen ruptured, exploding a line of blood and viscera across the pavement. Then the man and his Lexus were gone, speeding away, oblivious.

Michael looked at the robin, which was not entirely ground into the street (only the legs and lower back had been compressed), and experienced an odd sinking sensation. The poor creature stared blindly back through bulging, grotesque eyes, a crimson bubble ballooning from its beak. When it burst,

Michael was overcome with the sensation of falling. He leaned forward and steadied himself with his hands on his knees. He shut his eyes, but the image of the bird's dark *eyes* remained, leering forth from the black of his vision. And the strange sensation became a strange word, an awful whistling refrain that seemed to Michael to echo from the very soul of the dead thing as it dissipated into the air: *falling, falling, falling*. And, faintly, he heard footsteps behind him, felt a soft hand grip his arm.

It was Greta. He looked up at her and saw concern.

"Are you okay?" she said.

"I'm fine," he said, and stood up. "Just feeling a little lightheaded."

"You sure?" She put a hand on his shoulder and he managed a smile.

"I'm sure." He looked at her face, at eyes that were beautiful and haunting and mysterious, long enough so that their image replaced that of the bird's and his feeling of falling, of dying, was replaced by one of refreshment.

"Anyways," she said, "I'm glad I caught you. I wanted to give you this"—she produced a small note on which was written a phone number—"in case you'd like to see me before Sunday."[7]

A FEW weeks later, Michael sat alone on the floor of his bedroom, blinking in candlelight. This was his ritual: He played guitar to clear his mind, perhaps read a few Psalms, then turned out the lights and lit a single candle and began to meditate, not quite in the lotus but near to it, sitting there communing with the small mite of Cherokee blood that swam inside him, thinking of who he was, what he was, of the man he hoped to become, and praying, speaking his mind to his God. This was an escape and

---

7 It's not often we happen across strong omens, especially ones whose interpretations are so simple. When mine came, I recognized it immediately. Then I shoved it down deep to somewhere it couldn't bother me.

a silent, personal declaration of what his religion should be, a protestation against what it was not. As a teenager he had been told a story by a missionary who had served in Russia. A few years after the fall of the Soviet Union, a small group of American students had come to visit for a time and serve with him, to see and understand the quiet and hidden faith that had suffered under communism. They were all together, Russians with their American brothers, in a circle at night, around a fire, attempting fellowship despite the language barrier. The Americans were singing and laughing, praising their God as they would have at home, smiling, merely existing in major tonality, as if all were light and lithe and could never be any other way. The Russians were quiet, for their faith was different. They were not indignant with the others, rather, they were perplexed. Faith was something somber and beautiful, something lived out in the quiet of night and pursued underground where perhaps persecution might not touch them. When this was explained to the Americans, they were startled and ashamed. Michael was entranced with that image of faith: always serious, always sincere. And so he would light a candle on certain nights, in the quiet of his room, and struggle to experience his faith as something real.

But for so long it had been a shadow, the lingering ghost of past experience. He felt nothing sitting there with his candle, trying to be reverent. There was no question now: He had sunk completely into the dark night, into the purgation of the sense. He could not remember the last time he had felt anything identifiable as the presence of God. It was as if God had simply ceased to exist, or had at least fled Michael's small corner of the universe and left him with the inescapable suspicion that he would never be returning. He imagined that he now knew two separate worlds, the one of his past, of the faith of his youth, possessed of a wondrous metaphysic, inhabited by a God who both understood and loved him, and the one of his present, into which he had been involuntarily thrust, a world where there was no God, a nightmare land inhabited only by a hideous barking absurdity that threatened always to snatch away any joy or hope or truth that Michael managed to discover, a world that would cycle on forever in utter chaos, that would not tolerate reason or beauty or goodness or sanity, that catered only to depravity, temptation, and the slow burning hells of indecision and irresolution, a fever-sleep from which there was no reprieve or waking.

Michael breathed and exhaled and the flame rippled and shadows danced about the room. He closed his eyes and thought of Greta, of the time they had spent together since their first meeting. Their second encounter had gone well. Somehow the terror of being with someone so attractive, of exposing himself to the intrusion of intimate discourse, had not touched him. They had met at a small pub they both enjoyed and, once warmed by a few drinks, shared more of their histories. It was strange to Michael how naturally the subject of sex had arisen and how open they had been about their pasts. Michael had less to share, of course, a mere two experiences, the most recent of which had been over five years ago, and the latter was unflattering, hardly romantic. He had been visiting a friend at his university in northern Indiana and met a girl there who, unbeknownst to Michael (or her), had, through years of nymphomaniacal acumen—and despite possessing what could only be described as a blistering, exotic beauty—acquired the moniker 'Superbeast.' It had been a long, awkward night of mutual masturbation that ended in umbrage when Michael refused to have intercourse with her and she refused to finish what she had started. Lying next to her, enduring the dull ache induced by three hours of foreplay, he had fallen asleep thinking of a girl for whom he actually gave a damn.[8]

8 I will not mention her name, she of the true and tested character; suffice to say that it is Gaelic for "dark one of the north," a meaning that is nothing if not alluring. What a foil she plays to the fool I fondled in Muncie. In accord with her name, I met her deep in the north of Michigan and spent a night holding her on the shore of Lake Huron, auroras glowing above us, stars falling every few minutes, the moon hovering just above the dark water—a combination of elements that rarely occurs outside of daydreams. A pity I was too afraid of intimacy to allow her any traction in my life.

Greta, in her turn, described to him the night she lost her virginity to Landon. It was the middle of her senior year of high school and a Saturday night—she remembered that clearly because of the wrenching guilt she felt the next morning at church. It was no accident: His parents had left town for the weekend and she had contrived, through a delicate logistical finagling, to stay with him. What she remembered most clearly was not the pleasure of it, nor the weight of his body, nor the first quick bite of pain, but the stillness of the room, how she could hardly even hear their breathing, how they had said nothing during or after but had merely held each other in the quiet.

By the end of the evening Greta and Michael's interaction had become decidedly flirtatious, she pinching or punching him at every off-color comment, he reciprocating with nonsensical insults or maneuvers of his own. Smelling her and thanking her for not showering or deodorizing. Accusing her of trying to intoxicate him with her pheromones. Foolish things laughable only to the mutually inebriated. For the first time in perhaps four years Michael was becoming infatuated. He felt none of his previous apprehension or embarrassment around Greta and managed, quite naturally, to exist in the moment, in the fluid present. Then it happened. In the wake of many smiles and laughs she had laid her head against Michael's shoulder, and everything for him went silent. His body seemed at once to become cold, save for the warmth pulsating from that point of contact. He found her hand and interlocked their fingers. They sat that way for some time, at peace in themselves, in their shared warmth, Michael concentrating only on the sensation of her breath breaking lightly against his neck. He surprised himself by kissing her.

Michael held his palm above the flame. Grains of carbon collected against his skin, forming a dark patch that he rubbed and spread out in spirals with a finger. He lingered for a moment on the symbolism inherent in the act: a source of light, of goodness, also sullying, his indulging in both the warmth and the pollution. He knew where his relationship with Greta was leading, or, rather, the knowledge was present somewhere inside him, threatening to come to the fore and end the brief snatch of joy that had entered his life. Since the night at the pub, their interactions had grown increasingly physical. They were sharing, growing in their awareness of each other, sure. However, Michael sensed that around Greta he was somehow not in control of himself. Things that until now had been unthinkable felt only natural with her.[9] Time spent with Greta was sheer dissonance. The warm rush of emotion as she caressed his neck, the tickle of her tongue inside his mouth, her body folded against him, the mysterious thing shifting behind her eyes as, sitting together on the plush couch in her loft apartment, they would silently dare each other to go further; these things, these delightful things, were always pitted against a voice shouting somewhere behind and above Michael—the invasive clarion call of morality, issuing from the mouth of a God who seemed not to exist. How he longed to mute that voice, to surrender to Greta the way she was surrendering to him.

---

9 Like so many young evangelicals, I had been indoctrinated with a philosophy thatinextricably linked the notion of sin—and hence death—with the image of sex. It was not merely that fornication was sin, but that all sin was in some sense fornication, a false intimacy with the world, adultery committed against God himself. (Read Ezekiel: Idolatry as Adultery. Oholah and Oholibah spreading their legs for the Baals of Canaan and Egypt. *She [allegorical Israel] lusted after her lovers, whose genitals were like those of donkeys and whose emission was like that of horses.* This is the Word of the Lord. Can I get a Hallelujah?) And don't forget the Apostle Paul: "Flee from sexual immorality. Every other sin a man can commit is outside his body, but he who sins sexually sins against his own body. Do you not know that your body is a temple of the Holy Spirit who is in you, whom you have received from God? You are not your own; you were bought at a price. Therefore glorify God with your body." Theological truth aside—and this is orthodox theology—such thinking had instilled in me a biting apprehension of my own sexuality. Well, that's not quite right. Biblical allegory is one thing; its application within American evangelical culture is quite another. But even when the fault lies in the application, the damage also gets emotionally wedded to the allegory, wedded to faith. It's a theologico-hormonal quagmire.

Christ she was intoxicating!

Michael found no deficiency in her, save for the faint desire that her sexual ethics match his own. And was that a deficiency? Did he want her to be shut off to reality, to be dishonest about the things she desired, to be forever denying herself? For how long would he deny himself? Had he not, while drinking with her, achieved a genuine sobriety, a moment of uninhibited emotional honesty? He wanted to make love to her, to feel that consummation of emotion. But even that was an untruth. Making love? Impossible. Love was a necessary ingredient in love-making. And Michael was merely in love with the idea of being in love, with the idea of her, not with her, which is to say he was not in love at all. No, Michael did not want to "make love." He wanted to fuck. And he hated himself for wanting to fuck, for wanting to throw away his virginity. He also hated God in this moment, not merely for abandoning him, but for blessing him with lactose intolerance and then setting a fucking Klondike Bar under his nose.[10]

Michael groaned.

"Where are you? Why is this so difficult? Why so fucking difficult?"

---

10 What would *you* do for a Klondike Bar? Would you keep it in the freezer, taking it out to hold briefly a few days a week (but not too often, mind you—that could sour the deal), eventually having a "Determine The Relationship" talk with it where you explain your intention of someday (but *not today*, you stress, not until Scorpio and Cancer are properly aligned) tasting its sweet vanilla filling, and then wait and wait and wait, probably for years, just to one day come to the freezer and reach into the back left corner where you have hidden your innocent Klondike Bar behind the ice-trays and frozen broccoli to find it's gone, that someone—your brother, your dad, your friend, anyone with teeth and gums—has eaten it, or, even worse, that someone has taken a bite out of it and then put it back to test your goddamn allegiance to what was a glorious confection and you discover that, yes, you will still eat it even though god-knows-whose mouth has been on it, and when that day comes at last you remove what's left of the wrapping and begin to eat it, only it has been somewhat-unfrozen-then-refrozen so that it melts quicker than it should, giving you a handful of sticky mess instead a lifetime of marital satisfaction? Would you do this?

So many nights Michael had pursued his religion, burying himself in the darkness of his room, seeking after some hint of God in the absence of distraction. But where was God? Secretly ministering to Michael's soul in ways imperceptible to the physical sense? Yes, and denying him his presence so that he can stand on his own feet, suffering under the bearish burden of righteousness without the sensuous reinforcement. Or so St. John of the Cross would have him believe. And Michael wanted to believe it, desperately so. Without God his world would crumble. Was crumbling. Where was God when he prayed and pleaded for relief, for affirmation that his pursuit was not in vain? Michael imagined him sprawled lackadaisically over a couch of constellations and nebulae, blinking into oblivion.

For reasons he couldn't explain—reasons residing within some dark recess of his soul inaccessible to his conscious mind—Michael lowered his hand against the flame, matching his emotional masochism with something tangible. He held it there, the silver screen of his imagination instantly bleached by the pop and crackle of flesh. He did not remove it until he could smell what he had done cloying the air. The pain was intense, but quickly dulled to a background static as Michael held his palm to his mouth.[11]

The Dark Night of the Soul lay on his bedside table, the blue cover nearly black in the room's dimness. A yellowing receipt lolled out from between the pages, marking his progress. Three-quarters done, but he feared he would never finish it. Before lighting his candle, Michael had reread a section discussing the temptations that are sure to befall anyone passing through the *night*. According to St. John, sexual temptation of a ferocious nature will certainly arise and in all likelihood coincide with the peak of the night, with the darkest, lowest hour. In order to pass through the night this temptation must be mastered. "Sometimes," explains the Carmelite reformist, "these

---

11 I still have the scar. It's the size of a pea, a white knot in the center of my palm.

spiritual people, when speaking of or performing spiritual devotions, are seized with a certain sort of exaltation and wildness of spirit caused by some reminiscence of the people nearest to them, whose intimacy they affect with a certain sort of frivolous relish; the which likewise springs from spiritual concupiscence (as we use the expression here), and sometimes excites in the will a *pleasurable* sensation."

A pleasurable sensation. Time spent with Greta was nothing but pleasurable. The very air she exhaled shivered with a freshness formerly alien to Michael. If she was this sure temptation, this clever and irresistible agent of the devil, could he refuse her? And if he could, would he choose to? A decision was necessary. This much was clear; however, Michael refused to acknowledge its immediacy. He closed his eyes and let his head fall back against the edge of his mattress. A pleasurable sensation. Only three hours ago he had been with her, lying in her apartment, whispering with her. They were spooning on the floor of her front room, telling stories, each waiting for the other to do something. This time it had been Michael. She had divulged to him days earlier that there existed a spot on her body that, when caressed, drove her insane. It was unusual, not something typically so erogenous, as if by some genetic quirk she had received an additional nerve bundle placed at random in the left side of her neck. He had touched her hair lightly, drawing it behind her ear, exposing the tender stretch of skin he hoped to exploit. He breathed lightly there and felt Greta register a shudder that spread down her body, even passing into him where her buttocks rested against his crotch. He caressed and then kissed her neck, his cock hardening as her breathing quickened. They had proceeded in that vein for several minutes, until Greta was overcome and turned to Michael, kissing him fiercely and climbing on top of him.

He imagined, and not without guilt, that she was with him now, straddling him as she had earlier, but now lifting off her shirt and allowing him to unfasten her bra, to fondle and kiss her breasts, to slide his hands gingerly along her sides, summoning gooseflesh, becoming lost in the way she was losing herself in him.

Michael leaned forward and blew out the candle. His fantasy continued, well beyond the point at which he had truncated the actual encounter.[12] Unknowing, he chose to continue as he had with her since their second meeting, to dissolve himself in the moment, in the fluid present.[13]

A WEEK later, Michael lay in bed, trembling.

He pushed forward through darkness as the dream raged around him. He was lost in a vulgar, labyrinthine mess of corridors, rooms, and subterranean passages. The sound of water rushed somewhere near, but he could not see its source. Soon the sound dissolved into the slithering of blood through his head. He was disoriented. The hallways seemed to feed back on themselves and, though he crossed and re-crossed his path, he was somehow always walking downhill. The sensation was of circling into a void. Suddenly, the maze opened and he was in a single, sane hallway. It was dim and contained medical paraphernalia strewn at random down its length. Lights the color of jaundiced children hung in five-meter intervals for a significant

---

12 As odd as this may seem to me now, it was an effort to even imagine myself having intercourse. Even in fantasy, the act seemed forbidden, as if the dream of penetration should somehow yield to the actual. I remember sitting back against my bed and indulging what had long before become a favorite fantasy. She (then, Greta; before, whatever face most fascinated me) would grind herself into me and we would dryly simulate what we actually desired. But this would not be enough. Wordlessly complicit, we would undress and she would resume her position, only now with her back to me. She would take and wedge me between her buttocks and lean back against my chest, trapping me inside the triangle fold of her cheeks and my abdomen. And she would rock and shake her ass, resting her head on my shoulder, turning and breathing against my neck, until I would come and we would sit motionless, feeling the wetness between us.

13 Then: sleep. No dreams of gray goatish creatures shuffling through pale mists in a reek of shit and sulfur. No fever-sleep with guilt painted in terrifying, incomprehensible patterns against the *eigengrau*. No. A sweet dreamless sleep to follow a sleepless dream. Then: shame over the absence of shame.

stretch until everything terminated in abrupt darkness. Michael continued forward until he came to a viewing window, the sort found in postnatal wards. He stood there transfixed, absorbing an abomination.

The window looked into a room with two collapsible steel beds. The one to the right was covered in rust and the sheets were torn and stained the color of old urine. On the bed lay Christ, buried in agony. He was naked with tubes and lines feeding into his body at every possible access point. The insides of his elbows were black, boiling with edema where the IVs hung dry and stagnant, their bags long emptied, the only fluid in the lines whatever happened to leak out from his body. His legs and sides were covered in bedsores and his face was obscured by a defunct oxygen mask. He looked steadily at Michael, his eyes graying, and Michael knew he was dying.

A man dressed in all black reclined on the bed to the left, propped up by an excess of pillows, eating with a spoon from a tin of cherry preserves. He was intensely attractive, yet Michael found it hard to look at his face. Something about him was deeply unsettling. He was staring at Christ, slowly eating his cherries. Christ turned his head toward the man and Michael could discern his lips moving beneath the mask. "Please," they seemed to say. The man simply continued to eat, a glossy redness slipping down from the corners of his mouth. Then he became aware of Michael. He looked at him and rose from the bed, setting the cherries carefully on the bedside table. Michael realized what was so unsettling about the man's appearance. His irises were completely black.

The man walked to the window and flattened his palm against it. And his eyes began to change. The sclerae were darkening. Black vessels like roots shot out from the corners. Behind him Christ's chest heaved and the useless oxygen mask clouded with his quickening breath. A monitor switched on. Jagged blue lines tore the screen. The heart rate was climbing. 189. 201. 212. 234. 289. 306. 392. How fast should God's heart beat?

The man in black began to laugh.

Michael woke up screaming.

HE CALLED her. It was only a quarter past midnight.

"Hey, Michael." Her voice was soft and refreshing as usual, but merely hearing it brought Michael no peace. He didn't know where to begin. He was slick with sweat and could feel the nipping precursor of a panic attack sidling up to him.

"God is dead."

"Friedrich, is that you? I'm sorry, I thought I was talking to Michael Catherwood."

"No, dying. I mean, God is dying." Michael took a steadying breath and let the phone rest against his neck for a moment. "I don't know what I mean. I think I'm losing my faith."[14]

"Do you want to come over and talk about it?"

"I don't know. I should pray, but I have no desire to. Does that make sense?"

"You should come over. We can sort it out together."

"Alright. Yeah. Give me about twenty minutes." He stood and stretched. His room was dark and silent save for the occasional murmur and glow of traffic from the window. He cursed the vividness of his dreams and began to get dressed.

SHE WAS wearing old sweat pants and a charcoal T-shirt when Michael arrived. This was a regular look for her, casual and carefree, and Michael always took comfort in it. He adored her for

---

14 As I look back, I don't believe anyone ever *loses* his faith. Once you know, once you experience Him, you're marked. It becomes impossible to believe in His inexistence, regardless of how militantly you may cry it out. You simply stop believing in his goodness. And this, this conscious rebellion, is so much worse than mere unbelief. You wish that your life had been different, that you hadn't been tested in certain ways. You wish and you wish and you wish. You never know what to do. Because this is Hell. Or a foretaste: to feel all the weight of theology, to move forward with the shadow of what can never be fully abandoned keeping pace behind you, to be yourself and not yourself, only and ever the shadow of a self.

never adorning herself, for merely existing. She smiled as she opened the door for him and then led him to the couch.

"What happened?"

Michael told her about the dream, watching her expression as he spoke, expecting to read disgust in her features. But her face never changed from that pacifying cast. He told her also about the pain of the last year, the feeling that God was departing—had departed—from his life. He had discussed this with her before, but never in great detail, never sharing the full depth of the feeling of loss. Never sharing his anger. Never using that apt word: forsaken. He had been afraid to discuss spirituality in much detail with her, terrified that he would discover that her faith was only a byproduct of southern culture. But none of that mattered now. She was here with him, a comforting presence, this bright intrusion of warmth.

He finished and there was a burning silence. He waited for her to answer, to explain away his troubles, to tell him that God was there with him, that this too would pass, as her own hurt was passing. But she said nothing. Merely sat watching Michael. Seeming to wait on him. Perhaps because her pain was not passing, because she still felt the sting of betrayal, needed comforting just as much as Michael. Can you swallow the pain of another when you can't swallow your own? Michael didn't know. Suddenly Greta looked intensely sad. Tired. He imagined the scenes playing in her mind. Sweet moments of simplicity and love, probably moments of shared and accommodating silence with Landon, the two lost in each other. She had told Michael of how Landon could take away any of her worries, even if just for an evening, with only a touch. Oh, to have that currency. To wipe away her grief.

He knew he could not. He did not yet love her and she did not love him. They would probably never be in love. The timing was all wrong.

They remained motionless together, the silence weighing on them. At last Michael gave expression to his emotions. His eyes moistened and a tear sprang.[15] Greta leaned forward and kissed him. Then she kissed away his tear. Michael rested his head in the crook of her neck.

They fell asleep together, neither able to touch the hollowness in the other.

IT WAS an unusually cold Sunday morning, about two weeks later. Michael entered church coughing and shivering. He was to meet Greta and sit with her, as they had been doing for the past few weeks. He strode to the coatroom and slipped out of his jacket and happened across a close friend of his father's. "Good morning, Lew."

"Ah, Michael. How are you?"

"Shitty," he said, with a touch of humor. Lewis Mackey was among the few men at church who appreciated such bluntness. "Yourself?"

"No complaints." Lew was positive in a way that made Michael envious. If he was in Lew's boat he might have responded tersely with something like, "How the fuck do you think I am?" or "Life is shit." Lew and his wife, Sarah, had spent the previous year as missionaries in the Sudan, Lew having taken a sabbatical from his professorate. Shortly after returning to Terre Haute they had decided to move back permanently to Khartoum to continue their work. Once Lew had finalized his retirement—a replacement having been promptly hired—Sarah was diagnosed with terminal ovarian cancer. Lew saw this as a hurdle, yes; however, his faith was such that he considered it an opportunity for God to demonstrate his sovereignty. Certainly Sarah and he would not be called to abandon their life of comfort for one of poverty in the Sudan, only to have their

---

15 This is a lie. I have not cried since I was thirteen years old. God knows how I wish I could cry.

ministry thwarted by cancer. No, faith would prevail and their ministry would thrive regardless.

Michael was less hopeful. Sarah would die,[16] along with the dream of continued missions work. The idea left a bitter taste in his mouth. "How's Sarah?" he asked.

"Oh, no real change there. She's continuing treatment, pushing along in faith. She's been learning conversational Arabic. Which has been great. It's given her something to focus on, take her mind off it all." Lew smiled and patted Michael's shoulder. "I know things are pretty stagnant for you right now, Michael. Things will look up. The Lord is faithful."

"I know he is, Lew."

"Tell your dad hello for me," Lew said, and went on his way, meeting and greeting.

Michael left the coatroom and began to scan the atrium for Greta, trying not to think about God's faithfulness, about cancer. He circled the room, dropping hellos and smiling at everyone, annoyed that Greta wasn't turning up. He passed through the sanctuary, but it was almost empty and she was not among the early birds, chasing their gospel worms. He left and walked through a few hallways, checked classrooms, eventually making his way back to the atrium. But she never came.

Dejected and annoyed, Michael found his father and mother and sat with them. They were seated three rows from the front, next to a couple with three children, one boy and two girls, all under the age of five. Michael hated sitting in the front. He always felt that people were watching him. Also, the pastor made eye contact with you when you sat in the front, and it was nearly impossible to occupy yourself with something other than his words. But Michael had brought nothing with which to distract himself today. For the past several weeks, Greta had been his distraction. They would hold hands, slyly tickling each other's palms. His thoughts were with her constantly while in church,

---

16 Sarah did soon die.

she made the whole thing—the monotony, the bad music, the empty sermons[17]—so much more bearable.

Someone was touching his hand.

He looked to his left and found the little boy seated next to him gripping his hand with both of his, shaking it, smiling up at him. People had begun to greet one another and Michael had been lost in his own mind. He couldn't help but smile at the little boy. Finally achieving some recognition, the boy dropped Michael's hand and turned to harass his sister. Michael stood to join in the greetings.

"You alright, Son?" his father asked. He was speaking over the top of Michael's mother, who stood between them. "You look distant."

"I'm just dragging. Should have gotten coffee."

"You want my sunglasses? Donnie will never know if you fall asleep." He took off his glasses and reached around his wife to poke Michael in the ribs with them.

"Quit it," said his mother.

"I didn't do anything. Tell your son to stop being morose."

"Are you being morose, Michael?"

"No, Mom."

"Where's that girl of yours you never let us see?"

"You saw her last week."

"Oh, we *saw* her," said his father, "in the strictest, most literal sense of the word."

"You're not in high school, Michael," said his mother. "You're not supposed to be embarrassed by us anymore."

"Is that so?"

"It's in the Bible," said his father.

"Is that so?"

"It's in the back somewhere."

His father smiled and Michael smiled, too. His parents were always good at encouraging and distracting him from his brooding. But his father was right, he did feel distant, and despite his

---

17 My emptiness.

parents' presence, despite being surrounded by good people, he felt lonely.

Worship began again and those congregants who had not stood for the greeting stood now. Michael, however, remained seated. His singing had begun to feel false. They were embarking on a contemporary chorus now, the refrain containing the phrase "You are more than enough for me, Jesus." Michael could not in good conscience sing this, not when it was an untruth. He felt nauseated in his dissatisfaction. He wondered how many people standing near him were lying through their teeth to sing that song. The next song was a hymn, "It is well with my soul." But it was not well with Michael's soul, and so he kept his silence. He wondered if perhaps Sarah Mackey was keeping her silence as well.[18]

The pastor rose to speak. Michael closed his eyes. He felt so out of place. When he leaned his head forward, hoping to rest his forehead on the back edge of the pew in front of him, he bumped into someone. He opened his eyes to see a large, densely bearded man judging him. "Grow up," the man muttered under his breath as he turned back around.

---

18 I think of Horatio Spafford, of the circumstances during which he wrote "It is well with my soul": on a ship in the Atlantic, just two years after the death of his only son and mere weeks since the great Chicago fire ruined his legal practice, sailing to meet his wife who had just survived the sinking of the *SS Ville du Havre*, which had claimed the lives of the couple's four daughters. *When sorrows like sea billows roll . . .* I try to imagine myself in his place. Rocking back and forth, head between my knees, hidden somewhere in the ship's hull, ripping out tufts of hair, screaming, cursing the name of my God. And yet Spafford let his loss be transformed into one of the greatest poems of the Christian tradition. He saw past his *night*. Clung to that greater reality. Christ. *Hath shed his own blood for my soul.* Through some unfathomable alchemy of spirit, Spafford claimed comfort. *Thou wilt whisper thy peace to my soul.* I have known pain—but I have yet to know this kind of pain. What was my hell compared with Spafford's? Compared with Sarah Mackey's? Latent adolescent angst? A pinprick on the foot of a giant?

I now see two ways to approach singing praises such as these: Sing because these things are true, or sing because they should be true. I believe the latter is what Spafford did. He declared the reality of what he could not feel. Declared it until it was true. This is art. True art. Getting out of your own way, pushing in earnest toward a wider understanding of truth. What am I? What is this? Coldness. A mere pantomime.

As the pastor dismissed the children to "children's church," Michael rose, stepped past his confused parents, and went home.

MICHAEL GOT home a little before noon. He went straight to his bedroom on the second floor, passing his younger brother who was passed out on a sofa in the living room, reeking of burnt chemicals, an empty forty of Cobra on the floor beside him.[19] He lay in his bed and fought against the glacial tide swelling within him and managed to achieve a pathetic half-sleep that lasted most of the day. He awoke feeling at once dry and unclean, having slept in his clothes, and upon looking at his phone discovered several missed calls. They were all from Greta.

"I need to see you," she said when he called her back.

"Is everything alright?"

She exhaled and told him that it was now, but that she had had a difficult time that morning and the night before. She had met a friend for dinner and happened upon Landon and his most recent conquest in the restaurant. It was too much for her and she had canceled on the spot and gone back to her apartment. All those emotions from the early fall had revisited her with a force she had not expected. "I just need to keep my mind off everything. Can you come over?"

THEY SAT on the floor in front of her sofa, the evening's second bottle of wine between them, half-empty. They had abandoned Greta's stemware and begun taking swigs. On his way over, Michael had brainstormed how to cheer her up, help her dissolve into forgetfulness. But all those affirming words he had prepared became unnecessary as soon as he stepped foot in her apartment. His mere presence was enough. She had thrown her arms around him and kissed him, swinging enough of herself

---

19 I've not mentioned him before and only do so here because he caught me off guard. Discussing how my faith nearly burnt away is one thing, but my brother is another. It simply hurts too much.

into the action that they both fell back against the door and began laughing. “That’s all I needed,” she had said. “But you can stick around if you like.” That had been two hours ago.

“You had me a little worried this morning,” said Michael.

“Aw. You were concerned for me?”

“No. Concerned for myself. That I was going to have to endure that whole service on my own.” He grinned foolishly and she punched his leg, nearly tipping the wine.

“Did you find someone else to entertain you?”

“I just left.”

“Skipping church now?”

“You’re one to talk.”

“I suppose we’re heathens together then.”

“I suppose.” He raised the bottle of wine to his lips and, as he was tilting it up, Greta pushed up on the bottom, spilling wine down the front of his shirt. “Hey!” he sputtered.

“You were flushed,” she said. “You looked like you needed cooling off.”

“Oh really?” Michael lifted the bottle over her head. Greta tried to wriggle away but Michael reached an arm around her and held her in place.

“You rotten bastard,” she said, giggling uncontrollably as he threatened to upend it on her. “Don’t, you’ll waste it!” He let her seize the bottle from him. She threw her leg over his waist and straddled him as he leaned back against her sofa. She made him tilt back his head and poured the last bit of wine into his mouth. Then she mashed her lips against his, kissing him until all the wine was either swallowed or spilled down their chins.

For a moment she lay against him, and the spilt shiraz crept from his shirt to hers. She no doubt was aware of his erection pressing against her thigh. He moved her mouth to his and they kissed again.

She leaned back and began to unbutton his shirt. “You’re all wet,” she said.

Once she removed Michael's shirt, she removed her own. She had not been wearing a bra and it was the first time, outside of his imaginings, that Michael had seen her naked breasts. They were glorious, sprayed with freckles, each half again the size of his closed fist. She guided his hands to them, closing his fingers around her nipples, and then his head, pulling him into her, telling him to kiss them. And he did. He slowly dragged his lips across her, delighting in the quickening of her breath, in the dry-sweet flavor of wine still clinging to her skin.

Greta ran her fingernails down Michael's chest and his skin grew taut in tiny eruptions of gooseflesh. She rested her hand between his legs and rubbed his cock. She unfastened the clasp at the top of his pants and slowly unzipped him. Then she stood abruptly.

"You're such a tease," he said. His emotions were all bleeding together in a fluid crash that painted his body in dissonance, hot and cold all over. Apprehension built quietly in the back of his mind, but he paid it no heed.

Greta looked down at him, wisps of hair, moist and glowing in the warm lamplight, draped across her face, her lips parted slightly. She appeared unkempt, wild and wily. She slid out of her jeans and then kicked them aside with her bare feet. She turned her body from him, a smile and flash of blue eyes lingering over her shoulder, and walked like a ballerina on her toes—her thighs long and curving, calves tensed in gorgeous, lean knots—toward her bedroom.

As he followed, a rush of romanticism he did not know he possessed overwhelmed him. He quickened his pace and caught up with her, twirled her around and kissed her, and lifted her into the air and carried her the rest of the way to her bed. Michael fought to get out of his pants and crawled into bed beside her.

She grabbed a fistful of hair at the back of his neck and pulled his face to hers so forcibly their teeth clicked. Soon they were wrestling. Greta, laughing, fought to straddle him. She guided his hands to her breasts and slid her ass down his stomach until she was sitting on his cock. He imagined he could feel her every fold through the fabric of his boxers. Then she bent forward and began kissing his chest. She trailed kisses down past his navel and grabbed his waistband. "Can I do something for you?" she said. But before Michael could answer she slid his boxers to his knees and began to fellate him.

He watched her, frozen, afraid to move, afraid to do anything that might result in her stopping. She gripped the base of his cock and squeezed. He felt himself thickening as she coaxed more blood into him, as if to read his pulse with her tongue.

After a minute she stopped and brushed her hair from her face. She crawled back beside him and kissed him and pulled him on top of her. She interlocked her fingers with his and led his hands down the length of her torso to the lacy ink of her lingerie. Michael sat back on his knees and hooked his thumbs through the sides and slowly pulled them up over her knees, revealing her beauty in its fullness. A dutiful egalitarianism seized him and he lowered his face to her cunt. Her odor was warm and feline, the taste of her keen, saline.[20] He had only just begun to get used to it when she stroked his hair with her fingers and spoke his name. He looked up at her. "Come here," she said.

For a moment he was worried he'd done something wrong, that he was too rough or had offended her by seeming startled at the experience. But then they were kissing and it seemed to him that she was inflamed by the taste of herself on his lips.

Michael pulled her beneath him and she grabbed his cock and pressed him against the soft down of her mons. Her eyes were black in the warm semi-dark, the only light leaking in from the living room. He took her in, long hair spread in a gold nimbus over the embroidery of her duvet, skin that was perfect in its glistening imperfections, those delicious peach slices that were parted lips, the line of neck disappearing into his periphery,

---

20 It's wild how sensory experience cauterizes itself into memory. I'll never forget how she tasted: like the wet kiss of a woman with a watch battery under her tongue.

the tack of her nipples digging against his chest, the warm heavy smell of her, the dark swirl of emotion that emanated from her, pouring over and through him, all the howls of conscience dragged to the silent floor of the sensuous sea that was Greta.

"Are you sure?" she asked.

"Yes," he said.

What had swam shivering (made him shiver) in the years since his first prepubescent interest in sex through the waves of his imagining now lay shivering beneath him in the pleasure he was inciting, conducting like a dark, empyrean symphony, blowing its breath into him, scenting him, his mind reeling in the revelation that was her, this tenebrous coalescence, this concrete, lucid tangling of all those years of images and longings, this sensation that was sex, that was fucking, only not fucking, he could see that now, feel it in the compress of their skin, the faint rush of air through their teeth, the joy in her eyes, no, this was making love, this was the frightful union on which God had exhausted twenty-four crashing hours of omnipotence, the thing for which men the world over livedslaughtereddied, which Michael had denied himself for so long, but not now, oh not now! that the sensation was building and she was moaning against his neck, her muscles tensing, her body tightening around him, his name released emptily into the air from silent lips, and he was there, on the brink of something wonderful, yet he didn't want to be there, not yet, not this quick, but he was, wave after electric wave billowing through him, his mind emptying into that lilting jazz crescendo, and, in the wake of that powerful emptiness, in that exquisite unbearable tenderness, he kissed her cheek and spoke, his words ringing in the clarion silence, three words, which, once they were gone and irretrievable, he knew to be wretched:

"I love you."

Greta looked at him with a faint quizzical smile. He lay beside her and buried his face in her neck. "Did you come?" she said.

He was silent.

She turned on her side and pulled him close to her, entwining their legs. "Of course you did," she said and kissed his forehead. He pressed his face back into her neck. He dared not open his eyes. They rested that way for some minutes.

"What are you thinking about?" she said.

("I love you.")

He felt a fire build behind his eyes and work down into his cheeks. He feared he would cry out. More than anger or regret or shame he felt anxiety. Soon he would have a panic attack. He had amputated a part of his identity. Who was he now, this not-virgin? What would he say when he came before his God?

"Michael?"

"This can't happen again," he said.

"What?"

"I need to be alone tonight," he said. "I need to think. I need to pray."

Greta pulled away and sat at the edge of the bed with her back to him. Michael sat up as well and tried to move nearer her but she stopped him.

"I'm sorry," he began.

"You want to *be alone*?" she said. "Why did you have to say that?"

The fire had spread from his eyes and cheeks to his ears and neck, down his back. He could feel his heart thumping in his chest like a speed bag.

"This isn't how it's supposed to be," she said. "I opened myself to you. You're supposed to hold me. We're supposed to . . . bask."

"I'm–"

"You're sorry. I know. You said that. We're not supposed to think. We're supposed to just *be*."

Michael stood. His pants lay crumpled on the floor with his socks. He picked them up and went into the living room to retrieve his shirt. He dressed quickly and looked once into the bedroom. She was lying on the bed, her feet flat on the mattress, knees at angles, hands together behind her head. She was looking at the ceiling. Michael left the apartment and leaned his forehead against the door after he shut it.

("I love you.")

(You stupid fucking fool, you've never loved a woman in your life, you don't love her, you're incapable of love, God what did I just say what did I just do)

("I love you.")

(Is this what it is to be outside faith, to be alone, embracing myself, why can't I just enjoy her, what–)

He raised his hands, clenched in fists, to the sides of his head, took a deep breath and exhaled. Now that he was dressed and away from her bed the panic seemed to be subsiding. The insides of his thighs were slick with semen and the fluids she had left him. He felt his boxers riding high, cemented to his legs. He turned and walked down the hallway, which was well-lit and whitewashed, and found the stairs.

OUTSIDE, NOT even the bitter wind could induce the tears he longed to cry. He was downtown, only a block from the university, staring down Wabash Avenue–silent and empty at one in the morning–at the amber lights blinking away toward some lost focal distance, at the particles of falling snow briefly highlighted in their illumination. He walked towards his car, a rusted '90 Camaro, parked in front of Greta's building. He found the keys in his pocket when he remembered that he was drunk. Unable to drive in good

(fool, where is your)

conscience, he decided to walk the city. He passed by his car and stepped into the street, walking briskly, the ghosts of the day's traffic spurting past him in an unending stream, filling him with dread. A weight lay on him, a sentence, as if Greta had spoken a terrible judgment over him and ordered him into the void to drown in its emptiness. He found the opposing sidewalk and walked east. The wind scorched his flushed skin, the semen in his shorts chilled quickly and pricked his flesh, and yet he pushed on past bars and cafes, businesses fledgling and defunct, storefronts filled with useless miscellany, feeling all the while that his city was burnt out, that it hadn't seen life since Capone contracted syphilis from it. Michael had always hated Terre Haute, but hated it most of all now.21 He gritted his teeth as he tracked through the fresh snow. He came to a parking garage and walked inside, not to escape the wind—no, the wind he deserved—but to escape the emptiness of the street.

The garage was dim and mostly empty, vaguely cylindrical as opposed to rectangular. A vagrant slept in a sprawl against a concrete pillar, moaning quietly and fouling the air with his breath. *Here,* he thought, *here is my city's filth.* Michael made to walk past him, but stopped, something odd having caught his eye.

The vagrant's long black coat was partially folded back and trapped beneath his body, providing an unobstructed view of the man's denim-covered ass. Something long and fleshy protruded from a hole at the base of the back pocket. Michael's first thoughts were that it must be an elephantine phallus, and that it must be cold. Then he noticed the vertebral notches of bone beneath the skin.

He felt as if he had stumbled upon a sideshow in the remains of a long-dead carnival. Only there were no tents, no smells of

---

21 See this city as Michael sees it. See its men. (Again I must pilfer *pensées.*) See a sprawling line of men in chains, all under sentence of death, some of whom are each day butchered in the sight of the others; those remaining see their own condition in that of their fellows, and looking at each other with grief and despair wait their turn. See this. See their eyes. This is the human condition.

But it is more than this. Imagine those same chained men completely naked. See the horror in their eyes as they watch their fellows cut down, felled like rotting trees, but know that this is not simply a horror of blood, but a horror of their own arousal. Their nostrils are full of the warm heavy smell of dying flesh and yet each one wants desperately to bring his chained hands together for one last tug before the blade falls. See this. See these spirits spent in a waste of shame.

old spilled beer and rotted popcorn, no animals, no mothers with screaming children, no clowns with megaphones crying, "COME ONE, COME ALL! TO THE GROTESQUERY HALL! DON'T LET THIS TRIP BE IN VAIN! SEE THE PAGEANT OF THE TRANSMUNDANE! OH THE STORIES YOU'LL TELL, ONCE YOU'VE SEEN A MAN WITH A TAIL!" No, just silence. Just a real-life monstrosity, three sheets to the wind and passed out in an empty parking garage. Michael felt a deep nausea take hold in his bowels. He wanted to turn back, return to Greta's, face whatever awaited him there.

The vagrant shook and moved his jaw as if chewing something. Michael could hear the faint scratching of the man's stubble against the concrete. As Michael recognized the ache in his bowels as a species of pity, the man awakened. He coughed and moved so that he was resting on all fours, looking up at Michael, malice glittering in his hard eyes. He looked bestial, like something from another world. Michael could not move.

More of them came. Some scuttled on hands and knees, others walked upright, though bent forward, like crones. They were circling him, closing him in. Soft language poured incomprehensibly from their oversized mouths. Michael wanted to scream, to run. He thought of Greta, wrapped in the warmth of her loft, and longed to be back there, to be anywhere but frozen in the midst of these foul lumbering things. He was like a stone idol that they circled in the performance of a rite. They were dressed like ragmen. Some wore nothing more than knotted lengths of burlap. They were covered in excrement; even their long hair was matted with stale crusted dung. The odor was heavy and warm and filled Michael's mouth. He felt a rush of vomit threaten his throat.

They circled in, closer and closer, their long fleshy tails leaving execrable trails of effluvium in their wake, their terrific faces glowering at Michael.

Life returned to his limbs and he tore through the circle, running deeper into the garage, ascending,[22] up and up, past a scattering of cars, a scattering of trash, until he reached the wide-open roof. He turned back, expecting to hear the howls of pursuit, but heard only the murmuring of that dark language and the slow shuffle of feet. He ran to the enclosed stairway, but upon opening the door he heard the smack of bare feet on the steps below. He was trapped. There was nothing left for him but to wait.

When they reached him their numbers had increased. They filled the entire roof, save for a small semicircle where Michael had pressed himself against the concrete lip at the building's east side. It was several moments before Michael understood what was happening before him. The creatures were undressing, exposing bodies that were gnarled and deformed, covered with tumorous growths that swelled and shrank like lungs. They turned to one another and began kissing and clutching viciously at their partners' tails. Spittle frothed from their mouths. Soon they were fucking. Michael didn't understand how this was achieved and didn't want to. He sank to the concrete and buried his face between his knees, shaking violently in the cold, as the heat of the creatures' movement turned the snow into a brownish sludge.

He did not know how long he kept his eyes shut.

When he looked up he knew that the last of his mind had left him, for the sight of all that writhing meat made him hungry. Absurdly hungry.

When at last their orgy was finished the creatures fell all at once into a great heap. They squirmed against one another, moaning contentedly. Soon they were asleep and Michael was left alone as the snow fell and began to cover their bodies.

He stood and peered out over his city, watching the silver snow falling faintly in drifts everywhere, watching the city disappear in a sheet of white. It was deceptively beautiful, as if all that snow could somehow cleanse his city.

---

22 Descending.

He turned back to the mass of dreaming monsters and found that he could barely discern the contours of their tangled bodies, so thick was the snow that covered them. Not even a hint of the brown slush remained. Even their smell seemed to be gone. The entire roof was a whiteout. Michael's stomach leapt within him. The hunger began to hit him in waves.

He thought to eat some of the snow and dropped to his knees and began scooping up handfuls and shoving them into his mouth. He swallowed and swallowed but the hunger only grew. He needed meat. He crawled forward and pawed through the great mound of snow, trying to grasp hold of one of the creatures. An arm. All he needed was an arm. He would even settle for a tail.

But they were gone. Michael stood and jumped through the steadily growing drifts, swiping madly, cursing. Nothing. The creatures were no more.

And yet he felt a presence with him on the roof. In the white dimness he discerned shapes that were not there. Wraiths. Drifting otherworldly in the gloom. There was one in particular that stood horridly at his back, the shadow of a shadow.

(*"I love you."*)

The wraith waited behind Michael as he stood motionless in the center of the roof. He felt it there watching him, refusing to approach, merely existing as a passive, contented malevolence. Michael turned to confront it. But it was not there. In its place stood a robin, shivering nervously atop a pile of snow. Michael watched it, his stomach growling, demanding he capture and eat it. The bird began to prune itself, picking out the filth from between its feathers.

Michael threw himself at it.

The robin squawked once and flew away.

(*Fool. Faithless fool.*)

Quaking violently in the cold, Michael allowed his mind to fill with white. He looked down and found his hands. He began with the fleshy webbing between his left thumb and index finger.

It hurt less than he ever could have expected. Once this choicest cut had been swallowed, he rolled the skin back like a glove, dragged his teeth down the edges of metacarpals, phalanges, stripping the meat like bark from birch trees. And he thought of the birch trees he stripped as a child, how the white bark curled like a scroll. He would write on these scrolls with his mother, after they collected them from the woods, write verses in ink, sometimes paint. They were beautiful, his mother's scrolls. But his were sloppy, only the work of a child, better used as kindling.

WORSHIP IN THE LAND OF THE DEAD (A Briefer Epic, Part II)

TIME AND SCENE: *A snow-capped mountain peak overlooking a green alpine tundra covered in wildflowers and bathed in sunlight. The sounds of a snow-melt waterfall can be discerned in the distance.*

MICHAEL *stands alone, feet planted firmly in the snowpack, the cold air quickening his mind.*

MICHAEL:
Come, oh Tempter. Resume your infernal labor.

PAUL, *in the form of a small blue man, emerges naked from the snow and presents himself with a bow. His head is elongated front-to-back, sitting atop the neck like the blade of a pickaxe.*

PAUL:
Why the formal diction, Mister Catheterwood?

MICHAEL:
I thought I'd preempt your further attacks on my pedantry.

PAUL:
I'm no longer interested in your pedantry. Your pederasty, now, that's another matter.

MICHAEL:
Will you never tire of the gay jokes?

PAUL:
Never. Although I was speaking less to the Greek gentleman's predilection for puer-poking than to his penchant for pedagogy.

MICHAEL:
"Puer" is Latin, not Greek.

PAUL:
I'm aware. But it's à propos, nonetheless, as the Romans also enjoyed ramming their rugrats. And don't get me started on the Roman Catholics! Their altered altar boys are legion.

MICHAEL:
You're getting far afield from pedagogy.

PAUL:
Ah, yes. Pedagogy. As if using art for therapy weren't despicable enough, you insist on teaching us with your stories. What profound arrogance. Haven't you learned the lessons of the age? Art is art, man. It's inviolable. Art isn't "for" anything but itself. Fuck

your allegories. We want nothing to do with your bourgeois intellectual and moral utility. No one gives a shit about John Bunyan and his big blue ox. Look at the moribund legacy of D.H. Lawrence and his sodomitical jouissance. Or take any of the bloviating excrescences of Ayn Rand. From moralism flee, Christian Pilgrim, flee! Even if such Popish methods could produce art, what then? What could one possibly learn from these dreadful creations of yours, these miscarriages of your "tortured" psyche?

MICHAEL:
Truth in fiction is not propositional. Hell, truth in general is rarely ever propositional—

PAUL:
Easy now, you're tempting the Gates of Hell. We devils are all positivists, after all.

MICHAEL:
When it suits you.

PAUL:
And it always does. Most people would be amazed at what arch-materialists we spirits are. Even in our most starry-eyed and Gnostic temptations, we proceed within a strict, programmatic regime efficient enough to make even the most anal managerial liberal more than a little hot and bothered. In fact, nothing pleases us more than a consummately "spiritual" person. So long as the body is ours, the mind can soar in the air all it likes. The air, of course, belongs to us as well.

MICHAEL:
I suppose even the enemies of truth can't get by without affirming it on occasion.

PAUL:
As you said, when it suits us.

MICHAEL:
And when does it not suit you?

PAUL:
I don't know. Ask me when I'm in a different mood and maybe I will. In the meantime, please elaborate on your "non-propositional" meanings.

MICHAEL:
I mean the same thing Flannery O'Connor meant when she wrote that the truth of fiction is experiential. The encounter of art is its own form of knowledge.

PAUL:
It's just an endless cavalcade of leached credibility with you, isn't it?

MICHAEL:
I can't help but love the woman.

PAUL:
If she weren't rotting in a Georgian grave, I expect she might love you, too, but not as a human loves another human. No, she'd have you caged on her property with the rest of her peafowl, sweating and strutting in the Dixie humidity. Maybe she'd give you a noble name once you pecked her ankles enough to distinguish yourself from the other birds.

Speaking of the grave, it's time we made our descent. No matter how brief or briefer, an epic isn't an epic without a trip down-under. You ready to harrow Hell, honey?

MICHAEL:
If we must.

PAUL *lifts his hands to the sky, which darkens and solidifies and rushes down upon them. Everything that was land—snow, rock, dirt, and stream—becomes air, and everything that was air becomes dark and rocky soil. A complete inversion is effected, and* MICHAEL *and* PAUL *find themselves standing at the bottom of a mountainous crater. Pale fires flare in the distance. A gray mist, neither smoke nor liquid, rolls over everything in great, waving skeins.*

PAUL:
Welcome to the Land of the Dead. Flannery must be around her somewhere. Maybe we'll find her and you can burn down the rest of your days fawning over her shade.

MICHAEL:
I've imagined worse ways to live.

PAUL:
But have you imagined better?

Begins to walk aimlessly in the mist. MICHAEL *reluctantly follows.*

That's what this is all about, right—showing people how to live? I once heard you say that great fiction is a splintered mirror, each shard offering a strange new vantage on the reader's soul. It's a nice metaphor (even if you did steal it from Joyce).

However, insofar as your writing is a cracked mirror, it has also been further vandalized by the spray can of a moralizing miscreant. There is nothing to be seen here, no insights to be gained. Nothing that hasn't been better expressed by any of the crooners of post-modern lament who precede you.

MICHAEL:
If I have no message, why accuse me of didacticism?

PAUL:
Because I know your heart. This vacuum of meaning didn't result from a lack of effort. You want desperately to move others to live lives of virtue, to proffer some shape of goodness they might participate in. But you've accomplished no such thing. You lack the vision. These pages are filled with pain, loneliness, and resentment. How do you expect anyone to recognize themselves in them? In your eagerness to render sin you have failed to affirm life. This is nihilism at its worst: crass, naive, triumphant in its despair. You've made the world a more lonesome place.

MICHAEL *is silent for a long while. Then he puts his hands behind his head and looks up at the dismal roof of Sheol, smiling, almost laughing.*

PAUL:
What, pray tell, is so amusing?

MICHAEL:
Everything. You. This exercise. I needed to hear it, actually hear it, from the mouth of my accuser to know it isn't true.

PAUL, *inly wracked, struggles to maintain his haughty composure and resorts to glowering.*

PAUL:
Whether it's true or not is beside the point–

MICHAEL:
That right there is the point.

PAUL:
Excuse me?

MICHAEL:
Forget it. Do continue. . . .

PAUL:
Whether it's true is beside the point. It doesn't matter what your message is or isn't. I suggested a moment ago that you have a good heart, that you hope to ennoble others. That was a lie–a flattery-unto-despair, if you like. Your desire to instruct is a matter of pride. You've already admitted your terror over the possibility that you are insignificant, that this self you ceaselessly construct with words and deeds is just a house of cards, concealing only emptiness. You accused those who deny a text its power of being cowards. That was quite clever. Provoke them to bravery like a cavalry officer swinging his saber atop his mount to rally his troops. If your readers follow you–that is, if they are moved by your words, if their world changes even a fraction because of what you've written–then that emptiness becomes less weighty, your identity seems less fragile, you are made real. More than that, you become a god. I'm reminded of the famous concluding lines of Rilke's "Archaic Torso of Apollo": "For here there is no place that does not see you. You must

change your life." If the viewer does change his life, then the statue was indeed filled with light. Apollo is justified.

Now, do you expect me to believe that you've never fancied yourself an Apollo?

MICHAEL.
Of course not.

PAUL:
Then you admit this is all for your own glory, all for the pride of life?

MICHAEL:
I admit everything. My terror. My deceitfulness. My self-loathing. My pride. My thirst for justification. My belief that if even a stranger can know the smallest portion of my mind, I will feel less alone.

PAUL:
Who doesn't want to be loved? To be known? If you want this, if you truly want this, you can have it, easily. It is in my power to give it to you. Only bow down and worship me. That is, bow down and worship yourself. You've done it before, now do it again—in a sense, you're already doing it. Worship me and they will worship you. Look deep inside yourself and see that I am there, that I am truly a part of you, even if only your shadow, and accept me. Accept yourself. If you would have others follow you, do this. All anyone has ever wanted is to be affirmed as they are, accepted without qualification. The self, in all the grand conglomeration of its idiosyncrasies and desires and dispositions, is to be affirmed and loved. So go ahead, Michael, allow yourself to love.

MICHAEL:
What is love?

PAUL:
Shit, Mikey. What is love? Are you kidding me? Love is affirmation. The joyful embrace of another for being just what they are. Think about all those times after your first with Greta, after your initial, protracted self-shaming. How you didn't care what she was, what she believed, only that she was with you and you with her, in stillness and absolute freedom. That feeling, that openness—that is love.

Soft music begins to suffuse the air, wimpling the gray curtains of Hadean mist, stirring in MICHAEL *memories of exquisite, aching tenderness. A thousand scenes take shape in the mist and, at their heart, Greta's features condense in a shimmering of white and gold.*

MICHAEL:
This is really beautiful sophistry, Paul. I mean that.

PAUL:
You're rather fond of that word.

MICHAEL:
I am. It's seductive. And a wonderful pejorative, praising while it denounces.

PAUL:
And just what are you denouncing?

MICHAEL:
What you've been calling love is worse than hate. There is no love that is not founded on truth. There can be no love without

discernment. Love embraces the good, the true, and the beautiful. It can affirm nothing else. Insofar as you are a part of me, loving myself without qualification can only mean your destruction.

PAUL:
Such close-minded drivel. You need to learn to listen to the universe, baby.

Immediately the visions vanish.

MICHAEL:
Oh, I have learned. I have listened. And the silence is deafening.

PAUL:
So where does this leave us?

MICHAEL:
This is where you drop the charade. You're a lousy tempter. You're much more interesting as an accuser.

PAUL:
You want accusation?

MICHAEL:
Give me your best.

PAUL:
Then let's return to the issue of pride. Say what you will about the nature of love and self-affirmation—your words are voided by hypocrisy. This very moment you're engaging in the purest, most absolute vanity. Casting yourself as Christ in your own temptation narrative? How fucking disgusting. Milton was able enough to depict "deeds above heroic," but you? Pah! The only quality this exercise shares with *Paradise Regained* is its sublime dullness. Much as you would love to be known as the Hammer

of God, you are no Milton. You're nothing but a blunt instrument, beating your plebeian morality into the ground.

PAUL*'s head transforms into a hammer. He whips it back and forth gleefully on his neck.*

MICHAEL:
I will admit I'm nervous about this little intertextual experiment. But have you considered the possibility that I'm only highlighting my failure to perform "deeds above heroic"? My desire to imitate Christ, along with that desire's seemingly ceaseless frustration?

PAUL:
And is that what you're doing?

MICHAEL:
I don't know. It's certainly possible. I never know about these things until I've finished doing them.

Exeunt omnes.

PAGES FROM THE EFFECTS OF ARTHUR WAYNE PRINCE

To whom it may concern,

It used to be that when your reason left you, or rather, when your children or executors or what have you decided that was the case, you were run to an asylum and laid in a white bed until your eyes rolled back in your head and your soul rolled up to the clouds, or down to someplace less respectable. Now, in this, the twenty-first century, wonder of wonders, they bring the asylum to you. It's called hospice. I'm lying on a white bed in the living room, hospital covers up past my waist, writing this on a bunion-yellow legal pad. In the next room the nurse is reading some Harlequin romance novel with a cover to make Venus squirm in her clam. She's waiting for a little amber light to flash on the monitor by my bed, which will mean I've passed on and she can pack up her things and go wait for some other old fool to quit burdening society.

It's an odd thing, watching someone watch you die, or rather, watching someone grow increasingly exasperated that you haven't died yet. She's been here over a month and brooded her way through a couple dozen of those books and a few others, less trashy, which she seemed to be reading out of obligation. I've been reading myself—old philosophy mostly. Started with a survey of the pre-Socratics and just finished *The Republic* yesterday. I kid myself that I'm a late-to-the-game intellectual, but I'm also reading these books because I know it makes my nurse embarrassed of her glossy, Thor-covered drivel. Her name is Quintessa, which is an awful name.

I've tried telling her she needs to get used to being here, that I'm a stubborn bastard and my body's no different. But her exasperation only grows, as if after thirty-some years of living she's seen every manner of dying man and I'm just another character pulled from the stock. When I told her about the farm burning in '39 and what happened to me, she rolled her eyes and snorted, even called me a liar under her breath. But the farm did burn (it was my fault, actually, butted a cigarette near some spilt diesel—I was only fifteen) and I was out fooling around in the field when it happened. The flames came on pretty quick and ate the field from the outside in, exploding cornstalks like matchsticks. I was trapped in the center, like a little cherry bullseye, with nothing to do but roast or walk out through the flames, which is just what I did. I came away with little more than a healthy tan. To Quintessa it's just a crock stewed up by an old codger. She hasn't noticed the scar on my wrist—my only enduring souvenir, the farm having been rebuilt and replanted.

But how can I hold it against her? It's a law of nature: A man spends the first seventy-one years of his life gradually building respect, becoming that wizened sage, and then pisses it all away in less than a decade. This has nothing to do with the mind losing its moorings, but has everything to do with honesty, and a little with the loss of inhibition. Old men say crazy things not because they're crazy but because some fool door has been opened in their mind that gives them the freedom to say all those things they were too uncomfortable to say earlier. Too uncomfortable or too damn fearful. I'll admit that I tend toward the latter category, which is why I'm writing this now. I won't bother you with an apologetic for my own rationality. Whether or not you believe what I have to tell means precisely squat to me, unless of course your name is George Prince.

This is for him, so that he'll no longer question his sanity, so that he'll know someone else was there and saw Him too. I know why he never spoke to the investigators, why he withdrew into himself in silence. I'd have done the same thing had I been eight years old at the time and not sixty. I'm writing this so that someday, when he's an old man in a hospice bed discovering this same freedom—the freedom to remember, and to vent—he might know that he wasn't alone. Most people will read this and think it's a sick joke, not the least of which will be my brother's family, those who cared about Kevin. So be it. George was always my favorite. Falling out of esteem with the rest of the family is nothing if it means he'll have even a little peace of mind.

And doubtless, there are people out there still curious about the disappearance of Kevin Prince. In all my years of relative geographical seclusion, my grandnephew's disappearance is the only thing to have happened in Grant County which made the national news: a locked-room mystery without the lock or the room.

After all the alibis and what have you were cleared, the state police had very little to go on. Once the extraneous footprints (those of Kevin's father and his wife, the paramedics, etc.) were taken out of the equation, what remained were two pairs: Kevin's size-ten Nikes (monstrous for a ten-year-old) and George's size-seven Keds. The footprints ended in the broad stretch of mud near the barn. George was discovered unconscious, on his side in the muck under the noonday sun. Kevin was never found. The investigators deemed it impossible that he just walked off, or even that someone came and took him—either scenario would have meant prints in the soft mud. It was as if Kevin had been simply lifted out of existence.

George never spoke a word to the investigators, despite many hours of interrogation. Even at the age of eight he had the sense to know that there are some things people will never believe, whether coming from an eight-year-old or a member of Congress. Had the whole occurrence been videotaped, and the tape confirmed as legitimate by every specialist in this country, still no one would believe it. The mind reels at such things. I've been stuffing down the memory for these twenty years because I just don't want to deal with the implications. And trust me, sitting around feigning ignorance when your family is grieving is no easy thing.

Before I recount what took place, I must explain a little about what sort of boy Kevin Prince was first. In my experience I've found that there are really only two sorts of bullies: First there are those who have been abused, neglected, or in some other way had their self-esteem busted, and try to fill up that need by dominating others; then there are the sociopaths, who have no such need, yet thrive on the suffering of others. Kevin was the latter sort. Even at the age of ten his life was a charade. Adults loved him. He was courteous, helpful, respectful, and, above all, friendly. Yet, behind all that there was something else. I saw it even before the first time I caught him bullying another child—a strange coldness behind his eyes. If my theology would permit it, I'd call him soulless. He treated other children as insects, but only when he believed he could get away with it. He was careful. If he learned that any of his cousins, or even siblings, had a special fear, Kevin did everything in his power to exploit it.

To my knowledge, the worst thing he ever did was dump a jarful of spiders on George. It used to be that in the summers the whole family (Michael, my brother's son, with his family, and even my two boys with theirs) would come to the old farm, where I still live, and stay for a few weeks. The adults enjoyed the country air and the quiet; the kids, well, what don't kids enjoy on a farm? Anyways, it was about a week into their stay when I found Kevin plucking spiders from webs and drain pipes on a Saturday afternoon. I didn't give it any thought. I hated spiders, and if Kevin was going to pull their legs off, great. Later that night, George's screams woke the whole house. The spiders were still in the room when we opened the door, scurrying under rugs and into cracks. And they were huge—mostly wolf spiders and funnel-web bastards—several dozen in all. What caught my attention though was what George had crushed against his neck and wiped on the bedside table: a thick, shiny, black thing with a red hourglass on its belly. George didn't know what a black widow was or that it had bitten him when he crushed it. All George knew was that he was arachnophobic and got panic attacks. He was shuddering on the bed, knees to his chest, rocking back and forth, his eyes spinning. We rushed him to the hospital where they administered antivenin. Later, I told Michael what his son had done. Kevin has despised me ever since.

That is the sort of boy Kevin Prince was. Nasty, calculating, and in my estimation, irredeemable. His disappearance occurred during an act of bullying.

It was late morning and I was out working in the garden. The sky was cloudless and the air was warm, but far from humid, which is surprising the day after a summer thunderstorm in Indiana. I had stopped growing crops several years back, just after my wife's death, and began renting out most of the acreage. There was still the plot the house was on and the red barn, rebuilt after the fire, and the small wood and my garden. I grew all my own vegetables back then; all I bought was meat. I had made breakfast earlier that morning: red-pepper eggs, hot sausage, and bacon. Now red-pepper anything is a terrific recipe for gas. Kevin loved my breakfasts, despite hating me, because it gave him an opportunity to blow a little steam at his siblings and cousins. The boy passed the foulest wind of any ten-year-old to have walked God's earth. It was as if all his sociopathic evil were somehow concentrated in his large intestine. The kid was noxious.

The storm had blown away the looser soil around my onions and beets and I was shoveling in some fertilizer to cover the bulbs. I happened to look up and see Kevin chasing George out of the house and out toward the barn. Kevin was a full head taller than George—who was not short for his age, but a little skinny—and had no problem catching him up about thirty feet from the barn. Kevin caught the collar of George's shirt and yanked him back. George's feet slid out from under him and he crashed into the mud. Kevin immediately sat down on George's face and began farting. He taunted, "Eat it, slut! Suck it in, fill up your lungs!" I was about eighty yards away and could have shouted, but instead I just watched, wanting to let George sort it out for himself. Having finished, Kevin stood up and turned around, then sat down again on George's chest. He started smacking George's cheeks as if he needed reviving. "It's not so bad, is it? Are you passed out?" His voice had an odd quality, rebounding off the barn. George struggled and cursed at Kevin. But every time he cursed Kevin smacked him on the lips. Finally, Kevin began to scoop up mud and try to put it in George's mouth. George cried out for help. He yelled out to every power he could think of: his mom and dad, Uncle Mike, Grandpa, God. I finally dropped my shovel and made for the barn.

And then his prayer was answered. I stopped running and just stood, mouth hanging, dumb.

God rounded the corner of the barn, stooped down real low so that the top of His head was below the crest. He was wearing a white robe, not the blinding white I would have expected, but off-white, sort of a cream color. His hair was long, down to the middle of His back, and shone such a brilliant white it made His robe look filthy. His beard bounced like a windsock. And He had a runny nose, *God* had a runny nose. The stream of fluid glimmered in the sunlight over the thicket of His beard. Kevin turned to look at Him, and even from that distance I saw all the color leave his face. God reached out His great hand and seized him by the back of the shirt and lifted him off of George. Having been freed, George scuttled back and gaped.

Pinched between the thumb and forefinger of Almighty God, Kevin was rather helpless. But he still tried to look defiant and spat a few nasty words at his maker. God held him near to His face and studied him with eyes that were deeply wise, sad, and amused. Then He opened His mouth so wide I expected Him to swallow Kevin whole. The boy flinched and kicked his feet pathetically in the air. Then,

God belched.

If Plato, in all his dreaming of Forms, dreamt of the essence of a belch, it could not have been more flavorful, nastier, or louder than what issued from the mouth of God. Kevin could not scream. He could not kick. He just hung limply, his face bloodless, in awe. It was as if all thought had been wiped from his mind. God held him out a little farther and then flicked him with the middle finger of His other hand. Kevin soared eastward through the air and disappeared beyond the horizon.

It didn't take me long to give up on rationalizing what happened. It would require a thorough reworking of my Methodism and I just haven't been up to the task. Probably, that is foolish, but I suppose it is how most people deal with traumatic experiences. It's what's easy.

Writing this has been good. Already a weight has been lifted off me. But I don't intend to dwell on it much more. I've achieved a fairly delicate balancing of my condition. Some days I feel healthy enough to ditch hospice altogether. Other days I expect I'll just die outright. And I'm not ready to go just yet. I've only touched the surface of Plato and there are plenty of other books I'd like to taunt Quintessa with. And, if I'm to be entirely honest, she is a rather attractive woman to have changing your tubes.

I have no idea where Kevin is today. If I had to guess, I'd say he's drifting in the Atlantic somewhere, bullying fish. George is currently finishing law school in Ann Arbor, and I am very proud of him. If he hasn't repressed everything that happened that day, I hope he finds this encouraging. I hope he remembers what was said to him. After sending his cousin only He knows where, God grinned at George. His lips moved and comprehension shone on George's face, but I heard nothing. Then He turned and strode off into the woods.

I haven't seen Him since.

SCENES FROM A LONG GESTATION

Jillian imagines she will one day tell the child about how it had a name before it had a name. They will be sharing a cup of coffee on a porch somewhere—God forbid it be *this* porch still, with its splintery trellis and rusted iron grating; no, there will be new porches, new places to know. She looks down at her belly and speaks to the tangle of life thudding behind her navel as if it were older, "I never could think of you as an 'it.' It's a cold word. And to think of you as 'he' or 'she' would have been premature. So I found this beautiful genderless name and used it as a sort of holding place. Rowan. You were Rowan before you became—" Possibilities flick through her mind. She finds it hard to imagine her child grown to maturity, so she focuses on the features that can be made indeterminate. Hands that might equally be those of a woman who enjoys outdoor work or the hands of a slender man who spends his time with books. Skin that will be smooth and olive-hued, like hers and James's. Tough or supple? You'll only know when you touch it. Brains? Tangled writer's mess or the spreadsheeted gray matter of a financier?

Eyes, now, the eyes could be all hers, no telling gender in those isolated disks. The child's eyes would become familiar as her own, why shouldn't hers fill the blank space? She traces the infinite shapes of what may be, merging her features with her husband's, combining pigments from their kaleidoscopic palettes, chromosomes as colors, chromo- and chroma-, blessed similarity, mo and ma. Mama. Odd title, she thinks. Somehow old, dumb (hickish), theatrical, but undeniably endearing. Did it come somehow from mammary? Old Mama and her jangling mammaries. Jangling 'dugs,' to use that lovely arcane literary word. Warm bells for ringing.

It occurs to her that she has failed in her fantasy to give a shape to a future-self who would speak, coffee in hand, to future-Rowan. She would be older, wiser, a respected academic, those warm bells a little warmer and a little lower in pitch, and that is harder to imagine than the soft putty form of a genderless child. She palms the swell of her belly and wonders how much longer she'll be able to wear bare midriffs without looking like white trash. She stands and yawns and the porch swing bounces with the absence of her weight. The October morning tastes thick and wholesome as the unbroken skin of an apple.

"YOU REALLY want to?" she asks, supine in bed, her elbows winged out, hands folded beneath her neck. She looks at James, nestled between her legs, and then past him to the bookcase. On the bottom shelf, wedged between the larger of her course books, are two antique hooch-jugs, each half-filled with pennies.

"Of course," says James.

"Doesn't it make you nervous? Knowing he's just inches away?"

"*He*?"

"Sure. He."

Silence. James drags the stubble of his chin against her thigh. Then, "Is that what you want?"

"It's what every woman wants," she says, still looking at the jugs, imagining them as the bulbs of a broken hourglass. Their marriage counselor had told them weeks before the wedding that if you put a penny in a jar every time you have sex during the first year of matrimony, and then take one out for every time after that first year, you'll die with pennies left in the jar. They decided that that was bullshit. So they bought two jars at a fleet market, filled one with pennies during the first year; after that they transferred the pennies into the other jar. A year and a half passed and they had emptied the first jar and had to start filling it up again. It went on that way for years. They made tallies each time a jug was emptied, so that some cold day, when they were both withered and impotent, they could quantify their bliss.

"No. I mean a boy. Now you want it to be a boy?"

"I think so." She closes her eyes a moment before looking down the length of her naked body and meeting his eyes. "He'll be like you. I adore you, you know."

"I know," he says.

"But he'll have my wits."

"May the Lord save and protect us."

"Don't be mean."

"Who's being mean?" James bares his teeth, growls, and makes to bite her leg.

She flinches her legs and thwaps him on the forehead with a finger. "Naughty little pup," she says. "You're all bark."

"I've got your pup right here." James shoots a hand beneath her and pinches a cheek. She tries to pull away but he grabs her hips and holds her in place.

"Careful," she says. "You're outnumbered."

"Am I now?"

"It's two to one."

"So sure he'll take your side?" says James.

"Secret trans-uterine telepathy. You wouldn't know about it."

"I know about this. . . ."

"Well." She lies back and watches him. "Let's hope he doesn't reach out and grab your tongue."

"JILLIAN, I have to apologize. It seems our machine is having some problems." Dr. Sidney turns the display on and off a few times and then tries disconnecting and reconnecting the inputs. "Bizarre."

"What's bizarre?" The word seems to Jillian to float down and stick in the cool ultrasound goo smeared on her stomach.

"Oh, it's nothing. The image isn't coming out right." Dr. Sidney concedes defeat and turns the display off a final time. She turns to Jillian with a mild frown. "How about we reschedule for later this week? In the meantime, I'll have this fixed or replaced."

"That's fine."

"Everything is good though. All his numbers are healthy."

Jillian watches Dr. Sidney roll the leather stool out of her way and walk to the door of the white room. She removes a manila folder from the box affixed to the door.

"Dr. Sidney?"

"Yes?"

"Is it weird to think you can feel your baby's thoughts? I mean, do other women mention that?"

"Oh, sure. It was like that with my two. You wonder about it enough and I suppose you start projecting all sorts of things. It's easy with something so intimate."

"What I mean is a bit different. Sometimes I feel certain I know what his emotions are. As certain as if I had seen him smiling or frowning or sneering."

Dr. Sidney is silent for a moment, considering. "You know, I've never seen a baby sneer. I think I'd like to see that."

Jillian laughs.

"Not yours, of course."

SHE HEARS the words Dr. Sidney is speaking, she recognizes them, knows their definitions, words safe enough in isolation, but in concert, now, in this precise order, they are alien sounds, the black music of a forgotten race older than man. Dr. Sidney traces a finger over gray ridges in the shadowy ultrasound image, showing her again where the fetus has passed through the uterine wall and begun to adhere to her spinal column. Jillian stares at the dark curled thing as if it were a solar eclipse seen through foil. The two women are silent and Jillian feels the nausea steal over her.

"I wanted to believe it was the machine," says Dr. Sidney. "What I saw, what I'm seeing, it can't be real. But there it is."

"I LOVE you," James says.

"I know."

"And I want you. I want us to try. I don't care how strange it gets." He strokes her forehead and then stands up next to the bed and unbuttons his striped lavender dress shirt. "Do you remember when you bought me this shirt? You said you wanted to test me, see how comfortable I was in my own skin."

"I was nervous you were in the closet."

"Really?"

"I worried that all those muscles and flannels were affectations."

"Such a frightening word, 'affectation.'"

"Wouldn't be if you'd read more," she said.

"I thought we had a deal. I make the money for now and you read the books for the both of us."

"You and your deals, you big wanker."

"Hey!" James puts a knee on the bed and grabs for her side-ribs, the ticklish ones.

"I said *banker*! BANKER!" She rolls onto her back, cackling, and James cuddles up next to her.

"I'm just your wanking banker, is that it?" He goes from tickling to caressing her side over the satin nightgown. "Nice baiting me down a rabbit trail, you naughty little bunny."

And, just as quickly as it came, the joy is gone. She feels the anxious, itching rush of neurotransmitters as if they were in her skin and not her brain. As if her brain were smeared like cream cheese beneath her dermis.

"I suppose a wanking banker is about right. It's not like I'm any good to you." She feels James tighten against her and knows she has hurt him with her self-deprecation. She is silent, struggling under the weight of seven sexless months.

"That's not true," he says. "What I was trying to say about the shirt is, it was the first of many things you've done to help me feel more comfortable with myself. I know it's silly, but changing my style made me disregard how other people saw me. I felt so safe with you. And this," he breaks his speech and gropes her belly, distended by fourteen months of pregnancy, with his right hand, "this doesn't change how I feel about you. You will always be beautiful to me. I want to help you be comfortable with yourself again. It's been months. It may never be like it was, but we've got to start somewhere."

She is quiet and the emotion percolates behind her eyes. She wants to look at him and wants to continue looking away in equal measure. She feels moods changing through her body, colors dancing through her hormone-harried flesh. She retreats from her husband, from the heavy unbirthable fetus growing ever more fused to her person, and navigates the halls of her head, longing for those times she left her husband panting, felled like an oak.

After several moments she says, "Okay, James. Let's try."

The sex feels medical. On her side, it is too much effort to squirm, to eye him over her shoulder, to give the act character. She is too aware of the body inside her, bones that have consolidated with her own, like a tree become one with a barbed-wire fence, too aware of the child's nerves insinuating into the fibers of her own, of the terrible intimacy of mother and son becoming one flesh, each dependent on the other.

She gasps and pretends that the pain she feels is pleasure.

He finishes and remains there against her warmth, letting himself grow small inside her body as their child, slowly, grows larger.

"THE PROCEDURE will be quite simple," explains Dr. Matheson. He is a somewhat grizzled man, a specialist, with a bearded smile that shines like a flashlight through a sweater. "Very much like a cesarean, only the wound will not be closed. We will fold over the skin of the opening and cauterize some of it, though not all, as the scar tissue will need to be flexible down the road as he grows. Your body has already formed a cavity of sorts. We just need to make the best use of it." Dr. Matheson indicates on the MRI image where the incision will be made and how the child will be allowed to protrude.

"Like a joey in his pouch," says James, squeezing Jillian's shoulder.

No one laughs.

Jillian glimpses Dr. Sidney shaking her head softly in the corner, and then she returns her attention to the display. She expects that seeing these images will get easier with time, but it has not begun to happen yet. She looks at the small white hips set within hers, the legs like ridges down her own bones, the length of spinal cord they share, the arms folded in the great cave of her belly. Birth, she thinks. This will be like a birthday. His birthday. She will finally see her child's eyes.

"MOMMY," ROLAND says, bending his head as far back as it will go, looking up at her with his giant hazel eyes. He is five years old, fused to his mother's lap. Her little spoon.

"Yes, my sweet?" she says, staring down at him.

"Can we play outside?"

"Sure. But not for long. Your father will be home soon with dinner."

She wheels the chair, *their* chair, out of the living room toward the kitchen and rear door. The chair is motorized, but she insists on using her own strength, taking joy in the firm lean muscle of her arms.

"Open the door for Mommy?" she says.

Roland reaches forward and twists the knob. Once the bolt is out of the jamb, Jillian pulls back on the wheel-grips as Roland holds on and, with only a minor strain where they are conjoined, together they swing the door open. They roll onto the back porch and ease down the ramp.

It is a large yard, about an acre, sparsely populated with willows and sycamores. Three years ago James installed a wide cement path that winds through the property, around the trees and bushes and the goldfish pond at the far end. The breeze is mild and smells of damp cut grass. For a moment Roland is content and quietly distracted with surveying the outside world, and Jillian closes her eyes and feels the breeze move over her brow. She hears the sweet susurrus of the willow strands and inhales deeply.

In this quiet moment she could be anywhere.

"WHAT DOES my name mean?" he asks one afternoon, months later, while Jillian is reading in the living room, by the large front window. She lowers the volume—Schleiermacher's *Monologen*, an artifact of her abandoned dissertation—and rests it on her belly.

"Roland means *land of fame*."

"Is that good?"

"Certainly."

After a pause, he says, "Why? I'm a person, not a land."

Jillian scratches his shoulder blade and he leans back against her so she will stop. "Of course you're not a land. But Roland is a famous name. And it comes from one of my favorite poems." Roland, Rowan, she thinks. Rol and Row. Land and wan. My wan little roe in a famous land.

"Tell me it."

"I don't know the whole thing."

"You said it was your favorite."

She imagines his brow furrowing as he says this, but she can't see his face.

"Well, it's long. I never memorized it. But I can tell you what it's called. It's called 'Childe Roland to the Dark Tower Came.'"

"I'm child Roland?"

"Sure. But in the poem, Childe doesn't mean a kid, it means a young knight. You're a warrior on a quest."

"What's a quest?"

Jillian laughs but finds she is growing tired in the warm sunlight. "A long trip with a very specific purpose. Often to rescue someone. A prince goes on a quest and battles a dragon to save a princess."

"I have a quest?"

"Not yet. Just a lot of quest*ions*."

He turns quickly and gives her the stink eye. Something pops deep in the confusion of their groin. "Ouch," they say at once.

"Is HE asleep?" asks James. The lights are off in the dining room, except for the small reading lamp attached to the back of the wheelchair.

Jillian looks up from her journal and nods. She is jotting ideas for a personal essay, ways to narrate the years she spent overseas as a teenager, with her father in Hertfordshire, England.

"How about these?" says James. He is holding Roland's sketches in one hand, feeling about with the other in his jacket pocket for his reading glasses. He finds them and slips them on. "Wow. Just, wow. How can a seven-year-old do this?"

"Isn't it something?" She feels her voice is too even, so she tries to sound more enthusiastic. "We've been doing simple shapes this week. Shading and such. Then we started looking at dimensions of the human body. You know, using shapes as guides. He's so natural with it."

"You're such a natural teacher." James bends down and kisses his wife's forehead. "I'm going to make a drink. Do you want anything?"

"Yes."

"Yes?"

"Take a mistress," she says. "I want you to take a mistress."

James grabs a chair from the dining room table and moves it next to Jillian and sits down. He removes his glasses and leans forward and rests his head against her shoulder. She cups the base of his skull with her right hand and tangles the soft hair with her fingers. She feels the fabric over her shoulder dampen, but her husband is silent. Roland stirs, twitching in his sleep.

"I want you to take a mistress," she whispers, her voice dry as her eyes. "I want you to be happy." She listens to his troubled breath as he weeps against her.

"I am, Jill," he says, steadying his voice. "I have. I did. Six months ago."

She lifts his head up so that he looks at her. "Who is she?"

"You remember Kim Sylvan? The new analyst we took on last year. You met her at—"

"I remember," Jillian says. "I like her."

"She—"

"I don't need to know any more," she says, and smiles. "Nothing will ever be easy about any of this. Don't judge yourself. I love you."

He kisses her quickly on the lips and stands, rubbing his eyes. "I need that drink," he says.

"Could I have water?"

"Sure."

"And James? Encourage this, the drawing. He'll need something. I think this might be it."

THE STUDIO, when it is finished, opens into a new foyer that sits where the porch behind the kitchen once was. It is perhaps larger than is necessary, but she knows James is proud of the studio, the seamless way it extends their home, proud that the idea came off so well. She loves the way the light from the broad bay window is doubled by the mirror that covers half of the south wall, how despite the clutter of ever-accumulating canvases, frames, cloths, spools of wire, plaster molds, and other creative appurtenances the room is always warm and bright. Roland, now fourteen, loses himself easily here, disappearing into his projects. Sometimes she will watch him for hours bringing something to life from his mind, absorbed as if she were not even there. Sometimes she will work on a project of her own—add to her private memoir, compose a poem. But today she does nothing but gaze out the window. She asked James to install a feeder there and now an assortment of winged life is always hovering, always there is some soft movement for her to relax her eyes upon.

She feels Roland shift uncomfortably against her as he adjusts the height of the easel. Their legs have hurt as of late, a kind of roving arthritic burn. The doctors say they are suffering growing pains, each of their lower bodies becoming more distinct from the other. They are hopeful, the doctors, that in time their bodies will each reject the other as alien, that at last a separation will be possible. She knows she should rejoice in such a possibility. But she cannot imagine freedom without a deep sense of melancholy. Will there always be an awareness of absence, or worse, psychosomatic winces, as in a phantom limb? What fears, she thinks. Irrational. The ghost of an ungainly teenager haunting her lap.

Jillian finds herself dreaming, so vividly it is as if her son painted it himself. They are in a nightclub filled with young adults near in age to Roland's sixteen years, mostly women, dressed for carousing. The scaly mass of short sequined skirts flashes in the throb of lights like a school of herring. Roland strides through them, a dark giant matching his steps to the crunching industrial beat of music, as women try to grab hold of him and feel the tumid muscle of his arms. She hangs off the back of him like the unworn top half of a jumpsuit, her eyes wild, absorbing the bacchanal. Everywhere, people: thick in the unmeasured space, braying laughter and cutting wicked smiles. Everywhere the pheromonal reek of booze-inflamed flesh. Bodies jiving, grinding, jostling, hands discovering young glistening tanned thighs that sway slowly like hanging cuts of meat. She feels herself, loose-dangling, swinging side to side into strange moist skin, feels her long hair sweeping the sullied floor as if to clean it. Then they are climbing a wide, spiraling set of stairs, also filled with milling jades, each of whom stare at her thunderous Samson-son, and she longs for him to keep climbing, to only go up, never down, because down would mean her head dragging, thudding against the raised steps of the tower. And it is a tower, she sees that now as Roland shakes his hips and her head swings out over the rail. She stares into the obsidian nautilus of stairs receding into nothing. And the music's beat is growing stronger, vibrating into her very bones, a steady, concentrated beat, the feral thumping pulse of the tower itself.

She wakes to her son masturbating. They are in the large, four-post bed she shared with James before sleeping together became an imposition. After ten years she can still discern the scent of him on the mattress. Sweat and cardamom, familiar and unsettling. Across the room, still anchoring the bookcase, the hooch-jugs catch the moonlight like a pair of dusty glass eyes. She wonders now, after sixteen years of sexless nights, what the memory of all that exuberance is worth. It's not the pleasure she misses, but the knowing, the being known. Will her son ever have that? Privacy is all but impossible, except when one or the other is sleeping. How terrible it must be, she thinks, for a teenage boy to wade through puberty with his hands tied behind his back. She controls her breathing so that it will seem to Roland that she has not awoken. She will not rob him of these moments.

FRENZIED WORK, a canvas winking out its white existence before a daring carnival of color. A landscape of flesh, a torso oozing the good things of the earth; a thing is never itself, always partly another. A sorcery of surrealism. Fata morgana of the incarnadine created copse, or a greening thicket of corpses. Exhaustion. Roland lies against her now, drifting to one side, arm slack and swaying over the floor, the brush still gripped in his hand and dripping magenta on the hardwood. She studies their twofold form in the studio mirror. A living Pietà, motionless as a waxwork grotesquerie, yet ready any moment to spring monstrously into movement.

The long oily hair of her son sweeps down his neck and onto his pimpled back. She can smell the unwashed strands, odors of wax and fennel and well-diluted ammonia. An odor like poison. She could wring that sullen mess and dip arrowheads in the drops. Would there ever be anyone to shoot? Emotions that strong, directed, mated to a concrete object, have not visited her for a while. She knows them now by proxy, in the wild effusions of her boy.

SHE HAS never known the precise pain of childbirth, but when at last, after nineteen years, the separation comes, she believes the experience must be comparable. In her memoir, days later, she writes, *Imagine slowly removing an enormous rocky scab that covers you from the waist down like a pair of chaps. It clings tightly to the tender new flesh beneath, and although you want to tear it off all at once, be done with it in one nightmare instant of blinding pain, you cannot. You are at the thing's mercy. It is as if gravity itself is pulling it from you and your efforts are merely theatrical. A great feat of endurance, long enough that there are moments when the pain moves you outside yourself and you can take pride in your own strength. When at last the great stony sheet is cast off, it's as if all the air in the room rushes to needle across oozing flesh that is fresh and pink as a baby mouse. You will never know the precise moment when tears of pain become tears of joy. Maybe they were the same from the beginning.*

LIGHTING IN A CLOUDLESS SKY

Michael imagined knocking on the door hard enough to shake the house to its foundation and then pushing past whoever answered and trying not to touch their sallow skin because they always have sallow skin, these people, these whores, methheads, wasted high-school beauties, soma-addled slack bodies, all with the same seeping sallow skin carrying Christknowswhat proud strains of plague in their milky sebum, their eyes blear and mucolated with knowing and seeing too much of themselves, their kind, their unfolding fallow futures, the women always holding womb-reeking farrow like it matters that these things are loved when it's always the same, son like felonfather like mother to drugdoxy daughter, so he'll push past them knowing he'll wash his whole body after this and he'll delve into the leaning hallways, splinters from the ancient hardwood lodging in the soles of his oxfords, and he'll find him, Dane, his brother, smell him out like a hound hunting quarry in a burnt-out forest, find him sitting on some stained mattress, propped against a wall and picking over his arm for a workable vein, the narrow hypodermic held between his teeth, a smell of ash, chalk, and vinegar suffusing the air over the torn-off bottom of an aluminum can coated with the drying paste of an opiate cocktail, the bottles and baggies nearby, the bottles always with names of people his brother has never met and the names of pharmaceuticals his brother couldn't spell if his next fix depended on it—fentanyl, codeine, meperdine, butorphonal, dextromoramide, all the synthetics and semi-synthetics ending in -done—this all for the joy of cooking that hot methahydrooxycodone soup and sluicing it mm . . . mm good into a cold and hungry vascular sewer, and his brother will look up at him like a teenager caught jerking off to sacrilegious porn, and he'll be angry and defensive, act irrationally wounded, because that's easier than swallowing shame, and he'll spit the needle out of his mouth and try to get up but older brother's fist will put him back down limp and unconscious and he'll be carried out of that hellhouse of one-way streets, out to the rented car parked at the curb and laid gently onto the backseat, to be driven home to food and a shower to scald the drugfilth out of his hair and skin.

Fury furled around Michael's heart, but he did not know this place, try as he might to reduce it to trope, and he would not allow himself to act on emotion. He had been to similar ratholes when Dane was in a bind or needed a ride back before he had moved away, but not this tall blistered Victorian set a good piece of lawn back from South Fifth Street and waiting like a spider with its legs hunched against its abdomen, its many window eyes staring out junk-hungry at the chill November world. He shouldn't have to be back here, at this house, in this city, this state, playing Dad now that their parents were dead. Handling the estate alone was more than he thought he could manage.

That he even found where Dane was hiding out had been a fluke. He had gone to haunt after haunt, getting the runaround from distrustful assholes who could smell the sobriety on him, until by dumb luck he met someone in a dilapidated duplex on the east side of town who assumed he was after Dane to settle some score or other. Michael had played along.

"When you get what's yours, you tell him Black Rob's waiting for his. Tell him Black Rob ain't going to wait much longer."

Black Rob was a full foot shorter than Michael and wore an oversized faux-athletic outfit that should have been a parody of itself but wasn't. Black Rob had one of those eternally round, immature faces that put him anywhere from nineteen to forty years old. He was not even approximately black.

Michael tried the doorbell of the Victorian but he could tell by the way the button offered no resistance that the thing was dead and so he took up the tarnished brass knocker and let it fall a few times. After a minute he heard a muffled voice and then the door wasn't so much opened as made decidedly ajar and whoever had done it didn't care enough to stick around and see what had been let in. Michael stepped over the threshold and looked around for whoever had admitted him, but the heavy blinds were drawn against the bright morning and it took a moment for his eyes to adjust to the gloom. A tall, spinning-top-shaped androgynous figure in a black sleeveless T-shirt stood by a doorway at the far right of the large front room, chewing on something held with both hands, ignoring Michael.

"I'm looking for Dane," Michael said.

The androgyne loped through the doorway and disappeared. Michael shut the front door and followed it into a kitchen made claustrophobic by refuse. The room was the rotten nexus of a house where people didn't seem to live but only visit and thus didn't care to confront the defecatory odor that hung so thick in the air that Michael could feel it sweep like dust across his face as he stopped before the androgyne to wait for it to finish what he now saw was a burrito.

"I'm here for my brother. I understand he's been staying here for a few days?" He tasted the foul air as he spoke and felt his gorge rise.

The androgyne, looking at him with its large deep-set eyes, balled up the fast-food foil and tossed it onto the counter before raising its arms over its head, interlocking fingers and stretching hard enough for its sternum to pop. Michael saw that one armpit had been shaven smooth while the other was a dark fibrous bush. The asymmetry increased Michael's already growing nausea. He was about to press the androgyne for an answer when it abruptly turned and walked out of the kitchen.

A moment later came the sound of a fist pounding a door and a caricature of a deep baritone voice calling, "DANE! DANE!"

"The fuck?" was the slow answer.

"DANE!"

"Goddamn you faggoty motherfucker!"

"DANE!"

"We're asleep, the fuck you want?"

Michael made his way to where the androgyne continued to pound and shout his brother's name. It was all but laughing, struggling to maintain the marvelous false-voice that shook the pit of Michael's bowels. When the door opened his tall jackal-thin naked brother shoved the androgyne back a few steps and then started when he saw Michael.

"The fuck are you doing here?"

Michael was long accustomed to the slow ceaseless degeneration of his brother's speech into stranger and stranger gorilla vernacular, but this, the compression of "what the fuck" into "the fuck," seemed extravagantly stupid. He looked past his brother into the bedroom and saw an amorphous female form moving under a sheet on an otherwise bare mattress.

"Taking you home," Michael said. He was surprised by how softly he spoke, how the hate had gone out of him the instant he saw his brother's lankwasted body, ghostlike with grief and darkened in a wearied affectation of toughness. "We talked about this. You insisted we do this together. I've been back four days and this is the first I've seen you."

Dane looked at him silently, his smoke-blue eyes half closed and stony as rainless thunderheads.

"Come on. There's time enough for this later." Michael made a gesture to include the skag on the bed and whatever else had been transpiring in that Victorian flophouse.

After twenty minutes of cajoling, Michael had Dane in the passenger seat of his rented Volkswagen. Dane was scrolling through the list of missed calls on his phone. Michael noticed. "They add up when you don't answer for a week." He had even tried calling from unfamiliar numbers to get him to pick up.

"How'd you find me?"

"Sleuthing."

Dane said nothing, started opening and closing the glove compartment.

"Some guy named Black Rob," said Michael.

"Fuck Black Rob." Dane slammed the glove compartment shut and sat back in his seat.

Michael started the engine, put the car in gear, and swung away from the curb. Michael laughed. "Black Rob said to tell you Black Rob isn't going to wait much longer for what's his."

"The fuck."

"Please, no more *the fuck*."

Dane snorted.

"What do you owe the guy?"

"Not a goddamn thing. I don't want to talk about it."

Michael turned from Fifth onto Ohio Boulevard and cruised down the empty street, watching the houses fade by, until they stopped at a traffic light. There was a gas station at the intersection and Dane told Michael to stop and buy him cigarettes, but Michael ignored him and drove on when the light changed to green.

"Fuck you then."

"Who was your friend back at the house?"

Dane was silent, looking out the window, holding his hand by his mouth as if he had a cigarette pinched between his fingers.

"Your 'faggoty motherfucker.'"

"Shit."

"No, seriously. What the hell was that thing?"

"Charlie."

"Okay, but, what I want to know–"

"I know what you want to know and I sure as fuck don't want to talk about it."

They were silent until Michael turned the car into the driveway that wrapped around to the back of their parents' home, a two-story brick affair that had been built just before the close of the nineteenth century. It had been a farmhouse with a modest acreage not far outside the city limits, but the city had grown and engulfed it like a brown amoeba. Still, it sat at the front of an acre plot, hedged in by ancient maples, sycamores, and a few pines. In the center of it all was a giant persimmon tree that each fall covered the ground with small, blandly flavored mauve fruit. The property afforded its own sort of peace, and Michael had always been thankful for that. Growing up there, he and Dane had been able to escape into their backyard, which was surrounded by a small wood, and, together, imagine they were anywhere.

It was Dane who had found them dead two months ago. He had been gone for days, swimming in the bright ether of his habit, and returned home on a Wednesday afternoon. The smell of unmoving flesh flooded the air. He found them in their bed, peaceful under the covers as if sleeping. In his mind Michael saw pale stones wrapped in cloth. He would not let himself see anything else. They say carbon monoxide is odorless, but he knows that if you are attentive, if you are patient, a scent will emerge, a spiritual essence, a smell of smoky bile, of bloodflint, brimstone. When Dane called Michael, he had been in Texas working the job he hated, playing big brother and wrath of God to a rabble of teenage boys with drug and behavioral issues whose parents cared too much to simply let their children be eaten by the world but were much too wealthy to do the work of reformation themselves. Michael had to leave off supervising a group therapy session and went outside to find an open, lonely place to sit and listen to his brother's frantic voice. Even in that first moment he found himself assigning blame. The family home had seen a slow physical dissolution during the eight years of Dane's addictions, their parents becoming increasingly weary and apathetic, their souls' energy poured into what was not yet, no, could never quite be, a lost hope. It was no surprise that the furnace's disrepair had gone unnoticed. The temptation to believe their parents' death was somehow a logical consequence of his brother's life had been there with him in Texas two months before and it was here now, cowling his skin like a fine mist of spider silk.

Michael parked the car behind the house and got out, but Dane stayed inside. He watched him for a moment, sitting there, forlornly staring at his knees, before going to the house and unlocking the back door. The air was stale inside, even though Michael had tried opening the place up each day since he had returned, even though Dane still ostensibly lived there. Michael made his way through the kitchen, past the boxes of pots and utensils he had already sorted, and into the dining room, where more boxes sat, filled with china and glassware. He went to the bathroom and began to relieve himself, letting his head rest against the cabinet that hung over the commode. He heard the car door shut through the wall of the house. Then there was a howl. The howl became a scream and Michael's first thought as he pinched off the flow was that his brother had trapped his hand in the car door.

He found Dane pressing both hands against the side of the Volkswagen as if to roll it over. He didn't seem to be hurt, just screaming, the scapulae knifing beneath his shirt. Michael came closer and saw that Dane's face was flush. His nose was wet and his eyelids were clenched like jaws. Michael put a hand on his shoulder, but instead of acknowledging him, Dane slumped down to his knees and pressed his face against the side of the car. His screaming muffled into something harsher and metallic. Then it died altogether and Dane just panted. Michael lowered himself onto the pavement and leaned his back against the car. Dane sobbed.

It disturbed Michael, as he held his brother to him, that he was unable to cry himself. His grief, though rotting his soul like a cancer, felt unreal because he couldn't express it. He hadn't shed a single tear over them, and he felt indicted by his brother's cries. This was just another burden, another stone tied to his neck. It broke his heart to feel this way.

THROUGHOUT THE following week, Dane worked much harder than Michael had expected. They were mostly silent around each other, but the boxes continued to be filled, the property sorted—soon to be donated or sold along with the house itself. The rooms were not emptied so much as thrown inward to their centers in organized cubes. The basement and attic were the most troublesome, teeming with insectile life, their walls curtained with mildew. Most of what they found in the basement—heaps of old moldering clothes, primarily—was stuffed into trash bags and hauled to the curb. The attic, however, yielded forgotten camping equipment and an old Remington rifle with a crooked bolt. In the days he had sorted alone before finding Dane, it became clear to Michael that his brother had already picked over most of the house since the funeral, that the most valuable objects—their mother's jewelry, a collection of classic LPs, a cavalry saber that smelled like it had actually participated in the Civil War—had been pawned or fenced. Michael felt a bitterness over this, but he would not bring it up with Dane. It was a small miracle that Dane was doing the work at all, and Michael did not want to break the spell. Even when his brother would lock himself in the downstairs bathroom in the evenings, and not come out for more than an hour, Michael restrained himself. He knew Dane was shooting up, but he also knew that to say anything was to provoke a fight. So he would sit in his childhood bedroom in silent exhaustion or else work alone, remembering the many times in the last year when he had called home to speak to his parents and the conversation had been interrupted by the sound of his mom or dad, whichever wasn't on the phone with him, beating on the bathroom door, screaming how they knew Dane wasn't constipated, that he was in there so long because he was doing fucking drugs. If it was Mom at the door, Dane would yell at her to fuck herself and not be such a cunt to him, whereas, if it were Dad, Dane would try to reinforce the lie while scrambling to hide whatever implements he had out, anything to avoid the *real* fight that sat always on the horizon like a flicker of distant fire.

Michael found the videotapes on an evening at the end of their first week together. He was sorting his parents' room alone—Dane had sworn he'd not go in there until Michael needed him to help move the heavy king-size mattress—and while clearing out a closet he discovered a lone wooden drawer beneath a pile of his mother's shoes. In the drawer were four VHS tapes. His first thought was that they must contain some matrimonial monkey business that would bleach his mind if he watched it. But the tapes were labeled: "Michael & Dane." Beneath their names on each tape was a list of dates. He took the tapes downstairs to the living room.

The television, an old nineteen-inch Samsung with a built-in VCR, sat on a too-large stand in the corner of the living room. It had been around since Michael was in middle school. He put in the first tape, pressed play, and sat down on the threadbare sofa. He had not rewound the tape and it began to play from somewhere near the middle. The tube lit up for a moment with banded static and then settled into a living memory.

Michael and Dane, seven and four years old respectively, were playing together on the living room floor with their mother. In her arms was an enormous, gray long-haired rabbit.

Michael and Dane were silent, but it was clear from their awed expressions that this was a new addition to the home. Their mother was explaining how they should hold it so as not to frighten the thing.

"We understand," Michael heard himself say, the voice so high and gentle, every syllable threatening to curl upward into a question. It was an alien sound and represented a way of orienting himself to the world that Michael had lost. He knew it was there inside him, a winking dour light sealed in a lonely cage.

He thought suddenly of Texas and his work at the treatment center. How had he become such a fascist asshole? He knew he had crossed a line during his year and a half there, but he could not pinpoint when. He had been gentle and patient at the start, never trusting himself to advise a kid unless he had spent many days walking alongside him in empathy, gaining trust. Now, that patience was gone, seared away by watching too many of them fail, by battling too many young egos, knowing that in the end he was powerless, that his care was wasted unless they cared for themselves, seeing in each of them a younger version of Dane.

On the screen, Mom released the rabbit and it hopped to the center of the room, and he and Dane went for it. Michael got there first and held it in his lap.

"Let me," Dane said.

Michael set the rabbit on the floor and patted its tail and it jumped toward his brother. Dane grabbed its fur and the rabbit kicked out, trying to escape.

"No, like I showed you," said their mother.

But Dane continued squeezing with his small hands, seeming not to understand why the rabbit was afraid. Michael scooted over to his brother. *"Like this,"* he said. Dane opened his hands and Michael repositioned the animal on his brother's tiny lap and showed him how to hold it without pinching. The rabbit became pacified and Dane smiled brightly at his brother.

There was a muffled sound as the handheld camera was repositioned. *"There you go,"* said their father. His voice was magnified because he was so close to the microphone.

"What are you doing?" asked Dane from the doorway.

Michael jumped at the sound of his brother's voice. The door, which opened into the short hallway with the bathroom, stood just outside of Michael's peripheral vision. There was no telling how long Dane had been watching him.

"Watching us," Michael answered.

"Why?"

Michael observed the way Dane held both his elbows and stared at the television. He supposed Dane was trying to look imperious, but his eyes remained only half open, dreamy and pink.

"I don't want to see this," Dane said.

"Then don't see it."

"Turn this shit off."

On the screen, their mother collected the rabbit and carried him into the dining room, Dad with the camera following. She placed the rabbit on the dinner table inside a large, open aquarium with a bed of wood chips.

"I said–"

"Do you remember his name?" Michael interrupted, trying to bat down the great froth of anger rising inside him.

"What?"

"Our rabbit's name. Do you remember?"

Dane closed his eyes and sighed. "I just want to fucking watch TV and fall asleep. I don't need to think about this. You know that's where I sleep." Dane had always preferred the old couch to his bed, if only for the white noise of the television. But now that preference had become a mandate; his bedroom was next to their parents' room and he could not bear to sleep in it.

"It's all yours if you can tell me his name."

"You're a fucking monster." His voice was quiet and wet.

"Just say his name and I'm gone." Michael felt sickened by his reasonable tone, but that didn't stop him. "I can't remember his name and I intend to stay right here until I do."

Dane opened his eyes and looked for a moment at the television. "Hoppity," he said, and walked across the room and out the opposite door.

Michael heard his brother sobbing in the other room.

THEIR WORK continued. But Dane's enthusiasm flagged and more and more he confined himself to the bathroom, before disappearing for many hours each night without a word to Michael of where he was going. Inevitably he would turn up late at night, always dropped off by different cars (or so it seemed to Michael), and come in weary-eyed and darkly emotive. Michael was always awake when his brother came home, but he couldn't admit to himself that he was waiting up for him.

One night he opened the front door to find a young woman standing on the porch. There had been no knock, but Michael had heard a car pull into the driveway. She was facing the street but turned when the door opened. The porch light was burnt out and he could only see her by the light of a tall lamp behind him in the living room.

"Oh," she said. "I'm waiting for Dane."

She looked familiar, Michael thought, as did all of Dane's girlfriends, as do all people who have been eroded by the same experiences. He thought of the woman he had found Dane with more than a week ago, the woman under the sheets. Was this her? He hadn't seen her face.

"You're welcome to wait inside," he said. "Or on the swing."

The woman stepped toward the door and stopped, eclipsed by Michael's shadow. She smiled. "Thank you, but I'll wait out here. It's such a lovely night."

As he closed the door, Michael wondered why he had invited her in. The last thing he wanted was a member of Dane's tribe inside his parents' house. Could he be that lonely? There had been something sympathetic in her face, something warm and maternal, something human.

Something human? he thought. He felt sickened by his own inhumanity, his assumption that anyone associated with his brother was necessarily sub-human, a creature of pure appetite. As if he were any different. He too sought escape, in books, in film, in daydream, but above all in denial. In his cowardice he had built a shield, the weight of which was becoming unbearable. He felt himself lowering it more each night as he sat in front of the television, meditating on his past. But perhaps that was an illusion, perhaps it was just another means of escape. He imagined rolling up his sleeve, pulling the silky tape out of a video and feeding it into a vein. He saw the film circulating through his body, frame by frame, cell by cell, his flesh flooded with the light of memory.

He had taken to watching the videos every night, for hours, shutting them off only when he heard the bolt moving in the backdoor. He longed to press his face to the screen and pass into that other world, to live there, even if he was allowed only to observe, to hide in the shadows, a contented ghost. Michael had come to see the world of drug use as purely deterministic, governed by a fierce Calvinism void of its strange God, a world where free will had been reduced to a choice of dead ends cut into the wet stone of the frontal lobe, a world robbed of transcendence, save the false transcendence of junk. But seeing his brother and himself so small, so untouched by the world, and their parents, likewise unjaded, so intensely hopeful and delighted in their children—seeing these things Michael could believe that back then all things had been possible. And perhaps they were possible still. Even as that small voice of innocence continued to resonate in the walls of his consciousness, might it not be the same for Dane? As he watched a four-year-old Dane opening Christmas presents, dancing around the house dressed as Spiderman on Halloween, or riding a Big Wheel down the driveway, his shaggy blonde curls blowing out behind him,

Michael tried and failed to map onto the soft round face the face he now saw daily. It was much easier the other way around, to look at the older version and imagine those haggard contours softening, the sallow skin becoming rosy, the opiate-rheumed eyes washing to a pure and startling blue.

Michael filled six nights with the wondrous misery of his nostalgia, hoping always that his brother might choose to join him and share in the experience. He knew it would be painful and uncomfortable, maybe ugly. But that didn't matter. Something needed to be broken loose.

On the seventh night, Dane came home earlier than usual, just before midnight. He was livid. His upper lip was swollen to the size of a garden slug and he had blood in his teeth.

Michael had been sitting on the couch watching his eight-year-old self and Dane in their backyard, in the playhouse their father was building for them. When finished it would be about twelve feet high, a canvas-roofed wooden box suspended in the air on four legs like a hut in a flood-prone village. But at the time, it consisted of just the legs and a platform. Their mother had the video camera and was interviewing the two boys playfully. Their father was either not there or off-screen and silent.

Dane rushed past Michael and into the bathroom. He didn't shut the door and Michael heard him kick the sink in anger and turn on the faucet. He got up and went to the bathroom door and watched his brother. Dane lowered his face and tried unsuccessfully to drink from the faucet and then resorted to cupping the water with his hands. He washed out his mouth again and again until there was no more blood.

"You should rinse with peroxide," said Michael as Dane patted his mouth with a hand towel.

"I hate that stuff," said Dane. "It burns." His gray long-sleeved T-shirt was soaked around the neck.

"It doesn't burn," said Michael. "It just tingles and foams."

"It tastes like a dry snatch."

They were both silent for a moment.

"What happened?" said Michael.

"Fuckin' Black Rob tried to jump me."

"That hobbit? How'd he even reach your face?"

Dane coughed and hung the towel back on its bar next to the sink. "Outside of Simrell's. Coldcocked me with a fuckin' .38. I'd'a fucked his shit up if it weren't for him holding that gun." Dane pressed his palm to his jaw for a moment. Then his face lit up as if registering a sudden epiphany. "That little wigger is dead. He's *dead*. I'll kill him."

"What's he want?"

"Fuck if I know."

"Seriously, Dane."

"A grand."

"What'd you do? Did you cheat him?"

"Man fuck you." Dane was shaking, looking hard at Michael, his hands vice-gripping the edge of the sink. This was all Michael needed to know that Black Rob's grievance was warranted.

"Does he know you live here?"

Dane didn't answer. He opened the medicine cabinet over the sink and began to root around in it.

"Dane—"

"Just leave me the fuck alone a minute. I'm having a fucking panic attack."

"You're not having a panic attack."

"And you'd fucking know."

Michael left the bathroom. He sat back down on the couch and stared at the television. *"Who do you love, Dane?"* his mother asked from inside the past. A five-year-old Dane, wearing a yellow- and red-striped shirt, looked into the camera and smiled. *"Who do you love?"* she repeated.

"Jesus!" said Dane.

"Good!" said their mother. *"Who else?"*

"Daddy!"

"And?"

Even at five Dane was coy enough to draw it out. He sat rocking on the edge of the play house, smiling with a closed mouth.

"And?"

"Mommy!"

"Who else do you love, baby?"

Little Dane looked shyly at his brother.

Then, an angry Dane, older by twenty years, stomped into the living room. "Turn it off."

"No."

"I'm having a panic attack and I'm out of fucking Xanax and I don't want to see them."

"Well, that's just tough, Dane. Because I *do* want to see them."

"Turn it the fuck off!"

"Go to another room, dammit." Michael took the remote from the arm of the couch and thumbed up the volume.

"Come on, Dane," said their mother. *"Now who do you love?"*

"Michael!" was little Dane's sudden, happy answer.

"Yeah, we all fuckin' love Michael," Dane said and advanced toward the television.

On the screen, Michael slid off the playhouse platform, and Dane was left alone in the frame.

"Don't touch it," Michael said, jumping up from the couch.

Dane didn't touch the television, but instead picked up one of the video tapes from the stand. He stuck a finger under the tape head and quickly brought out a few inches of the slick black ribbon.

Michael balled his hands into fists.

"Back the fuck up or I'll rip it to shit." The cassette was shaking in Dane's hand.

Michael stopped cold. "You wouldn't do that."

"I said I didn't want to see them!"

"They're not even on the screen."

"I could hear them. I don't want to hear them."

"You think you're the only one who's suffering?" said Michael. "I haven't been able to shed a single fucking tear over them. Do you have any idea how awful that is? Of course not. All you do is cry. Cry and stuff your veins with fucking bullshit so you don't have to feel anything. You're a coward."

Dane didn't say anything, but he let go of the tape and it fed back into the cassette. He let the cassette fall to the floor. He stood limply, as if all the fight had gone out of him.

"Did you hear me?" said Michael. He felt a charge building around him, as if the room were filling with static electricity.

At that moment, what was on the screen was very strange. The frame had become fixed, as though the camera were no longer held by a hand but secured to a tripod, and Dane was staring into it so intensely, it was as if he were watching their fight from inside the television.

"I want to die," Dane said quietly, looking at his younger self on the television.

"What?"

"I've wanted to die for a long time. I tried it, after the funeral. After you went back to Texas and left me here. I shot so much shit into myself. It should have killed three of me."

"What are you saying?"

"I tried it again," he said, the words coming in emphatic hitches. "And again. I even got the real thing, not just 'scripts. It just won't work. Something won't let me die. I always wake up."

"Am I supposed to feel guilty?"

"He's looking at me," Dane interrupted. "I swear to God he's looking at me." His eyes were fixed on the television.

Michael looked at the screen. It did appear that young Dane was staring right at him. "Listen," he began and then stopped.

Dane took his eyes off the screen and looked at his brother. Michael watched as Dane's wet and ragged figure flickered in front of him like a bad cable feed. Large bands of white static rolled up and down his body and he seemed to lift an inch or two off the floor. A blue thread of electricity arced between Dane and the television. There was a magnificent crash of thunder outside and then, quite suddenly, he was gone. Michael stared in bewilderment at the empty space his brother had just occupied. The air hummed with the stench of ozone.

He heard a sound in the adjoining room, a sharp intake of breath. He had to will himself to move, to break free from a powerful stasis. He walked hesitantly into the dining room, his skin tingling as if it had been asleep.

Michael didn't see the child immediately. He stood partially obscured by a stack of sealed cardboard boxes. But it was Dane, the same Dane who had moments before been inside the television, sitting alone on an unfinished playhouse. He wore the same long-sleeve striped shirt and corduroy pants. His face revealed curiosity rather than fright, as he looked about at a familiar place that had become unfamiliar. He noticed Michael, who was indeed very frightened. "Hi," he said.

"Hello," said Michael. He began to laugh, slowly at first, but it soon built to something near hysterics. "Hello," he repeated amidst the laughter.

The child looked confused. "Where's my mom?"

Michael bent forward and grasped his knees. He felt faint.

"Are you okay?" asked the boy.

"Hello!"

"Hi," said the child. He smiled at Michael, but then scrunched his eyebrows.

"I need air," said Michael. "I need to get air."

He stumbled into the kitchen and out the back door. He inhaled deeply the cold, fresh night air. It was a moment before he noticed the sky. Heat lightning pulsed in a vast ring over the city. There were no clouds and yet the light danced, yellow with sudden streaks of green, around a voided center in which the stars were visible. It was as if a great yellow eye had fixed itself over Michael's home. The pupil, he saw, was growing. The lightning retreated to the edges of the sky and then disappeared altogether. The night reestablished itself. Michael leaned against the house for several minutes, until his breathing evened out. Then he went back inside.

He found the child in the living room, standing before the television.

"Who's that?" the boy asked.

Michael moved him aside and looked at the screen. He saw Dane—*his* Dane, with his swollen mouth and sagging jeans—walking frantically around the backyard, hands balled into fists at the sides of his head, screaming.

ONCE HE mastered his astonishment, Michael was tempted to envy Dane's position, trapped in that other world he so desired. But the longer he watched Dane that night, the more he began to feel that his brother was simply trapped, and perhaps not even in a *world* at all. He watched Dane explore the borders of the yard, press his way through the thickets of summer growth. He would disappear beyond the trees, but never for long, always returning with a sullen look on his face. Michael wondered if the only world that existed for Dane was the world of their backyard, if beyond the edge of the property there was nothing but emptiness. Dane quickly gave up exploring and took to hiding beneath the unfinished playhouse. A few times Michael tried shouting into the television, hoping his brother could hear him. He had turned up the volume as far as possible, hoping to hear anything from his brother, even if only his private humming. But he could discern no sounds except those of the cicadas and birds hiding in the trees.

"Who are you?" the boy asked after an hour.

Michael chose to tell the boy the simple truth. "I'm your brother, Michael," he said. "I'm just older."

The boy watched him steadily.

"I don't expect you to understand, but this is the future. It's like you're in a different world now. It's just like yours, but everything is older. There was an older you here, but now he's in the past, where you're from."

"You're my brother?"

"I am."

"Okay." The boy accepted it simply, without further question. "What about Mommy and Daddy?"

"I'm so sorry. They're not alive in this world. They don't exist here anymore."

The boy was quiet and scratched his blonde head. "This world is no good, is it?" he asked.

"No," said Michael, "I don't think it's much good at all."

THE FOLLOWING morning they were both awakened by someone banging on the back door. They had fallen asleep together on the couch. The television was still on, the tape was somehow still running, and it was night in their old backyard. Dane was asleep on the screen, curled up under the playhouse.

Michael found Black Rob at the door, dressed in a plush baby-blue sweatsuit, arms crossed, looking both smug and confused. A backwards UNC baseball cap sat over his close-cropped brown hair. The black grip of a handgun poked out of the front of his pants.

"What are you doing here?" asked Black Rob. "Where's Dane?"

Michael didn't believe his life could get any stranger and he felt entitled to a little rashness. He bent his head down and looked squarely at Black Rob. He said, "You look preposterous."

"What'd you say motherfucker?"

"I said you look preposterous. Like a Smurf."

Black Rob looked startled. "I ought to shoot your ass."

"On what grounds?"

"What grounds? What the fuck is you thinking?" He put his right hand on the handle of the gun. "Where the fuck is Dane?"

"He's inside."

Black Rob patted his pistol. "Lead on."

Michael ushered Black Rob into the house and closed the door. He walked straight through the dining room and into the living room, where the child was still on the couch wrapped in an afghan, sleeping again.

Black Rob caught up with him. "Well?"

Michael motioned his hand toward the television and Black Rob looked at Dane, sleeping in the backyard under the playhouse.

"What is this?"

"You wanted Dane. This is Dane. Otherwise, there's no Dane here."

"Who are you?"

"I'm his brother."

Black Rob was silent for a minute. "When'll Dane be back?"

Michael sighed.

"Dane is gone. I don't think he's coming back."

"In that case," said Black Rob, "you just inherited his debt." He looked at Michael expectantly.

"And how much is that?"

"He took me for a grand five months ago. I don't give a damn about interest, so you don't have to worry about that."

"That's very generous of you, Black Rob."

"Excuse me?"

Michael laughed, humorlessly. "You should know, Black Rob, that I don't have any money."

The boy woke up, stirring under the afghan. "Who are you?" he asked, staring at Black Rob suspiciously.

"Don't mind him," Michael said. "He's just a wigger. Go back to sleep."

"My name is Black Rob." He glared at Michael and his hand twitched over the handle of the gun. "Enough bullshit."

"Why are you named 'Black Rob'?" asked the boy, sitting up on the couch, the throw falling off his shoulders.

Black Rob turned his glare on the boy, "Cause I got that donkey dick, bitch."

"Oh, Jesus Christ," said Michael. "Get out of my house."

Before Black Rob could say anything, Michael snatched the gun from his waistband. Neither could quite believe it had happened and they looked at each other for a moment, dumbfounded, before Black Rob threw a punch. It caught Michael on the nose and he took a step backwards. He dropped the gun and rushed forward and grabbed Black Rob by the neck and continued driving until he had him pressed against the wall. He reared back a fist and hit him once in the middle of the forehead. Black Rob looked immediately lost and, just for a moment, smiled. He seemed suddenly very young, and Michael felt ashamed for having attacked a man so much smaller than himself.

Holding him by the collar, Michael walked him to the back door and shoved him out. Then he watched from the window as Black Rob climbed slowly into his rusted Honda and proceeded to sit slumped against the steering wheel for several minutes. Michael couldn't tell whether he was crying. He felt anger at Black Rob's insolence, but he also felt remorse for tearing off his mask of machismo. He wondered what sort of damaged life demanded the construction of such a thin identity. He continued to watch out the window until Black Rob finally rallied himself, started his car, and left.

Michael returned to the living room and apologized to the boy. He picked up the gun, examined it, and found that it was unloaded and inoperable. The barrel had been filled with lead. He presented the gun to the television and saw that it was beginning to rain and Dane was standing with his face to the sky, mouth open. "You should have just fought the guy, Dane," he said, waggling the gun. "It's a prop."

"What?" asked the boy.

"Nothing. Let's go outside."

MICHAEL WALKED slowly into the backyard with the boy keeping pace at his side. They passed the persimmon tree and came to the middle of the open yard and stopped in the unkempt grass. A cold breeze ruffled their clothes and the boy crossed his arms over his chest and began to stare at him, not at his eyes but at his face. The child's mouth was open as if to speak, but he remained silent. Michael felt a warm stream winding out of his nose and down his chin. He licked his lips and tasted iron. He wiped the blood with his hand and then pinched his nose and held his head back. It made no sense that he was bleeding. He knew his nose was not broken. Black Rob's punch had been more startling than painful. But he didn't expect it to make sense. His was a world that no longer had to make sense, a world that had only to unspool itself according to whatever absurd logic it chose. But the unspooling itself, that was necessary. He knew this was so because he knew it was his responsibility to unspool with it, to move through the dense absurdity of his life, trusting in the Sense that would make sense of the nonsensical. He knew, beyond all sense, that this was just. These seething inconsistencies were of his making. They were his, as they were Dane's, his parents', even Black Rob's. They belonged to everyone, all who trespassed against that great unreasoned reason, all who chose the waters of chaos over the dry and fecund lands of order. As the oceans of this world belonged to no man, Michael knew, so all men belonged to the waters that were before the world.

Michael looked around him at the shivering trees and breathed the wintry air. Trees leaned against one another in the meager woods like the skeletons of tired men. The dry smell of their fallen leaves rose around them. In high summer these trees pressed together in thick bloom, shutting out the surrounding neighborhood, offering a glamor of seclusion that one could believe on certain days, when there was no traffic and the trains were silent. Now winter was waking and Michael could see through the bare limbs into the yards of other homes. The city of his birth stretched beyond them in every direction, tired and swollen with the melancholy of its years. He wished the crisp air could clean it, could clean him. He reached down and ruffled the boy's white-blonde hair.

He decided that here there should be a sea. A vast sea beyond which were undying lands. The water came on quickly and the city began to be eaten by the deluge. The homes and buildings were dissolving into gray sand, fine as powder, as the foaming tide swept in. It was a gray sea with flecks of indigo glinting in the dusklight. The water lapped at Michael's knees and he bent forward and cupped his hand and splashed his face to wash away the drying blood. He again licked his lips and replaced the savor of iron with that of salt. Michael felt his shoes sinking into the softening ground. He lifted the boy, whose face was less frightened than curious, over his head and set him on his shoulders and held his little legs against his chest. The boy clung tightly to Michael's head, his hands wrapped across his brow. The water was up past his navel now and deepening. His skin thrilled with the cold.

A boat drifted in on the tide. It was a sloop, about thirty feet long, made of bright rosewood. The vessel resounded with the slapping of the waves like a guitarist's knuckles rapping the box. The mainsail and jib were down, fully rigged, waiting. He lifted the child from his shoulders and set him in the boat. He looked back past the persimmon tree to the house as the water dissolved it like a cube of sugar. The house collapsed on itself, all those memories falling together, resolving into the same darkening silt. The television floated out of the mess and toward the boat. The water was deep enough now that each swell lifted Michael for a moment off the drowned earth. Michael grasped the starboard railing and pulled himself onto the boat, spilling over the rail like a thick wave. He shook himself and stood next to the child, who was fiddling with the starboard winch, spinning it and delighting in the ratchet sound. The television, its unplugged cord beating the water like a flagellum, floated to the side of the boat and bumped softly against the hull. Michael looked at the picture on the screen, which was still alive, and saw his brother shivering beneath the playhouse, trying to escape the torrent of rain pouring on the backyard. He lifted the television, his back straining with its weight, and held it for one moment at the side of the boat, letting the salt water drain out of it, then he brought it aboard and set it in the stern by the tiller.

Michael went to the child and stopped him from spinning the winch. "In another world," he said, "you learn to sail when you are fourteen. Younger than me when I learned." He took hold of the main line and began to pull. The sail rose toward the darkening sky. When it reached the masthead he cleated the rope and began raising the jib.

"Let me help," said the child.

Michael made the jib taut and showed the child how to pull the line through the cleat and tie it off. He draped the jib sheets around their winches and took hold of the main sheet and sat down by the tiller. He watched Dane continue to shiver beneath the playhouse, even though the rain had stopped and the day appeared to be brightening. Then he grasped the tiller and pulled it to the left and then much harder to the right, using the rudder to paddle them out of irons. He pulled in the main and the breeze caught the sail and they shot forward through the roughening water.

All around were the remains of the city. Uprooted trees drifted in the waves, their bare branches extending like calcified tentacles. Just beneath the surface were the automobiles, invisible and dangerous as shoals. But it was all disintegrating, an entire world worming through the water like paint. Night was coming on quickly. The sun was extinguishing itself far to the west and the whole horizon steamed and glowed like St. Elmo's Fire.

THE CRIMSON HEXAGON (A Briefer Epic, Part III)

TIME AND SCENE: *The Crimson Hexagon of the Library of Babel. It is midnight, or perhaps late morning. Eventide. Two orbs hang from the ceiling, dimly illuminating the gallery. Emerald moss spreads in patchwork over the stacks and their small, blood-writ volumes. The air is suffused with the smell of earth and paper.*

MICHAEL *sits in a thin leather armchair, an open book on his lap.* PAUL *circles the gallery, humming, fingering spines, sometimes seizing a book at random and flinging it over the rail into the air shaft at the gallery's center.*

PAUL:
What are you reading?

MICHAEL:
I don't know. I've never encountered such characters before. I suspect that it contains every word I will ever write, all of them secreted away inside some mad cryptography.

PAUL:
Why not set yourself to decoding it?

MICHAEL:
It's too complicated. And even if it weren't, the task would take me the same amount of time as actually writing it. For now, I'm content to stare at the pages and wonder.

PAUL:
It shouldn't be any great mystery. It'll just be more of the same.

MICHAEL:
Why have you brought me here?

PAUL:
Don't you like it? I admit it's grandiose. But it suits our vanity.

MICHAEL:
I thought we had finished with vanity.

PAUL:
One never finishes with vanity. I've stuffed Borges into Milton, the infinitely motile inside the inflexibly doctrinaire. One blind man inside another. Perhaps, in the interest of wedding form to content, we should gouge out our eyes as well. Vanity aside, I thought this a useful stage for your last temptation. It's no temple pinnacle, but the Library is also a place of decision, testing, the tight wire-strung abyss over which we all balance. The place

of infinite meaning or of absolute vanity. There is no middle ground here, though we walk our wires for all eternity.

MICHAEL:
We? Do you fancy yourself walking a wire too?

PAUL:
If I walk the wire I do so as a servant to the abyss. But I say "we" because our fates are bound. Where you go, I go, your ever-faithful shadow-dog.

MICHAEL:
You haven't abandoned hope of seducing me to self-worship or, as you bill it, self-affirmation?

PAUL:
I don't need to seduce you to anything. I have always already succeeded. In everything you do—every action, evil or good, in every step you take, on paths wide or narrow, in every word you write—you carry with you the abyss of self. "'Vanity of vanities,' says the Preacher, 'all is vanity.'" You will never outrun your own subjectivity. Even in your most intimate moments of private ritual, where you "empty yourself" like some bastard Bodhisattva, seeking to be filled by the Spirit of God, you remain mired in consciousness, in vanity. Even if there were some great and good Spirit that was more than the product of your vain imagination, even if that Spirit were incessantly filling you, the abyss is infinite. Even if that Presence intrudes for all eternity, there will always be more of the self underlying it. There is no escape.

MICHAEL:
Then why persist in tempting me, if the war is won?

PAUL:
I want you to face the facts. You're condemned to walk your wire. You might as well stand up straight while you do it.

MICHAEL:
Rejoice in vanity.

PAUL:
The only way to serve God with your whole being is by being God.

Stands before MICHAEL *and slowly becomes* MICHAEL. *His clothes begin to darken, to decay.*

MICHAEL:
Your logic is perverse.

PAUL:
Thank you. It's a rather tautological compliment, but I appreciate it nonetheless. Logic has never been anything but the purest perversion.

MICHAEL:
Why employ it if you don't believe in it?

PAUL:
Because, like truth, it's such a useful tool.

MICHAEL:
Is that "true"?

PAUL:
(Laughs.)

MICHAEL:
You can't have your cake and eat it. You can't affirm pragmatic value without also affirming value as such, higher order truth.

PAUL:
You can if you're a devil. But enough epistemological distraction. What I want to know is why you insist on believing in God when you know it's impossible to serve him.

MICHAEL:
Even the demons believe, and shudder.

PAUL:
Libel, I say! Libel!

MICHAEL:
You know very well why I believe.

PAUL:
Of course. I just want to hear you say it.

MICHAEL:
Why?

PAUL:
I'm helping you to become honest with yourself.

MICHAEL:
You believe in honesty but not truth?

PAUL:
Now you're just being evasive. What would happen if you didn't believe? Not more sinning, surely. You're already chock-full of

that. What would you do if there was no "Sense that could make sense of the nonsensical"?

MICHAEL *is silent.*

PAUL:
Perhaps the better question is not what you would do but how you will do it. Go ahead, tell me. How will you kill yourself?

MICHAEL:
I don't know. I haven't thought it through yet.

PAUL:
But you admit, at last, that at the bottom of everything, you believe in God because otherwise you're as good as a suicide?

MICHAEL:
I admit it.

PAUL:
That is rank cowardice.

MICHAEL:
No. It is neither cowardly nor courageous.

PAUL:
Fearing that a world without meaning would drive you to suicide–this isn't cowardice?

MICHAEL:
Suicide is not what I fear. My fear is that I would revel in such a world. In a way you're right, about vanity. My fear is that in such a world I would no longer be myself, that selfhood itself would

be extinguished, or at least this particular self. I fear a world where it is impossible to fear God. If I killed myself, it would be to prevent me from transforming into something alien.

PAUL:
Look at these rags.

Grabs at his decaying garments and tears away a strip of cloth.

All is impermanence. Nothing lasts. The self least of all.

MICHAEL:
Not on its own terms, anyway.

PAUL:
No, not on any terms. You are the kind of thing that comes to an end.

MICHAEL:
Might as well live it up, then, is that it? Revel in unreflective impulse?

PAUL:
Don't you see what's happening here?

Exasperated, tears off his remaining rags, and stands naked. His skin bears an odd, yellowish-green pallor.

Even the title you've chosen betrays you. Your faith is your prison, which you ceaselessly project on the darkness around you. You are your own jailer.

MICHAEL:
It is possible. But I refuse to believe it. Why is your skin that color? You look ill.

PAUL:
I am. Your stubborn self-loathing is making me sick. I can only imagine what it's doing to you. There is a way out, of course. Such a discovery doesn't need to end with your alienation from self.

MICHAEL:
And how's that?

PAUL:
We've covered it already. That alien thing you fear becoming is already a part of you. So much of you would survive the transformation. You have only to accept it. Accept me. This is your moment, what you've been writing toward all this while. This is your anagnorisis, your moment of supreme clarity. I am you. You know how infinitely variegated the self is. There are as many different aspects of you as there are books in Borges' Library. You contain multitudes.

MICHAEL:
What would you have me say, Meister Whitman, concerning these multitudes?

PAUL:

> Welcome is every organ and attribute of me, and of any man
> hearty and clean,
> Not an inch nor a particle of an inch is vile, and none shall be
> less familiar than the rest.

MICHAEL:
(Snorts.)

PAUL:
You've been singing the song of yourself all your life, love. So long as you have lungs, this is the only song you'll ever sing.

MICHAEL:
And how long until I can't stand the sound of my own voice?

PAUL:
You hold within you infinite voices and infinite listeners. You'll never exhaust the possibility of novelty.

MICHAEL:
No. I hold within me the exact number of all the possible combinations of everything I have read and experienced. If, like the Library, that number is infinite, it wasn't my doing. I am not my own possibilities. And I am not my own creations.

PAUL:
You expect anyone to believe that these characters of yours are not expressions of yourself? How foolish. They are all you. You are rapist, pedophile, child murderer, prisoner, avenger, mother and father, defiler of corpses, brother, addict and healer, Caucasian, Hispanic, lazy-eyed black man and blue-haired old woman, dying old man and child in utero. You are the Devil and Christ. Temptation and deliverance. You are demiurge to a universe of pulp. You are the white between your words and the penumbral din of every sign you've ever made. You are your own avatar. You are everything and nothing, god and abyss. And you are me.

MICHAEL:
No. You are not me, or even a part of me. You are not some vital potentiality buried deep within the void of self. You are a tool. You will only ever be a tool. And, someday, you will outlive your

usefulness, at which point you'll become only a memory, an idea I had in my youth.

PAUL:
Indeed, you are young. Someday you will come to be ashamed of all this. But tell me, what makes this "idea" useful?

MICHAEL:
You're useful now because I am not yet fully formed. My faith still requires doubt. I'm a skeptic so that I can believe.

PAUL:
This is why I exist, why you've written me?

MICHAEL:
Yes.

PAUL:
Then I wouldn't be fulfilling my function unless I told you that such faith is not faith at all. It is self-delusion. It's as if you only write so that you can believe. How can you call such a shallow, untested thing faith? Make it real, if it matters so much. Put down your pen and see if your God does not vanish with your words.

MICHAEL:
I cannot. It would be no test at all. I already know the outcome. This is the act of obedience that makes my faith possible. I create worlds in order to know that my world was created.

PAUL:
Look at me.

Skin pales to translucence. The crimson life within, infinitely racing its circuit, dilates against the skin, bright as neon piping. Blood fills the eyes to overbrimming and runs down to the mouth, painting the lips and cheeks clownish.

Look what you're doing to me.

MICHAEL:
I see well enough.

PAUL:
Yet you do nothing. Have you no care for your creations?

MICHAEL:
I'm exercising care even as we speak. I'm sending you away.

PAUL:
Where?

Skin begins to peel away in strips like wax paper. The blood darkens to a blackish blue. PAUL *rubs his arms as if cold. The sound is of pages tearing in a book.*

MICHAEL:
To your beloved abyss.

PAUL*'s skin rigidifies fully into loose scrolls of papyrus and the strange blood begins quickly to dry.*

You are a creature of paper and ink. And I am finished with you, for the time being.

PAUL:
How long?

MICHAEL:
You'll depart until an opportune time, I'm sure.

A wind howls through the Library and the infinite stacks respond with a chorus of groans. PAUL*'s body begins to disassemble in a hemorrhage of flapping pages that streams out and over the railing of the air shaft, disappearing down the throat of the chasm.*

PAUL:
All times are opportune, love.

The wind dies, passing on to other regions of the Library, and MICHAEL *is left alone in its wake. He rises, slowly, and closes his book and places it back on the shelf.*

ACKNOWLEDGMENTS

Writing is a solitary affair—until it's not. The artist, St. Thomas observed, concerns himself with the perfection of the thing made. And no art is learned, much less perfected, in a vacuum. To make art, especially literary art, is to commune with legions of the dead and, if one is lucky, some few living souls who labor in sympathetic parallel. David Foster Wallace once said that great literature is "an anodyne against loneliness." This is no less true of making than of enjoying it. To the extent that any of my writing has ever approached perfection, it's thanks to friends who have also made me less lonely.

I've dedicated this book to my parents, Larry and Debbie Lee, without whose encouragement, love, and faith this book, indeed my very self, would not exist. Mom and Dad, your faith—in me, yes, but much more so your unfailing faith in Jesus Christ, without whom there could be no art—is a beacon and a balm. Even now in your 70s you continue to grow, spiritually . . . and in your tolerance for the fictive monstrosities that pour from my head. I'm grateful. I love you more than words can express.

Many of these stories would never have been written without the encouragement of my mentors and peers at the Programs in Writing at the University of California, Irvine. My nostalgia for those three years of study is boundless. My cohort was legendary: Blake Kimzey, Tagert Ellis, Brendan Park, Kat Lewin, Eugenie Montague—you are all dear to me. I can't imagine better writers and readers—indeed, better *humans*—with whom to have braved the narrative trenches (not to mention the *emerods*!). Thank you for taking no excuses, toughening my hide, and forcing me to hone my craft.

I'm grateful to everyone I shared the workshop table with, and to the other Irviners with whom I've traded work over the years: Kris Dougherty, Lisa Horiuchi, Justin Jaeckels, Olga Moskvina, Alberto Gullaba, Jon and Tarah Keeperman, and many others besides. Most of all I'm grateful to Michelle Latiolais and Ron Carlson. You did more for me than you'll ever know by picking my work out of that stack of manuscripts. Michelle, I still hear your voice in my head admonishing me not to shy away from extremity, to let the work go where it will go. And I still strive to emulate your radical openness as a reader, your willingness to inhabit even perspectives you regard as anathema. I expect you hold the record for the "most acknowledged person" in the backs of contemporary works of fiction, though Ron must be nipping at your heels. Ron, you not only taught me to be faithful to the nuts and bolts of story, you provided a model for teaching that I use to this day. You also taught me to stay in the damned chair (and that "the wolf man doesn't want the moon"). You and Michelle have improved American fiction in lasting ways, through your own prodigious writing and your devotion to your students. It is a profound honor to be counted among them.

A heartfelt thanks to Jack Miles, for your wise mentorship, your incisive reading of my work, and most of all for your friendship. Thanks also to Brandon Fitzsimmons, Caleb Farmer, and Joel Looper for sticking it out with me like brothers for twenty years, even after slogging through my juvenilia. Ditto to my brother, Preston, who has stuck it out much longer. Thanks also to Dave Woods and Josh Mitchell, whose friendship kept me sane and relatively Christian amidst the sunny depredations of Southern California. Thanks as well to Jaspreet Singh Boparai, who helped with polishing edits for these stories.

To my editors at Passage Press, Jon Keeperman and Stace Maple, thank you so much for taking such care with my work. And thank you for creating a home for dissident literature at a time when both Big Five and indie publishers have cravenly capitulated to the Longhouse.

Last of all, thank *you*, dear reader. I pray in reading these pages you will have felt, however fleetingly, less alone.

ABOUT THE AUTHOR

Justin Lee is an associate editor at *First Things* magazine. A graduate of the MFA fiction program at the University of California, Irvine, he has been awarded numerous accolades for his work, including an Emerging Writers grant by the Elizabeth George Foundation and first place in the Passage Prize for Fiction. He was recently named a Claremont Institute Lincoln Fellow. His stories and essays have appeared in *The American Mind*, *FLAUNT*, *The Independent*, *Los Angeles Review of Books*, *New Haven Review*, *The New York Post*, *Return*, *The Saturday Evening Post*, *The Spectator*, *UnHeard*, *Vice*, *ZYZZYVA*, and elsewhere. He lives in Manhattan.